Mad Scientists and Feminization! Seven Erotic Stories!

The Great Gender Transformation Conspiracy
The Feminism Experiment
The Sexual Matrix
Feminized by Neuralink
National Lipstick Day
Boob Maximizer
Dr. Frankendick

Grace Mansfield
& one by
Alyce Thorndyke

Do you have all six volumes of The Big Book of Feminization?

https://gropperpress.wordpress.com

TABLE OF CONTENTS

The Great Gender Transformation Conspiracy

The plan to make men into women backfires!

PART ONE

"It's Voe-doe-pian-off.'

I repeated, "Wovopianov," using the pronunciation I had just been schooled on.

"That's right. Leonid Wodopianov. We just call him Doc Leo. Or Leo. He's got quite a history."

"Oh?"

The Jeep was bouncing up the trail, over ruts and through the dale. Driving in Alaska was like injecting hard rock into a six year old ballet class. It was rugged.

Beside me, Dana Lousch, pronounced 'lush, gripped the wheel tightly and drove like a man. She wore bulky over clothes, but I had had a glimpse of her in a regulation security guard uniform. Round butt, big breasts, and when her hair was down she was all woman.

Not that she let her hair down. She was Miss No Nonsense when it came to police work. Or security work.

"Yes. He actually paddled a boat across the Bering Straits. Braved giant seals and polar bears and made it to the 'Land of the Free.'"

"And he's a scientist."

"Top notch. Educated in the best Russian Universities. Let me tell you, Mother Russia was a bit unhappy when he showed up on our shores."

"And now he's in charge of the Alaska Scientific Studies Institute."

"Head doc."

"So what's the problem that you need an FBI agent?"

Dana gave a sound that might have been a snort, but it was soft, ladylike. "Better to show you. You wouldn't believe the spoken word, or even black on white."

I gripped my seat then, as she wound us through a corkscrew of a cow path. Over ruts so big they should have been classified as ravines, bouncing against the seatbelt harness so hard it hurt.

"Sorry," she said, glancing at me. "This is the only way."

"Strange place to put a scientific institute."

"Something about being free from the pollution of civilization."

A half hour later, two hours into our trip into the wilds, we found a paved road. Well, more of a chip seal paved road, and it had suffered from the seasons. It had potholes so big swimming pools would drown.

Dana pulled up to a cyclone fence with concertina wire on top. She

5

slid a card into a slot and the gate opened.

"Lot's of security. Doc Leo afraid the bunny rabbits are going to break in?"

"Something like that," grunted Dana. She drove through the gate and it slid shut behind us. Felt sort of ominous, like we had just entered a maximum security prison.

We rolled to a stop in a parking lot where all the lines had been weathered out of existence and she hopped out and lead the way into the big building.

It was long and low, nestled into a low peak just below the summit. It was painted brown and only had a few windows. And those windows were frosted and had bars on them.

We entered reception, and nobody was there.

"Huh," grunted Dana. She looked around, then went behind the round desk. I looked over the edge of the desk to watch her.

She picked up a phone and hit a number. Four. Watching me, she said, "Doc, I've brought the FBI agent up." She nodded, as if somebody could see her. "Yes. Okay."

She hung up and said to me. "Have a seat."

I turned to a cluster of squarish and very uncomfortable looking couches and picked one. I was right. It was uncomfortable. After that bucket ride up the mountain, however, it was comfy.

Dana sat down next to me.

Through the tinted front doors, the only windows in the whole place and they were too dark for easy looking, we watched a far peak. Snow on top.

"Storm coming."

I turned to Dana and she was frowning.

"You're probably going to be stuck here."

"I'll be spending the night?"

"Yes. But it's not too bad."

"Ring a round of roses, pocket full of posies..."

We turned to see who was singing, and my eyes widened.

She was six feet tall, Scandinavian blonde, naked as a new born. She skipped down the hall, making motions to the sides with her hands, pretending to throw out handfuls of poseys. Her large breasts bounced with every skip, and her voice was high and sweet.

"Oh, crap," muttered Dana.

"The doctor will see you, he he he..." she giggled as she went around our couches, throwing invisible posies and blowing kisses to us. then she went back down the hallway she had come down.

"Let's go." Dana said, and she moved after the naked woman quickly, and I had the feeling she was trying to get away from me before I could phrase a question.

No chance. I was right on her tail. "What the hell was that?"

"Naked woman," she muttered, not looking at me.

"And what is a naked woman doing prancing through the halls of a scientific institution?"

"Singing nursery rhymes."

The hallway was long, and Dana was reluctant to talk. My mind instinctively went to the nursery rhyme. It wasn't much, but it was all I had to analyze. My mind being somewhat orderly, and maybe even scientific, I sought logic everywhere, I considered the origins of the nursery rhyme.

Middle ages. The Plague. A ring of roses was a rash, the posies were a cure, everybody was falling down and dying. Fuck. What a weird thing for a naked woman to be chanting in a medical facility.

We reached the end of the hallway and turned up some stairs. To the top of the stairs, another turn and hallway, and, finally, a room.

The naked woman was waiting for us, holding the door open, smiling at us. She said to Dana, "Do you have any lipstick?"

Dana shook her head.

We entered the room.

It was a simple office. Nothing scientific or medical about it. Oh, there was a very small bookshelf behind a potted plant. The books looked like they were medical tomes.

At the back of the room was a desk, to one side was a small conference table. On one wall was a large picture of nature. Mountains and rivers, snow and in the foreground massive trees. The Alaskan outdoors. Just a few feet away, but only visible in picture. With naked women dancing in the halls. What a place.

"Doc Leo. This is agent Samuel Burns."

Leonid Wodopianov was short, maybe five foot six. He was in his sixties and had fringe grey hair around a lot of baldness. His eyes were an odd mix of sharp and rheumy. He had bright, white, false teeth.

He stood up and came around the desk, "Excellent. Excellent." He shook my hand. Mine was regulation FBI, hard and backed up by muscle. His was limp, soft, and felt sort of squishy, like he had doused it in too much hand lotion.

"Please sit down." We did.

The naked woman chirped, in a pouty manner, which made it a weird sort of a whine, "Doc? Can I have some more lipstick?"

"You know what it will do to you?"

"Yeah, but I really need to look good for..." she glanced shyly at me, "For Mr. Big Gun. He's got a gun! Did you know that? I could see it when..."

"Hush, Gwendolyn. Of course he has a gun. And you may have some lipstick."

7

Doc went back around his desk and opened a small wall safe set on a credenza. He extracted a tube of lipstick and handed it to Gwendolyn. Squealing with glee, the naked woman painted her lips. I watched in fascination. Just an aside, I have always been a lipstick man. Bright red lipstick was powerful, and it effected me. Hack. It gave me an erection.

I suffered my erection, and Gwendolyn handed the tube of lipstick back to the Doc.

"Off with you now," he had a slight accent. Hard to pick up.

"Okey dokey," Gwendolyn clapped her hands and pranced out of the office. We could hear her as she danced down the hallway. "London Bridge is falling down, falling down, falling down. London Bridge is falling…"

Her voice faded and the silence left behind was downright portentous.

"We've had more…more people have changed?"

Wodopianov sighed. "Yes. The workers think it's an outbreak."

"What kind of an outbreak?" I asked, suddenly nervous.

Sudden silence. I cocked my head and waited.

Wodopianov studied me, then told me. Straight from the hip. "I have invented something and I'm not sure what it is. Its effects, however, are…varied."

"Varied as in…?"

He changed pace on me. "What do you know about chromosomes?"

"A joke and there are two."

"A joke?" Dana wrinkled her brow.

I didn't even smile as I repeated the stupidity. "How do you tell the sex of a chromosome?"

She shook her head.

"Pull its genes down."

She looked blank for a second, then a quirky ripple twisted her lips. What went for a laugh in the world of the serious Dana.

Doc Leo, on the other hand, grinned. "That's funny."

I shrugged.

He said, "There are actually more than two chromosomes."

"X and Y is what I was taught."

"A woman is XX. A man is XY. The other two would be YX and YY."

"What?"

"And, to be honest, there are permutations beyond that. In fact, there are as many permutations as there are numbers in a binary code."

Binary code. The only numbers were 0 and 1. But one could count to infinite using binary code. It looked like this

$0 = 0$

01 = 1
10 = 2
11 = 3
100 = 4
101 = 5
110 = 6
111 = 7
1000 = 8
And so on.
It was a system that left out 2 through 9, A system that could be developed only by geniuses who built computers and wrote codes...or a man with only two fingers.

"I understand...but not really."

"XXX. XXY. XYY. YYY. And so on. Then XXXX. XXXY. XXYY ⸺"

"I get it. But what does that have to do with the price of tea in Alaska?"

Doc glanced at Dana. She glanced at him. They both watched me.

"The initial invention released constrictions on DNA."

"Huh?"

"We are now producing all manner of X and Y variant."

I looked confused.

"Dana, could you show him?"

Dana stood up and began taking off her clothes.

"What are you—"

"Patience, Agent Burns. Seeing is believing."

She took off her Alaskan over jacket, then her cop top, then her tee shirt. Finally, her bra. She had a nice set of jugs. Not as big as Gwendolyn's, but sizable. The tips were light, and they stood up as if excited.

Hell, they were excited. She was excited. I could see it in the gleam of her shiny eyes.

"I don't know what is..."

She unbuckled her belt and pulled down her pants. She was wearing boxers.

A woman? Wearing boxer shorts? What the—

She pulled down the boxers.

A penis. Not a big one, just three or four inches, but it was stiff. Erect. Pointing at me.

I could feel it then. The careful wall she had kept in place on the drive up, I thought it was professionalism, a lot of cops, security cop in her case, have wooden expressions.

But now, with her clothes off and her sex revealed, I could feel lust in the air. And it was directed at me.

I didn't feel like lust. I stared at it, at her, then turned to Doc Leo.

"No. She was not born a hermophrodite. She was infected. By my invention."

"So it's...it's airborne?"

I was stunned. Airborne meant I might be infected.

"Not to worry. You won't grow breasts, at least, not until you apply my invention, my lipstick, to yourself."

"Put on..." I stared at Dana, who leaned towards me.

I leaned away, fended her off, and turned back to the Doc, "What... is..."

"Technically, she is a hermaphrodite, be it one cultivated in a lab. Deep down, in her genes, because of the lipstick, she is XXY. Dana presents as a woman, with one slight Y addition."

"You call that slight?"

"I call it a penis. I suggest you measure your words carefully. While Dana is forgiving, she can also be emotional."

"Can I have some more lipstick?"

"Of course, my dear." He handed Dana the tube.

She turned the base and watched me with hungry eyes. The red column rose up and she touched it to her lips. She rolled it across her mouth and...I got an erection. Damn me. Why did I have to have that one, unique kink?

She rose up and took a half step towards me.

"No, Dana. Not now."

"If not now...when?"

"I'll let you know. Now, back to your duties."

Dana left her clothes on the floor and skipped out of the room. As she went down the hallway I hear her singing,

"Here comes a candle to light you to bed,
And here comes a chopper to chop off your head,
Chop, chop, chop, chop, the last man's dead!"

I sat and stared at the doorway. Then I turned and stared at Doc Leo.

"Would you like a whiskey?"

I nodded...then I shook my head. Hard.

He chuckled. "Only the lipstick makes change. The whiskey is pure Kentucky."

He didn't ask me again, he simply walked over to a small cabinet and took out a bottle of Yamazaki 12 year old Single Malt. He half filled the glass with ice cubes, then poured amber liquid over the cubes, then raised his eyebrows at me. "Would you like to ruin it with water? Or anything else?"

"Coke," I croaked.

He nodded, amiably enough. "Coke it is."

He took a Coke out of a small refrigerator and opened it, polluted my drink and put the half empty can back into the frig.

He handed me my glass, then returned to the cabinet and frig.

"I prefer Vodka." He poured Ultra Premium Vavoom into a glass. Straight. He might have no hair on his head, but he certainly had hair on his chest. And I wondered...

"Are you...have you..."

"Taken my own lipstick?"

So weird the way he said it.

"Yes. I happen to be XYY. I present as a man, but with an extra does of...how should I say it...manliness? Horniness?"

He sat down and sipped his brewski. He rolled the glass in his hands and looked over the top of it at me.

"The good news is that I am able to control myself. I want to fuck everything in sight, but...I don't." He shrugged. "I am a paragon of self control."

That made me think. "What...emotional characteristics do the various mutations present?"

"Good question." He nodded. "Thus far emotion is still presenting. The more X you have the more emotions you have, the less discipline you have. The more Y you have the more...forthcoming, you are. That 'forthcomingness' is usually tempered by the amount of discipline a person has. Discipline depends on what kind of a person you were in your 'pre-lipstick' life.

"Dana was a cop. His name was Dan. But as his DNA presented, as his chromosomes adjusted to his real desires, he became more woman."

"I thought he...she...was a cop and then grew a penis."

"No. No." He chuckled. The penis is shrinking. Not sure how much. Maybe all the way, probably all the way, and the breasts are growing."

"What about Gwendolyn?"

"XXX. Started out as a woman, became more womanly. Oh, you wouldn't believe how mousey and flat-chested she was."

It was hard to imagine that Valkyrie as flat chested.

"Now she is so womanly I have to inject her with estrogen blockers, and testosterone. If I hadn't done that she would have taken you to bed."

"I don't think so."

He actually laughed. "When she is not inhibited by my chemicals she exudes a pheromonic ambience. You would find yourself falling under her spell. You would be unable to resist her.

"I don't—"

"Let me make you another whiskey."

He stood up and did so. While he hummed merrily along, preparing libations, I was left to conjecture.

Men turning into manly women. Women turning into womanly men. And Doc Leo was a double man with just a trace of woman in him. How far did this go?

"So why am I here?"

He settled down behind his desk, sipped some more vodka, this time straight out of the bottle, and said, "Many reasons. First, there is science. We must observe experiments."

"I'm an experiment to you?" I didn't let out any of the disgust or bitterness in me.

"Tut, tut," he waved a finger, swigged from the Vavoom. "And then there's the need to share the wealth."

"Share the…you want to infect me?"

"I guess you could say that."

"Please, don't be ambiguous."

He smiled. "The downside of my being XYY, in your viewpoint, is that I want more and more women in the world."

Of course.

"So you want to make all men into women?"

"More or less. I need more women to satisfy my appetites, but I also need to reduce competition. What better way than to change the men into women. Eh?"

"So you're going to infect me, and I'm going to turn into a woman."

"Nope."

And with that brief negatory the conversation was over.

Oh, we talked some more, just not directly on the subject. And he told me much about the changes I would go through. He told me where to get women's clothes, there was a whole storeroom in the complex that would see to my outfitting, when I so needed it. He discussed how I should behave, how my behavior would change. He even talked about style and fashion and what would be best for me once I changed.

As for my part, though I didn't want to talk to him, especially about girly stuff pertaining to me, I did want him talking. I needed to learn more. I hoped he would say something that might give me a clue as to how to avoid the coming changes.

Changes which I knew nothing of, and especially how to avoid.

He said he wasn't going to use lipstick on me. So what was he going to use?

The only thing I learned, that evening was that he hadn't really invented his 'chromosome transferrer,' which is what he called it at one point.

Apparently he had received a sample of cosmetics from a place called Stepforth Valley. He had laughed, figured it was a mistake, and given the box to his secretary. That had started the ball rolling. He had noted men turning into women, traced it back to interaction with cosmetics, and began synthesizing the cosmetics on his own.

But as to how he himself had changed, he said nothing.

"Well, it is getting late," he finally said, "And my appetites are rising. One of the blessings, for me," he smiled, "is that my cock is quite large, and needs a lot of women to satisfy it. So I will have Gwendolyn show you to your room."

He used his phone and called the nubile Valkyrie to his office.

"Gwendolyn, dear. If you could see to Agent Burn's comfort for the night?"

I missed the nuance there, curse me.

"Surely, Doc. Can I have some more lipstick?"

"Of course, my dear."

I sat and watched while she rolled on a fresh coat of beautiful red, then she smiled at me, handed the tube back to Doc Leo, and led me out of the room.

"I'll take you the back way." She giggled, linking her arm in mine.

I let her guide me. "Gwendolyn? Do you know what the doctor has done to you?"

"Oh, yes," she chirped. "He has made me feel so womanly. I have never felt so nice and sexy. Wouldn't you like to feel nice and sexy?"

We were going down a flight of stairs. "Actually, no. Tell me, could you do without the lipstick?"

"Why would I want to? But I could. It's just that I don't want to."

Listening to her talk, she was a bubblehead. But i thoght under it she might be smart, just effected by her change and exploring a new life, new emotions, a new body.

But, bubblehead or not, she was having a strange effect on me. I kept seeing her roll on the lipstick in my mind. My penis was getting a little robust at the memory. And the way she held my arm, her breasts, her naked and large breasts, rubbing up against me...she was having an effect.

"Anyway, I'm taking you the back way because I don't want any of the other women to see you."

"Why not?"

"Silly. Because they're all women, and what does a woman want more than anything else?"

A man. Oh, crap. I suddenly realized I was the only man in the place. And all the women, according to what Doc Leo had told me, were going through hormonal changes. They were feeling their sex, and their sex was being denied simply because there were no men...and that meant...that meant they would want me. The only available man on the mountain.

Except for the Doc, of course.

The Doc. A scrawny, little piece of shit who was probably banging his way through the night even as I walked down the dark corridors with Gwendolyn.

We arrived at a room and entered. It was a simple room. Just a table and a bed. And a refrigerator. I looked into the refrigerator. TV dinners. But no microwave. Coke. Whiskey. What the fuck?

Gwendolyn locked the door and turned to me with a smile. If I hadn't been so numb nutted by my situation I would have perceived the lasciviousness of her sharp teeth.

"I'll just stay a while and make sure none of the other girls finds you."

She turned a switch next to the door and the lights dimmed. "Save a little electricity, eh?"

I stared at her.

She brushed her long, blonde hair back with one hand and said, "Let me pour you a drink. You must be tired after such a long day."

I nodded.

"Just sit on the bed."

I did. There were no chairs in the room. Just the bed and the table and the frig. I wished there was a microwave. I was getting hungry.

Gwendolyn handed me a drink. Apparently I would be drinking my dinner this night.

She didn't make a drink for herself. She came and sat on the bed next to me.

Naked.

Big breasts.

And my dick was getting harder. And harder. And harder.

"You're so handsome." She gazed at my face.

I smiled and drank. Heysoos. I was starting to feel a little a bit loopy. The Doc giving me drinks all afternoon, and now this Valkyrie babe giving me more.

And the way she held my arm, the way her breasts brushed against my arm.

"Isn't it getting hot in here?"

I nodded. It was hot. Or, at least I was flushed from all the bourbon…and from the overt sexual ambience in the room.

"Let's take off your jacket."

She helped me out of my jacket and we sat on the bed. Right next to each other. Me drinking.

"You look so strong. Can I see your muscles?"

I laughed and flexed a bicep. I felt like a school kid on a date with the prom queen. Would I get lucky tonight?

Somehow, she managed to get my shirt off, and I sat there in my teeshirt.

"You look so uncomfortable," she said. "Let's get you out of those pants.

She unbuckled them, her long nails fumbling with the buckle, then she gently pulled my pants off.

My penis was hard as a rock.

"Oh, my," she said, reached down, pulling my underpants down a bit, and stroking my tool. "This is big. I've never seen anything so big."

I grinned. I did have a big prick. I had had a big prick all my life. I liked having a big prick. Girls liked my big prick.

"And the head...it's like a tennis ball. Except, not green." She giggled.

I looked down to where her hand stroked me. My head was red, and pre-cum was leaking out of it.

"Honey," Gwendolyn said, staring at my monster. "How big is it?"

"Nine inches."

"Wow."

I could see the desire in her eyes.

And, I could feel my own desire. Man, was I horny. I hadn't felt this horny in...suddenly I got it.

I stared at Gwendolyn. "You're doing this."

"What?" she licked her red lips and stared at my cock.

"That ambience thing. You're putting out some kind of pheromones. You're turning me on."

"I sure hope so," she spoke softly. She pulled my underwear all the way off, actually ripped my tee shirt in uncovering me.

"I'm not going to get infected by...by..."

"By fucking me?" She used the word coyly, and in a way that inflamed me.

"Yeah."

"No."

I tried then. I tried to hold myself back. "But I shouldn't. We shouldn't."

"Why not?" she pushed me back on the bed, I was weak under her hands.

"I'm an FBI agent. I'm here on assignment."

"I'd like you to assign me...with your dick."

She was leaning over me, holding my hands down, and she touched her lips to mine. Such a gentle, soul searing kiss. I felt my dick roar with lust. My whole chest felt aflame with desire.

"Honey," she whispered into my ear. "I really need you."

"I shouldn't...I shouldn't..."

"You should. You should."

She held my lips down with hers. She stroked my penis. She fondled my testicles.

I could feel my heat rising, more and more. Heysoos, I needed

15

relief. I needed to put my dick somewhere.

"Do me, baby," she crooned to me.

My dick.

The pheromones.

Her naked body pressed against mine. Her large boobs squashed against my chest. I needed to...I needed to...

She brought her legs up, perched over me. She held my dick in one hand and began sitting down, lining my dick up and pushing it into her hole.

I felt the soft wonderfulness of her pussy surrounding my head. I felt her labia sliding down around my shaft. I felt the incredible moist warmth of her sliding down, down, until she was sitting on me. Her round buttocks against my upper thighs, her chest hanging over me. Pendulous, white globes in the dim light.

I reached up and grabbed her breasts.

She moaned and twisted, and it felt like somebody was wringing my cock out.

I sucked her nipples, and she leaned forward, and her pelvis tilted and slid along my shaft.

"Fuuu..." I whimpered.

I had never felt such a woman in my life. I had never known sex could feel like this.

"Oh, yes..." her voice was just a breath, but that breath scoured my soul, ripped me open and laid me bare. "Do you want to cum?"

Yet, I intuited that she was already cumming. I could feel little spasms happening deep within her cunt.

"Oh, yeah!"

"Then cum. Fill me up with your precious life. Fuck me. Take me. Squirt your big penis in me."

I began to jerk, my hips twisting and writhing, and I could feel my balls ignite, the fluid coming up the shaft.

"Fuck," I said. "Fuck."

I was gulping madly as my semen shot into her.

She ground down on me, writhed on me, took from me.

Joyously.

Like a real woman would.

"Fuck! Fuck!" I groaned, punctuating my pulsing cock, my shooting liquids.

She just held on, lost in the rapids of her own orgasm. Orgasms.

And, when it was all done, miraculously, I was able to do it again.

Of course. She was all woman. Of course.

PART TWO

I knew, immediately upon waking up, what had happened. I had become enraptured by Gwendolyn's XXX ambience, her pheromones, and had kissed her. Her lips had the lipstick on them. I had, inadvertently, applied her lipstick, the lipstick, to my own lips.

I knew upon waking because I could feel it.

Gwendolyn wasn't there. She had fucked me three times, I guess one of the benefits of screwing a triple X woman is that she keeps you overly horny. Horny enough to rise to the occasion three times.

So I woke up, and before I even opened my eyes I could feel changes happening in my body.

First, the hard on. If I thought I was horny the night before, it was nothing compared to now. Now I was a raging telephone pole of lust.

I wanted Gwendolyn. Or, for that matter, any woman. Or even a knothole in a tree. I was horny.

Second…why was I horny? Did men get horny when they changed into women? So when would these terrible lustful ravages stop? I mean, it was distracting!

I stood up, and my dick stood out.

I pulled on my underwear, and stopped when I found they wouldn't go comfortably over my penis. I put the underwear aside and was thankful that I hadn't worn tight pants. I pulled up my pants, took note of the obscene bulge in the front, then put on my shirt and jacket.

The room was unlocked and I simply stepped into the corridor and looked around.

Cement. A few doors here and there. Stairs at the far end of the hall.

I walked towards the stairs. I thought I would be able to find my way back to the Doc's office.

Up the stairs, down a corridor, and…lost.

This place was big, and I had been half drunk when Gwendolyn had taken me downstairs.

So, when in doubt, wander. I walked down hallways, opening doors and checking out the rooms.

Labs. Offices. Computer rooms. Storerooms. Classrooms. And so on. Everything the modern scientific institute needed to make synthetic Chromosome Transferrer.

I eventually found the lobby. Huh. There was the door. Could it be this simple?

I went to the door and pushed. Locked.

Frowning, I picked up a chair and threw it at the window. It bounced, nearly hit me on the rebound.

I went to the window, shaded my eyes and looked out.

Mountains. Wilderness. No snow storm. So the threat of a storm was just to keep me there.

I went behind the security desk and picked up a phone. A dial tone! Ah hah!

But I couldn't dial out.

I did, however, get a voice on the line.

"Section G."

"Hi. what's section G?"

"You silly. It's where I am! We make perfumes here. We used to isolate pheromones, but Doctor Wodopianov figured that out and now we make perfumes."

"Oh. I'm in the lobby. How do I get out of here."

I could feel the hush of thought on the other end. Funny how you can actually pick up emotions and other things on a phone line. "Are you...are you a man?" She spoke in a whisper.

"So far," I answered honestly.

"Just stay there. I'll come get you."

On one hand, I exulted. After a morning of wandering through empty corridors I was going to see a human being!

On the other hand, I worried. The way she had asked if I was 'a man,' was she...horny?

Still, nothing for it, I went to the waiting area and had a seat and waited.

I didn't have long to wait. A giggling, nervous woman came sliding around a corner. She was short, a brunette, and stacked. And naked. Her bubble cut flounced a bit, and her large breasts swayed a lot.

She straightened up to a walk, and she eyed me like I was a rabbit at a coyote convention. I could feel lust exuding from her.

"Hi, are you...who are you?"

"I'm Sam."

"And you're a man?"

"Last I looked."

She looked down at my crotch, her eyes grew wide and she giggled nervously. "And you've always been a man?"

"Would it matter?" I asked, curious.

"Not really," she breathed out. "But...I would like to think..."

"Well, I've always been a man. And...have you always been a woman?"

"Would it matter?" She was close to me and her eyes gleamed hungrily.

"Yes."

That stopped her. She was so horny that the idea that somebody wouldn't want sex, her sex, was odd.

"Oh." Then she brightened up. "I've always been a woman!"

"Excell—"

She was on me. Like a passel of coyotes on a rabbit. She flew through the air and landed against me, her arms locked around me. Her lips flattened against mine and her hips pressed against my obscenely bulging cock.

I found myself kissing back. I should have pushed her away, been the diligent FBI agent, but I couldn't. The lust in her soul ignited the lust in mine, and my dick wouldn't have it any other way.

Her mouth mashed against mine, her hands worked my belt, then she pulled it out of the loops and flung it away.

She grabbed my super erect cock and stroked it. She fell to her knees and gobbled me.

I moaned. I couldn't believe how good it all felt. I mean, sex is always good, but this sex, with super horny, super stacked women…it was enhanced. I mean, really enhanced.

I became the aggressor. I cupped her thighs and picked her up. I walked into her, my penis penetrating her, her mouth opening in a big O as she gasped with pleasure.

I walked, holding her onto me, until she hit the security counter, and then I pressed her ass on it and jammed hard.

My cock filled her all the way, and it never felt so big.

She grabbed me and held on. She groaned. "Oh, you're stretching me!"

I grinned and pulled back and rammed forward. Again and again. It was not subtle, it was not polite, it was a ravaging. It was lust unbridled. It was me taking what I wanted.

And her giving what she wanted.

"Oh…yes…yes…"

I tilted and twisted, and the big tip of my big dick rubbed against her inner walls.

I leaned my head down and took her nipple in my mouth. I pulled one nipple with one hand and sucked the other nipple with my mouth.

She was holding on, tight, and her hips ground into me and took as much cock as she could. And she could take a lot.

She reached down and squeezed my balls, and that did it. I began to spew. With a groan my balls unloaded and the semen surged through my shaft. I began painting her insides with my whiteness.

She whined, knew what was happening.

"Cum, you bitch," I commanded.

Maybe it was my polite language, or maybe it was my guttural growl, but she began to pop. Her inner muscles spasmed and gripped my cock, again and again.

She began crying. Tears actually streamed down her cheeks, and she humped and held on and cried.

I pumped my seed into her for a full thirty seconds. I mean, it was a lot, but eventually I emptied out. My dick sagged and went limp, and I pulled it out of her.

"Oh, God...God..." she whimpered.

I put her down, and she fell. Fortunately, I had placed her before one of the chairs in the waiting area, and she fell back and collapsed onto the chair.

"Fuck," she said. "You can really fuck."

"Excellent," I said. Now that I had cum my mind was already on to other things. "Can you tell me how to get out of here?"

"Out of here?" She was honestly confused. "Why would you want to leave?"

"I've got a job to do."

"Job? We all have jobs to do here."

"What's yours?"

"Well, I'm in charge of perfumes. But we're branching out into blush and concealer. So I'm doing some of that, too. Then, of course," she smiled proudly, "I make love to Doctor Wodopianov every Tuesday." She sighed. "I work hard. Maybe I can get promoted to two times a week. Wouldn't that be groovy?"

Groovy. Must have had a mother that was a hippy.

"Say," she brightened up. "Maybe I could do you a couple of times a week? I'm young, my pussy is tight...and I can do lots of things."

"What kinds of things?"

"Oh, I can give good head, and I swallow. I can also take it up the rear. Heck, I can do just about anything. I really want to be a good woman.

Her statement of abilities made me think.

Before lipstick she was probably plain Jane. Now she was hotter than hot.

If Doc was to be believed the lipstick did it all, unleashed the sexual monster within.

"Do you...do you put on the special lipstick every day?"

"Oh, no. I'm all changed."

"Do you want to?"

"Not really. Doc says a person will lose the desire for lipstick once he or she has completely changed."

"So how many men work here...and are they all women now?"

For the next half hour we talked. We had sated our desires, and I was able to get a lot of questions answered.

Half the work force had been men, but they had all changed. Now everybody was a woman. Except for the Doc.

"So when do I change all the way?"

"I don't know. Everybody is different."

"If I take more lipstick...does that change me faster."

"I think it does, but I don't know. Doc knows, though. He passes out the lipstick, and he keeps records of how much lipstick everybody gets, and other cosmetics, and what the effects are, and all that sort of thing.

Doc Wodo again. Hmm. Son of a bitch really had this placed figured out.

Or did he?

After all, I wasn't locked down, I was wandering around. Maybe there was something I could do...if I could stay free.

"Can you get me some lipstick?"

"Oh, no." But there was hesitation in her manner.

"What?"

"Maybe I could...like, kiss you when I get some on. would that work?"

"Yes."

It wasn't a bad idea, especially since my cock was starting to twitch. Apparently an orgasm, even a world shattering one like I had just had, was only good for a half hour or so.

And I wanted to see where this change was going to take me.

Believe me, I didn't want to be a woman, but the changes were happening, and...and something was compelling me.

I think underneath it all, I realized that change, the hormones being released, were compelling me, pulling me forward. Right then, on the surface, I just made justification and wanted to keep going.

In truth, I liked the horniness that possessed me. I liked my big dick being unleashed. I especially liked the way these women—I had only screwed two, but they seemed representative of the whole—wanted to latch on to me.

"What about other women."

Her eyebrows lowered slightly. "Are you going to be untrue to me?"

"Oh, honey," I smoothly stood up and took her in my arms. "There will never be anybody but you." Such a liar. Funny, I hadn't been a liar before, but this fire in my groin, it was making me do things. "But I need to complete the change. The more women I kiss the faster I'll change, and the happier we will be."

On the surface, and down in the depths, for that matter, it was not logical. But I was finding out a certain truth: women aren't logical. They are emotional. And I was in a such a position that I wanted to, had to, use that emotion for my own purposes.

So began my odyssey. I lived in the little room downstairs, and the women came to me. They brought me gifts. Little things to show their appreciation for my big cock.

They brought me food. Little viands they prepared specially for me. They brought themselves. Naked and wearing lingerie. And fully made up…with bright, red lipstick.

I gobbled their mouths. I hungrily kissed their lips. I smeared their lipstick onto my mouth. I absorbed that wonderful color into my soul, and I waited for the changes.

My cock, my wonderful cock, if anything, seemed to grow bigger, more stout, stronger.

And my semen came out in ever increasing floods.

But my chest remained flat. Relatively flat…I was gaining a little muscle. In fact, I think I had gained 10 pounds, and none of it flab, even though I wasn't getting any exercise.

The women came, horny and lusting.

The women went, satisfied and loose-legged.

When was the change going to occur?

I was starting to get desperate, and that's when Doc Wodo lowered the boom.

"Special Agent Samuel Burns."

I froze. I had been raiding a vending machine when the announcement had burped out form the loudspeaker system.

"Agent Burns. Please report to Doctor Wodopianov's office."

I didn't.

Several times during the day I heard the announcement, but I didn't want to see him. Instead, I hid in the laundry room. I curled up in the towels and sheets and white uniforms and took a nap.

Hmm. What did the bad doctor want with me?

I had been in the institute about a month.

I actually expected the FBI to send a team out to find out what had happened to me. But bureaucracies are notoriously slow, so…so what did the Doc want with me?

The next day. More announcements.

Then Gwendolyn found me.

"Here you are!"

She ran to me, snuggled into my arms, and we laid back in the sheets and uniforms and fucked madly. It was easily done because she wore no clothes, and I had given up wearing clothes, so I simply inserted and we bounced and, a while later, I spewed copious amounts of fluid into her.

"I've missed you so much!" she cried when we were done.

"What does the Doctor want with me?"

"I don't know."

"Can you find out?"

"I could ask, but then he'd know I knew where you were."

Hmm. I needed to know, but I didn't trust the doctor. He probably had a new perfume or something. I snorted. Weaponized perfume. How insidious.

"I think you're just going to have to go find out."

"Go see him," I stated without giving it much thought.

Yet, I was going to have to think about it.

"He's going to catch you, you know."

"Oh?" I looked at her.

"Yes. I heard he's forming a 'Catch Sam Corps."

"And how would he catch me?"

"He could threaten to withhold lipstick from the women until they found you."

Yeah. That would do it.

"Okay," I sighed. "Why don't you tell him I'll come to his office tomorrow morning."

"Okay," she sighed happily and snuggled into my arms. Her hand felt my dick. "Oh. It's soft."

"Another fifteen minutes. Then I can do you."

"Oh, goodie!" She snuggled further into me.

Eventually, after another tryst, she left, to go talk to Doc Leo, but she also talked to other women. All night long the ladies came to me. It was like they were sniffing me out, maybe it was me that was exuding pheromones, but they found me and they hugged me and they fucked me.

And what could I do? What's that old saying? 'Eat, drink and be merry, for tomorrow we die.' On the morrow I was going to beard the dragon in its den. I was going to see the man who had changed other men into women. Who had made regular women into super women.

Who knew what plans he had? What schemes he had concocted to...to what? Trap me? Ensnare me? Imprison me...to kill me?

And I didn't doubt that this was the case. What he had done... changing people's DNA, altering chromosomes...he was capable of anything.

At 10 in the morning I arose and kicked the women out.

They huddled together, some of them sniffling back tears, and stood in the hallway and waited.

I got dressed. First time in a month. Fortunately, my dick was limp, and would be for a half hour. I was temporarily drained and could wear pants without the obscene bulge.

I picked up my holster and put it on.

My gun.

Did I need it?

Would I need it to fight off whatever the nefarious doctor's plans were?

Whatever, I would be ready.

I stepped into the hallway and the women tried to hug me.

"No," I spoke firmly, loudly, and they contented themselves with touching me as I passed.

Over the month I had familiarized myself with the Institute, and I knew where Doc Leo's office was.

I walked down the corridors, climbed the stairs, and made my way to his office.

And stopped outside it.

The door was open, and I could swear I could hear him listening. Extending his perceptions and looking for me.

I stood, breathing deeply.

"Come on in," his voice didn't surprise me. For I could feel him.

I stepped into the doorway and looked into the office.

Same carpet. Same picture on the wall. Same conference table and 'frigerator and safe and everything.

Same doctor sitting behind his desk.

But, no. Something was different.

Sniffing the very air, suspicious, I entered the room.

Doctor Wodopianov watched me, a wry expression on his face.

No poison darts from the walls. No pit fill with poison dipped stakes. No vipers or pistols or other methods of cutting me down to size.

Just the doctor. And the look on his face, it was…wry. And rueful. And…satisfied.

"Agent Burns. How nice to see you. Though it seems you've been avoiding me."

"I don't trust you. Can you blame me?"

"Why don't you trust me?"

"Because of what you did, are doing, to everybody."

"So I do what I do. Why does that bother you?" He was actually curious.

"Because you never asked them. You just did it."

He nodded. "I understand, and you're right. But, in my defense, as I explained a month ago, I was compelled. The chemicals that changed people, they compelled me, altered my way of thought, made me do things I normally wouldn't have."

"That doesn't reassure me."

"No. I can see that." He sighed. Then: "that it would come to this…I never thought…"

I waited, but he said nothing more, then: "Would you like a drink?"

"The last time I had a drink with you I woke up a woman."

He looked startled, then he started to laugh. And laugh and laugh.

Put off by his belly laugh, I waited, a confused look on my face.

"You really don't know, do you?"

"Know what?" I asked.

"Know that…but, wait. It's obvious you don't understand, so let me explain it. Then maybe you can laugh with me."

"I doubt it."

"Then pour us some drinks. I'll take my Vodka on the rocks. And let us have a final chat before…before…" he started chuckling again.

Put upon, not having any real choice, I went to the frig and made drinks.

Me, bourbon and Coke. Him, vodka. I brought the glasses to his desk, placed his in front of him and looked at the chair waiting for me.

He laughed again, just a bark, and he said, "Come now. Sit. If I was going to trap you I would have chosen a better and more insidious method.

So I sat.

We stared at each other over the expanse of his desk.

He smiled. Rueful.

I waited.

"Do you know what happens when a Queen Bee dies?"

What the fuck? I looked mystified by this sudden non sequitur.

He smiled at the look on my face.

"The other bees select a fresh egg and feed it special jelly, a 'Royal Jelly,' and, voila, we have a new Queen.

"In this poor analogy I am building I suppose the Stepforth Valley cosmetics are the 'Royal Jelly.'

"At any rate, I missed one, little factor."

"What's that?" I asked. There was something in his attitude that was intriguing me.

"I thought," he said, "I thought I was immune. Maybe it was something as simple as age. Maybe I had superior genes. But I thought that, since I didn't change, that I was immune. That the 'Royal Jelly' didn't effect me like it did the others. But I was wrong. I just happened to be the first male to be effected by the cosmetics. I had been having an affair with my secretary, and she kissed me, and I developed into an XYY. More man.

"The other men…they came after, and there was no need for a 'King Bee,' perhaps I should say 'another' King Bee. So they became women.

"Or, perhaps I really did have good genes." He shrugged.

"Anyway, I was in charge, and I looked into synthesizing and making the world into a paradise for me, the most manly man around. Every one else a woman, designed to please me. Then you came along.

"I made sure Gwendolyn pleased you, and in the doing was able to apply the lipstick to you. I figured you would change into a woman, and I would have one more subject, and I would be closer to world domination."

"I don't…"

GRACE MANSFIELD & ALYCE THORNDYKE

He talked over me. "But you didn't change. At least, not into a woman."

"But what…"

"Instead, you were more manly than me. Even though I was XYY, you were more manly. Maybe my age, maybe something else, but you didn't change into what I wanted, you changed into what the 'hive'—I guess I can call our little enclave here a hive—wanted.

I still—"

"You are YYY."

I was silent.

Your dick is bigger. You can please more women than I can. Go on, look at yourself. Pull out your dick and let's measure up."

I sat, frozen. I couldn't figure out what this trap was.

He stood up and pulled down his pants, and took off his shirt, and I had my proof. His dick was shrunken. Limp. Useless. On his chest he had saggy tits. Old tits.

We stared at each other.

"So, my friend, who backfired on me. I am about to abdicate, to leave my desk, to turn it over to you. Before I do, however, before I do what my chromosomes are demanding, I want to tell you certain things."

He sat down and began speaking, and I listened. And, at the end, he stood up and walked out of his office.

I stood up, walked around the desk, and took his seat.

I was the 'King Bee.' I had the dick. I had the eternal lust. I would fill my women with seed and propogate the race, a new race.

Was this what Stepforth Valley had planned?

I thought not.

I thought that when Doctor Leonid Wodopianov had synthesized the ingredients of Stepforth Valley's 'Royal Jelly' he had made a mistake. He had deviated from a plan where certain men became women, and others didn't. And the new plan, according to the Alaska Scientific Studies Institute, was that only one man would be superior. And all the women would bend knee to him. And even the men would change into women and bend knee to him.

And I wondered what the original plan of Stepforth Valley was, and how this bizarre aberration would effect it.

Well, no matter. Someday I would find out.

But, until then, I would do what Doc Leo had told me. I would implement his plan.

I would continue his research into the Royal Jelly, and I would keep the institute running and supplied.

And I would gather people to us and expand our sphere of influence. I would change more and more men into women, and I would enhance more and more women.

We would take over the world, and I would lead...until another came along. A bigger YYY. Or maybe a YYYY.

Until then I would lead, and the world would follow.

END

Sissy Ride: The Book!

A giant saga of feminization!
Check it out at…

https://gropperpress.wordpress.com

The Feminist Experiment

If every man was feminized…

PART ONE

My wife thinks women should be in charge.
Her first argument is that women are smarter than men. She touts statistics about more women graduating from college, running companies, and so on.
Her second argument, and I think this is sort of insidious, is that women are smarter because they are more beautiful, and being beautiful, they can get men to do what they want done.
Hmm. Unfortunately, I think she's right. I mean, look what she's done to me? Or, maybe you shouldn't. I don't really feel like fessing up right now, and we'll be getting to that soon enough.
Anyway, with those two arguments to bolster her life, she charges around, making men do what she wants, and using them and discarding them, and now...well, you know. She's got that bill coming to a vote in Congress that will...let me start at the beginning.

"Honey, I'm home!"
I entered the kitchen, looked around, no answer. But her car was in the driveway.
Then: "I'm in here. Come here!"
Come here? Uh oh. What have I done now?
I entered the computer room and found her scribbling in a journal, which journal, upon my entering, she snapped shut.
"Hi, hon," I kissed the top of her hair. I would rather have kissed her on the cheek, or the lips, or maybe even the pussy. But my wife isn't that kind of woman. She frowns on extraneous and useless contact. Even between consenting adults.
"Go get me a drink. We need to talk."
Huh. This looked like it was going to be one of 'those days.' Well, the best way to handle one of 'those days' was to go with the flow and get it over with.
I went into the kitchen, searched through the bourbon, and found a half used bottle of 'The Boss Hog.' I smiled. $500 a bottle, and something I only dreamed about before Melissa was elected to the state senate.
Now that she was in charge of things, and considered a mover and a shaker and on the fast track to the US senate, we drank good stuff.
Well, I did.
I poured some Caliber Canadian whiskey into a glass for her.

I know, I know. What kind of a husband drinks the good stuff and palms off $5.96 whiskey on his wife?

I do.

And why do I do?

Because my name is Jerry, and I wear a chastity tube.

Yeah, one of those nefarious devices that strangles the cock and leaves it always horny and dripping.

Not only that, but when my wife does want to make love she...well, let me save that one for you. But when I do tell you, you'll understand why I take these silly, little 'revenges.'

Anyway, I splashed some Coke into the glasses, made sure to remember which hand held the good stuff, and returned to Melissa's computer room.

She was intent on a spreadsheet on the computer and didn't look at me. She did, however, lift her glass and take a good slug. And left her beautiful red lipstick on the lip of the glass.

I should tell you now, that though my wife can be a bit, uh...bitchy? She is a gorgeous woman.

She has a svelte body with just enough round on the hips, and breasts that, if they were for sale in a meat market, would go for $100 an ounce, and be sold only in twenty pound packages.

I mean, they were big! And...sweet! And they had large nipples that looked like they were cold in the hottest weather.

Of course, these days it was pretty much only hearsay for me. She still liked to have them sucked, but not by me. For me they were just for tantalizing and teasing.

I sat down next to her. She had summoned me, and it was best to be ready, at her beck and call, for when she deigned to speak to me.

As I sat there, lusting after her red lips and big tits, I should probably tell you that it wasn't always that way.

I met her in college. We ran into each other at a few mixers, and she wasn't interested.

I was a happy sort of dude, moving from relationship to relationship, getting a rep for being a little kinky, so it was fine with me if I didn't fall into the train of a real queen.

But, junior year, that changed.

Junior year she approached me, told me we were going to be a couple, and to report to her dorm that night at 8.

I often wonder why I reported. But I don't wonder that much. I was known as a footstool. Women went out with me, and I liked to kiss them, fondle their breasts, lick their pussies, suck their toes, and generally please them. And I didn't always please myself.

There's a greater pleasure in denial than there is in the act of sex.

At least for me there was.

So, though I didn't have much interest in her, I was intrigued enough to show up at her dorm at 8. I had heard a few rumors, she was the 'ice queen,' men loved her…until they hated her. Hmm.

It's sort of a wonder that I didn't see how we were made for each other.

So I showed up, and she took my hand and led me up to her room. In her room she commanded me to strip.

The door wasn't locked. Her roommate could come in at any time. Any of her dorm mates might come in at any time.

I started to walk out.

"Stop."

And, for some reason, I did.

Well, it wasn't for some reason. It was because all my life I had been drawn to strong women.

My mother was strong, and pushed me around like a shopping cart.

My girlfriends found out I was compliant, and they used me.

Oh, I got sex, a lot of sex, but it wasn't sex that I was after. It was that delicious moment of submission, when I gave up my will and became a hopeless, fawning puppet.

I liked being a footstool.

She told me to take off my clothes, and I could feel myself melting, giving up resistance, melting to her power.

I took off my clothes.

"Kneel." She lifted her skirt and she wasn't wearing panties.

I knelt.

"Eat me."

I moved forward, and now I was immune to the world. I was fascinated by the juicy folds of her vagina. I was hypnotized by her hairless slit. I was mesmerized by the moistness of her pinkness.

I remember the world going away as I dove into her. She was like a swimming pool, and I was completely immersed, holding my breath for ages, drowning in pussy.

She held my head at first, then she relaxed her grip. I was like a chicken put to the white line. I wasn't going anywhere.

Her roommate came in.

"Hey, Melissa."

"Hey, Sharon. This is Jerry, he's my new boyfriend."

I barely heard them talking. My ears were pressed by squeezing thighs. My mouth was sucking the nectar of the Gods.

"Can I use him when you're done?"

"Only if you haven't washed your pussy for a week."

They giggled, and I inserted my tongue, fucked her with my tongue, and she groaned.

"Long tongue?" asked Sharon.

"The longest."

"Oh, goodie."

"Hey, can you tell the girls to come here for a minute?"

There was something in me that perked up then. I wanted to stand up, to be seen, but she held my head again, wouldn't let me out of her folds. She thrust her hips into my mouth and fucked my face.

In a couple of minutes a bevy of young college coeds were in the room. I think that was the moment I realized something of Melissa's nature.

She was a mover, a shaker, a driven personality, and she commanded others. She was that strong.

Did I have any clue as to how far she would go? Nah. Besides I wasn't interested in that sort of thing. I was only interested in the pussy put before me, and the advice of my dear mother. 'You can take what you want, but eat all you take.'

And there seemed to be no end to the depths of this delicious cunt I was being swallowed by.

"Girls?"

The college kids all paid attention.

"I'm keeping this one, so put the word out, 'hands off.'"

There were a few giggles a couple of chuckles, and one outright laugh, then the girls were gone and I was left, and I came.

It was too much for me. The utter submissiveness, being told I was being 'kept,' my trigger clicked, the sperm shot up my dick and shot all over one of her feet.

"Ew!" And she pushed me away. "Did I actually…you did! What a disgusting pig!"

Yet there was a curious satisfaction in her. She liked the fact that she could make me cum so easily. It solidified her control over me.

"Lick my foot. And make sure you get in between the toes."

I had no problem with that. I licked her sole and sucked her toes, and shortly I had another erection.

She pushed me away and laughed. "We're going a long way, you and I."

And she dismissed me.

Over the next few days, even if I had wanted to break away from Melissa, pussy on campus dried up. Girls still talked to me, but not much. And none would go out with me.

I was claimed property.

The interesting thing was that Melissa ignored me. She didn't ask me to come see her, didn't demand to be taken out. She had put out the word, and was quite happy to let nature take its course.

And the course, in this instance, was that I eventually went to her and asked to be released.

She laughed. Told me to get naked, and had me lick her to an orgasm. This time hers, and not mine.

In fact, my days of orgasm became few and far between.

I would pleasure her pussy, and even her friends', and then be sent away.

I was horny all-l-l the time. I was erect and dripping. I was desperate.

I jacked off.

And, I don't know how, she sensed it.

I was commanded into her presence, and given a chastity tube.

"If you're going to be so selfish as to waste your seed...then we must control you.

She made me put it on, and it made me even hornier.

And everybody on campus knew.

Guys laughed at me. Girls 'accidentally' bumped their hands against my crotch.

Somehow, I don't know how, I managed to graduate, and the day after I graduated, and Melissa graduated, she moved in and shaped me to her needs.

First, she had me get a job. A good paying job, and she took control of our finances.

Oh, she was generous enough with me, with my money. She gave me an allowance that enabled me to go to lunches with the fellows, and even go drink a little beer on an occasional night out.

But she kept the lion's share.

She didn't work. At least, not for wages. She volunteered for the Democratic party. She went out recruiting voters, she stamped mail outs, she went to meetings long into the night.

The first time she came home with cum on her breath I could tell right away.

I kissed her, and I knew. I could taste the slimy substance on her lips. Heck, it was like she used that cum for gloss, and she smiled when she kissed me.

"Honey?" I protested. I had tasted enough of my own cum to known what she had done.

"What?" So pleasant.

"What? You come home with sperm in your mouth and expect me to...to..."

"To what?" And then she sat me down. And I grew to understand that whenever she sat me down, whenever she said, 'Honey, we've got to talk,' that I was in for it.

She sat me down, then had me get back up and go get her a drink, and when I came back and sat down again she apprised me of the facts of life.

"Honey? Baby? In this job I have to do things to get ahead. An hour ago I was on my knees, sucking Senator Johnson's johnson. And if he had wanted a fuck, then I would have been obliged. It's just the nature of this business.

I started to get upset, she listened for a while, then she reached out and slapped my face. "How dare you try to stop me! Is that what good husbands are supposed to do? Stop their wives from succeeding? How selfish are you?"

I rubbed my cheek in shock. It was the first time she had ever struck me. Oh, she had twisted my nuts, and played with my dick with a ping pong paddle, and one time she had even take a whip, a real live whip, to my fanny. Yes, she was gentle, at least that first time. But now she had actually, physically struck me. It wasn't that it hurt, it was the idea. I was properly cowed.

"Now, if you want to continue in this marriage in good graces, you have to eat me to three orgasms."

That was the key. No matter how bad it got, when she offered me her pussy to eat, I was a gone goose. I simply couldn't resist the lure of her womanhood, the moist smell of her snatch, the heady aroma of her dripping vagina.

And it did drip. And it dripped more and more, the more and more she shaped me to her will.

So I got down on my knees, and I ate till my jaw was aching, but I eventually felt the satisfaction of bringing her to three, count 'em, three, orgasms.

And so went our life. I became accustomed to being a cuckold, and even to licking her lover's sperm deposits right out of her cave.

And slowly we worked our way up the Democratic chain, and she got elected, and, suddenly, I no longer had to work.

I was more useful as a houseboy, a treat for her guests, or just a laugh for her perversions.

And now I was sitting down in front of her again. Well, to the side, watching her lips move slightly, so red, so plump, so moist. Her breasts, were so big they lay on the edge of the desk as she touched keys on the keyboard. And my groin throbbing and pulsing. My dick pushed outward, almost painfully, against the cage. My balls were big and full, and bluer than the sky. My heart was pounding. To be this close, even denied, especially denied, it was hard to even take a rhythmic breath.

Finally, she leaned back, frowned, then spun towards me...and smiled.

Uh oh. She wasn't a smiling type of girl, unless she had something she REALLY wanted.

"Honey, I have ordered some herbs and pills. It is very important that you take these medicines."

"Medicines? But I'm not sick."

"Not to your own way of thought, but you have a hopeless case of male-itis."

"That's not a sickness!" I laughed.

She frowned, and I stopped laughing.

She tapped a thick sheaf of papers sitting on her desk. "This is a preliminary medical report. Compiled by the CDC. Do you wish to read it?"

Oh, God, no! I didn't want to spend a week reading dry, medical reports! Whip me, beat me, but don't make me read medical reports! I shook my head.

She continued on, "Females, women, like myself, have two X chromosomes. We are pure, unsullied. With double the Xs we are doubly pure."

I blinked.

"Males, men, like yourself, have a virus. The so called Y chromosome." She tapped the medical report. "This report proves that the Y chromosome isn't a chromosome at all. It is, as I said, a virus. An invader. Something to make a man impure, less than he should be. A man."

"Hey, wait..."

She frowned. I wasn't supposed to interrupt her. But to be told that my whole sexuality was a mistake, a...a disease...you can imagine my confusion.

Then she did something that she almost NEVER does. She leaned forward and took my caged cock in her hands.

"Ohhh!" I groaned as she rolled the cage in her hands, gently twisted it, put her fingernail through an opening and tickled my slit.

I shivered. I felt like I was going to blow up and go to heaven.

And I should have realized that she was pulling out ALL the stops.

She said, "So I want you to take these herbs, these medicines, and we will cure you of your malady."

"But...but..." it had been so long since I had felt her hands, and I was becoming dreadfully confused.

Then she unbuttoned her blouse, and she wasn't wearing a bra. She pulled my head to her tit.

I licked the nipples and she groaned. I couldn't even remember the last time she had let me touch her breasts, and I was instantly transported to heaven. I sucked her nipples, and I actually put a hand up and felt her tits.

Oh. My. God! Such ambrosia, and my dick actually started to throb in its cage.

She stopped moving her hand on my cage. "If you do this for me, if you allow me to cure you, I will let you squirt. Only a few drops, but it will be a real squirt."

Way back in my befuddled head I realized something: for the first time in our lives I had an edge. If she wanted something this bad…I said: "I want to put my dick in you."

Her breath caught, and for a moment I felt a rage, and wondered if she was going to punch me, or even take a whip to me.

But she really wanted what she wanted, and she forced herself to be calm, and she said, "If that's what you want. Instead of just squirting, you get to put your penis in my vagina and…and have an orgasm."

"Oh…oh…" I was beside myself. To be given hope, to be given a chance to be in my wife's pussy, the greatest pussy in the world, it was too much. My dick began to drool. I didn't cum, but I was close, and my wife, instead of going 'EW!' and pushing me away, continued to milk me, to let my juices run out of me. Not an orgasm, but a milking, of which I had received a few over our lives together.

And she said, "Is it a deal?"

"Yes,"I blurted, unable to control myself any longer.

She let go of my dick then. It continued to drool and drip, but not as much, and the emission began to slow down, and then stop.

The following day we began getting small boxes. Some of these boxes were from Amazon, some were from pharmaceutical companies. I opened them up and took out a variety of herbs, and pills. I put them all in a special drawer in the kitchen, and that night Melissa gave me instructions.

To be honest, I was stupid. Of course, I was horny, so horny I couldn't think straight. All I could think of was at last being able to put my dick in my wife's love canal, to wiggle it around, and to shoot.

Heck, wasn't that what had been driving me all these years? Wasn't that the dream behind the licking of her pussy and the locking of my cock?

I thought so, so I followed the instructions and did my wife's bidding.

'Instructions for inducing galactorrhea'

(Whatever the heck galactorrhea was?)

Take 2 capsules of Metoclopramide with each meal.
Take 1 capsule of Domperidone each night before bed.
Take 2 capsules of sulpiride, breakfast and dinner.

And so on. I had a dozen pills to take, including Eglonyl, Dolmatil, Sulpitil, Sulparex and Equemote. the remaining pills came in bottles with hand printed labels.

Hand printed. And these were from pharmaceutical companies. Later I would figure out that Melissa had connections, and had had these pills custom made for me.

Or, rather that the companies were prescribing for me, and I was a guinea pig. I was the first human trial. If these drugs worked for me, they would work for the world.

And the instructions made mention of something called prolactin, whatever the heck that was.

So I began taking my pills. Every day. Every meal, as prescribed, throughout the day.

But that was only the start. Three times a day, before every meal, I had to make a herbal smoothie and drink it. All of it.

But, dreams of a real, live, wife induced orgasm, I did it.

Ingredients for increased libido

(Libido? Yeah! I wanted to be horny for when I finally inserted Mr. Penis into Miss Vagina. Ooooh, baby!

Anise Seed to aid digestion, dispel gas, stop nausea. Works well with raspberry leaves.

Borage Leaves (Borago officinalis)

Fennel Seed (Foeniculum vulgare) to reduce gas, stimulate blood blood.

Fenugreek (Trigonella foenumgraecum) as a digestive aid.

Goat's Rue (Galega officinalis) as a galactogue. (Another one of those stupid words I had no clue as to the meaning of)

Hops (Humulus lupulus) to promote relaxation and sleep. (Well, yeah! The better the hops the better the beer, right?)

Milk Thistle (Silybum marianum) is a poerful antioxidant. Good for the liver.

Nettle Leaf for easily digestible iron, calcium, vitamin K, and folic acid.

Red Raspberry Leaves (Rubus idaeus). Very nutritious.

Shatavari (Asparagus racemosa). An aruyvedic herb excellent for the reproductive system. And excellent for me. I wanted a good reproductive system. Hello, Mr. Dick!)

And that was it. Put it together with some almond milk, throw in a few things like bananas papayas, apricots, and so on, and the mess was palatable. In fact, two bananas and it was even tasty.

And, if all that wasn't bad enough, Melissa demanded that I change my eating habits.

Now, normally, I did the cooking. Many times Melissa was out for the night, and I was free to have a steak, drink a little bourbon, watch a little MMA, all things that Melissa frowned upon.

Now, however, she began to watch over what foods I cooked, and especially what I ate.

Oh, I smelled steak on her sometimes when she came home from a dinner meeting.

But I was doomed to such things as oatmeal and barley and berries and peaches and tofu and cruciferous vegetables.

Almost a vegetarian, and I began to crave meat. Protein. Caveman fare. Grrr!

But I was afraid Melissa would find out, and that I would not get my actually penis in a vagina cum.

So I made myself adhere to the pills and herbs and foods. And over the coming months I lost some weight. And, if that wasn't bad enough, I gained some bad weight. My hips grew rounder, my muscles grew slack, and...and one day I noticed something.

"Honey? Can you come here?"

I was in the bathroom. I had just taken a shower and noticed that my pecs were swollen. They were even tender.

"You come here," she yelled back. She was in the computer room and refused to be summoned by me.

I walked into the computer room, soft and flabby and my dick encased.

"What?" She was engrossed in a report about voting habits of single mothers.

"This?"

Irritated, she turned around, and then she wasn't irritated. She was fascinated.

"Oh, my." She leaned towards my chest and inspected my little mounds of fat.

Little mounds, just the size of round sponges. Very soft to the touch. And the nipples actually looked a little bigger.

But that was ridiculous. Nipples growing? That couldn't happen.

She touched one nipple with a fingernail, and it gave a tiny, little shock.

"Oh!" I exclaimed.

"Did that hurt?"

"Well, no. It just surprised me. It's very sensitive."

She nodded, and she seemed extremely happy. "Well," she said, "I don't know what you've been doing...but it looks like you're growing breasts."

"What?" My voice actually came out a little shrill. Growing tits? Me? I was a man!

"Here, let me taste. That will tell me." She leaned forward and, for the first time in our marriage, she put lips to my tips. And, ohhh, it made my knees weak. My legs began shivering.

She backed away, a smile on her face, a gleam in her eyes. "Yep. Tits. Real, live tits." She looked up at me. "What have you been eating behind my back?"

"Nothing! I swear!" And, funny, I suddenly felt close to tears. I felt all emotional.

Melissa saw this and stood up and took me in her arms. "There, there. It's all right."

"Okay," it felt so good to be held by her, to feel her flesh, to feel her actual and incredible breasts pressed against me.

She sat down, leaned back, and contemplated.

"What should I do?" I asked.

"Well, I would say keep taking those vitamins and herbs and things. They're good for you. And I can talk to some people, but..."

"But what?"

"But you're going to need some support."

"Support?"

"A training bra."

"What? I'm not going to wear a bra!"

"Well, maybe it is a bit premature, but if they get bigger, then you don't want a pair of big old saggers on your chest, do you?"

"No!"

"Then think about it, we'll keep an eye on them, and if you need to you need to." And that was it. She had laid down the law.

In the following days I began exercising. A lot. I did sit ups and push ups. I signed up for a gym, and I ran a lot.

But exercising a lot made me hungrier, so I began eating more. I began drinking two of the smoothies at each meal. And ran harder. All of which did nothing. I lost more and more muscle, got skinnier and skinnier, and the bumps on my chest grew larger.

"Honey?"

"What?" She was watching a documentary on the Republican party and didn't want to be interrupted.

But it had been a month since our last talk, and my breasts were not shrinking. In fact, they were twice the size. They were actually golf ball sized, maybe an A cup, though I'm not too sure about bra sizes.

"Look!"

She turned, and instantly lost her irritation. She smiled. "Oh, those look lovely. Come here."

I knelt in front of her and she examined my tits. She felt the nipples, and it was good that I was kneeling. I would have fallen for the weakness in my legs.

She palpated the breasts, move her hands, and the motion became sexual.

"Here, get closer."

I moved closer and raised up a little, and she sucked on my nipples.

Oh, it was heavenly. Her soft tongue drew out feelings of immense warmth and pleasure.

I almost lost my balance and placed my arms over her shoulders. I had never touched her like this, but now she didn't mind. She just bent her head closer, smashed her face against my breasts and loved them.

I was becoming light headed, couldn't breath, and then she pushed me away.

"Well," she said, showing a bit of satisfaction. "I guess you're going to have to wear a bra after all."

The following day Amazon delivered several bras. A couple were thick, designed to hold serious weight. I didn't think I would need those.

A couple of them were just plain old bras, nothing fancy. And a couple of them were...fancy. Frills and flowers embroidered into them. Colorful and sexy, designed to show the nipple over the top lip.

I didn't like the look or feel of the more utilitarian bras, so I slipped into one of the fancy ones.

Wow! I looked good. Well, they looked good.

And my body had shrunk a bit and reshaped, and I could see a potential for curves.

The potential was more plain to see when I opened a last box and took out...a corset.

What?

What the fu...?

I looked at it, then, feeling a bit naughty, nobody was home, I stepped into it and pulled it up.

Whoa! Now I had a true hourglass shape! And my boobs were pushed up and made to appear even larger.

I left it on and pranced around the house. I was a man, but I had a body that looked almost feminine. It was sexy. It was cool. And, I have to admit, it was horny.

Heck, Melissa hadn't milked me in months. And I was getting weird feelings and feeling emotional, and this feeling, this sexy feeling of having boobs, and butt, and looking a little feminine, it was getting to me.

Melissa came home that night, and she had big news.

I did, too. I was wearing the corset under my regular clothes. I was wearing a jacket to disguise the bigger boobs.

"What?" she asked, seeing the twinkle in my eyes.

"Nothing. You tell me first."

So she did. "I'm running for the US Senate."

"Wow!" That was big. Real big. It was what she had been shooting for.

"The only catch…I have to prove myself."

"Prove yourself? Haven't you done enough?"

"I've got a bill, I've been working on it for months. It has to do with chromosomes and making a purer race, eliminating viruses."

"Wow, that's a lot."

"It is, but if I can pass this bill, then I can get elected to the senate, and they will give me unlimited aid in getting it passed on a wider scale. A national scale.

"That's fantastic!" I was truly happy for her.

"So, chop chop, get out the bourbon and let's celebrate!"

Usually she just asked for a drink for herself, and I was left to fend. That she would invite me to drink with her showed just how important all this was.

I went to the kitchen and poured a couple of drinks. Boss Hog for me, Caliber for her. I brought them back and handed her one.

"So, what's the big news you have?"

Grinning, I placed my drink on the table, then took off my shirt.

"Whoa! Wow! You're kidding!"

She walked around me, sipping her drink, and eyeing my enhanced form.

She touched my tightly bound waist. She ran a hand over my bigger tits. Then she did something absolutely unexpected.

She came closer, moved her face closer to mine.

I was almost afraid. To have her face, those beautiful lips so close, I almost fainted.

But she stopped me by circling one arm around my waist. Then she actually kissed me! She pressed those gorgeous lips against mine, and she ground them against mine.

I grew weak, and she suddenly had to hold me up, yet she didn't stop kissing me.

I thought I had died and gone to heaven and God was kissing me.

Then she moved her head away and said those words I dreaded to hear.

"Honey, we've got to have a talk."

PART TWO

She poured us a couple of more drinks. She poured for us. Shock. It was always me pouring for us.

And she poured me the good stuff, not the Caliber Canadian. She poured the stuff she usually reserved for herself, the Boss Hog.

She tasted hers and said, "Hmm, doesn't taste as good." then she forgot about it and led me, by the dick, actually placing her hand on my cage, and we weren't even milking me, into her computer room.

We sat, and we sipped, and she contemplated me. She had a sleepy smile of satisfaction on her face.

"What?" I finally asked?

She didn't get irritated by my question. She simply said: "Do you remember the medical report I showed you? The one about the Xs and the Ys and how Y chromosomes weren't really chromosomes? They were viruses?"

"Yeah."

"Well, the big project I have been working on these last few months, it has to do with that.

I was puzzled. She explained.

"What if we could get rid of that virus?"

"The Y chromosome?"

"Yes. The fake chromosome. What if we could…delete it. Get rid of it. Return men to a more pure state."

"I don't see what that would do."

She sighed. She knew I was being obtuse, but she controlled herself. "Honey, what if we could get rid of the Y chromosome in you?"

"Get rid of my maleness? Make me stop being a man?" Light dawned on me. I wasn't happy nor sad by this epiphany, just stunned.

"Wouldn't you like to learn the truth of who you really are?"

"But…I'm me! I've always been me!"

"You've always been who you thought you were."

"But…I don't understand."

And I didn't. I was befuddled. On one hand I understood what she was saying, on the other, the consequences were too far reaching for me to grasp.

"Honey? Jerry? I've been working with the pharmaceutical companies on this. And what you've been going through these last couple of months, growing breasts, it's all coming together."

"How? What do you mean?"

"First off, we have to simulate the female body. We have to

rearrange fat, reshape the face, give you...boobs. We've done all that. Now it's time for the big step."

"What big step."

She turned and reached into a desk drawer and pulled out a little vial. She opened the vial and poured a single, small pill into the palm of her hand.

I stared at it.

She smiled at me. It was an innocuous smile, designed not to alarm, but rather to calm.

"What's that?"

"This is the pill that will erase the Y chromosome from your body."

"It will?" It was small, pink, round. Looked like baby aspirin.

"You already have sufficiently high levels of estrogen. You've been taking medicines and herbs that support a woman's structure. You're even been eating like a woman. Now it's time to go whole hog."

"But I...what if I..."

"Shhh, honey. Listen." She leaned close to me. We were inches apart. Her red lips were close enough to kiss, certainly close enough to enthrall. "If you take this everything will resolve. Your body will become pure, your mind will work differently. You will be superior, like a woman. You will be stronger per ounce, smarter per cranial capacity...it is the dream to end all dreams."

Several things went through my head. Whose dreams? Hers. But... look at me...I was changing. I had tits. I had the body of a woman. I couldn't deny it. And I knew that even if that body was shaped by her, through meds and herbs and foods, it was still my choice.

Was there something in me that wanted more?

Did I want to stop being a footstool? A second class citizen?

Did I want to be the ruling species...a woman?

I did, and my heart started to pound. But there was one thing I needed to do before I took that pill.

"I'm horny."

"Good. You'll be able to get all you want after you take this pill."

"But I want something before this pill."

She stared at me, and she knew. I could see the distaste in her eyes, but I could also see the hunger.

Here I was, the last stumbling block on her road to control, to being the senator who changed mankind, rescued it, made it into womankind.

"You don't—"

"Yes."

"But, I—"

"Tit for tat. You give me what I want, and I'll take all the pills you want.

"But...but..."

45

I stayed silent. For once…I was going to win. I was going to get my way.

Abruptly, she stood up and took my hand and led me to the bedroom.

I followed her, my mind in a daze, my dreams coming to fruition.

We entered the bedroom and she began taking off her clothes.

I had seen her body before, many times, but I had never felt it, touched it, like a man was supposed to touch a woman.

She, on the other hand was practiced. She had not only fucked any person on her ladder to success, but she had fucked me…with her fingers, with a dildo, milking me and relieving me of my less than desirable male attitudes.

"Get undressed," she snapped. I could feel her anger.

"Not like this."

"What?"

"Pretend you like it."

"Pretend I…I always pretend. I shouldn't have to pretend with my own husband."

Ah, what a twisted web. I folded my arms.

"Damn," she cursed, then she flipped. She turned her mean, irritation into calm and soothing, gentle and wanting. She pretended so well I instantly believed her.

"Come on, honey. Let's get those pants off." She unzipped me, unbuckled me, and pulled them down.

She was on eye level with my dick.

My dick, that I hadn't seen outside of my cage for years.

She took the little gold key off the chain around her neck. She inserted it into the lock and turned. the lock sprung open and she pulled it out of the device.

My cock fell out, and I looked at it in dismay. "It's smaller!"

"Oh, honey, it's a giant. It's going to fill me up!"

Yet the years of being caged, and especially all the estrogen pumped into my body, it was only a few inches long. Once it had been eight inches. Now it was four.

"Can I get it in you? Is it big enough to get in you?"

"Of course it is! I've had a lot smaller. Most guys are smaller than you. You're a giant."

Now she had all my clothes off, and she was working on the remainder of hers. She slipped out of her nylons, took off her garter belt, and then…those enormous, wonderful, sensational breasts were let loose.

She tossed the bra aside and I was left staring, speechless, at the grown up version of what I had. "Can I kiss them?"

"Oh, honey. They're all yours. You can do whatever you want to them."

I rushed to her and sucked and felt, and felt as if I had been enveloped by nirvana. And my dick grew. A sturdy…four inches. Hard as hot dog, bendable, would I be able to thrust it into her?

She fell to her knees and sucked me. Oh, God! That sexy mouth nibbling at my balls, swallowing my dick. I was in immediately danger of coming.

"No!" I gasped.

Thwarted, she gave no sign of displeasure. She rose to her feet and kissed me, and held my balls with one hand and played with them, and stroked my cock with the other.

For a long minute we just played with each other, loving, her probably bored out of her mind, me marveling at sensations I hadn't felt for a decade, not since college.

And I suddenly knew how much I had missed.

Yes, I loved the thrill of being chaste, the sweet torture of being nothing more than a servant, a footstool, a thing to be milked periodically and then most efficiently.

But I missed my dick. And I missed fucking. And I began to remember what I had given up.

In my quest for submission, I had…over submitted.

But, now was now, and now was my chance.

I pushed her back against the bed. She fell on her back, and frowned. I knew what the problem was. She wanted to be on top.

"I'm on top," I stated.

I crawled between her magnificent legs and licked her juices, sucked her clitoris, and then I moved higher, and I loved her breasts, and then I was ready. My tiny dick was as big as it would get, as hard as it would get, and it was poised at the door to her feminine mystique.

I pushed, and my dick bent.

I used my hand, and it sort of squiggled away from the ultimate destination.

She used her hand, and because she was more familiar with her anatomy than I was, she inserted me.

I froze, and my mind was stilled, and I felt myself in her. The warmth of her. The way her walls clung to my dick.

I was small, four inches, but that left at least a couple of inches truly penetrating.

I stared into her eyes, watched her face. She was blinking, and her mouth was open in an O. And her eyes were stark, staring, fixated on me.

And a thousand miles away. In the land where orgasms come from.

"Okay?" I asked.

"Oh, yes," and it was plain she was having a hard time breathing. "I always liked the big ones, I never tried the small ones, but this…this… I've never felt anything that…demanded so much of me."

"Can I move?"

For answer she ground her hips up, pressed hard against me, and…I squirted.

A couple of seconds of white hot pleasure, then I was done. My little balls, small as raisins, had emptied out. My dick instantly turned into a half sized worm and slid out.

"No! No!" she yelled, and she hugged me, and ground into me, but it was useless. It was over. And she finally just lay there and sobbed.

I got up and got dressed.

I had had sex. Real sex. With my wife. My mind was stunned, and overwhelmed. And underwhelmed. I had been too small. I had left her wanting. I was inadequate.

I went into the computer room, picked up the pink pill, and swallowed it. No more did I want to fuck her. I had not the tool, and I had not the desire. With my inadequate few droplets I had exhausted myself. Nothing of me left.

And the man in me? The Y chromosome? It was done. I was done. so there really was nothing left but the pill.

The next few weeks were interesting, to say the least.

On one hand, my wife was more solicitous to me. She kept asking me how I felt. She stopped going out on dinner dates and coming home smelling of other men's cum. And she kept looking at me. Looks filled with desire. And I knew she wanted me to lay down with her again. My penis had proved inadequate, but she probably felt that if she tried, then maybe…maybe…

On the other hand, I was imbued with a new energy.

I didn't feel like being a footstool. I let some chores go, and my wife actually took over in that department. I figured she was just keeping me happy while my body lost that dreadful Y chromosome.

Whatever, we began to take on a more happy existence. She was home more, starting to cook, and smiling a lot. When she wasn't pondering me and wondering whether she could get my dick into bed.

And we began to play with my budding new sexuality.

She bought me a carload of sexy underthings. Corsets and garters, nylons and bras. Everything.

And she bought me clothes. Dresses from expensive and exclusive shops. Skirts and blouses. Scarves and hats and everything that I had seen on a woman, but had never imagined myself as wearing.

And shoes. Oh, God! High heels! Boots that went up to the thigh, sandals, Mary Janes. And…more high heels.

My body changed, and my dick shrunk even more. My balls drew up, and sometimes it felt like I could feel things inside my groin. Weird things, the shifting of things male into things female. Testicles becoming ovaries. And the dick getting smaller, actually starting to invert. The slit widening and sinking in and...becoming a pussy?

And now Melissa looked truly discouraged. As my dick shrank into virtual non-existence, whatever plans she had for taking me to bed disappeared.

I began to be happy. There was something in her that was starting to be sad.

She signed me up for a class in make up. I learned about blush and foundation, eyeshadow and lips. I learned how to do my own nails, and I kept them long and red and sharp. I felt like a predator. I had never felt like that as a man, but now...now I felt like a shark, and people were... hors d'oeuvres.

I will always remember the day I was announced to the public.

The man who would be woman. The man who WAS a woman.

My dick had turned into a vagina, I had tits bigger than my wife's. And I dressed classy and wore make up like I had been wearing it all my life.

We announced me in San Francisco. We figured that the trans community would offer the most support, and we were right.

Person after person came up to me, hugged me, and wistfully asked what they could do to look like me.

"Vote for my wife," I suggested.

From San Francisco to Los Angeles. Another huge community that fell in love with me, promised to back me up. And the polls were looking good.

And I found that men were attracted to me. They sought out my company. While my wife was speaking on the podium, I would be talking to an endless line of men. Men who wanted to touch me, see me, hug me. And feel my breasts. And kiss me.

But I didn't want to be hugged and kissed. I wanted to be a predator. I wanted to be like my wife, strong and powerful, a mover and a shaker, changing the world.

My days of being a footstool were over.

The public was confused by the idea of a Y Chromosome being excess, and not needed. While the gays and trans and all those people embraced the idea, an explanation for whatever condition they might consider themselves in, the straights held on to their X and Y notion. Arguments burst out in forums, TV talking heads blurted ill conceived ideas at all hours of the day.

I didn't care about all that. I was in love with the new me.

I was no longer a weak male, hoping to impress a strong female.

Now I was a strong female, and males, with their pre-occupation with sex, were the weaker of the species.

Poor, Y diseased males.

Melissa was nominated for the US Senate.

Oh, we celebrated. We drank champagne. We danced. We partied. And something bad happened. Bad in Melissas eyes. Good in mine.

She was speaking, enthralling the crowd with her tales of a female led Utopia. Of males that were finally cured of being male.

I was behind her, standing in the wings, loving all the power oozing through the auditorium.

"Pardon me."

"Yes?" I turned to find a short man with a bushy mustache and a round face.

"My name is Oscar Brown. I represent Hegemony Software."

I had heard Melissa speak of this company. They were in charge of election software, and it was said that if you hired Hegemony…you got elected.

Well, of course. He who controls the computers controls the votes.

"How lovely to meet you, Mr. Brown."

"Please, Oscar."

"Oscar then. Did you come to hear Melissa speak?"

A far away came into his eyes. He nodded. "Yes. She seems to be a little busy."

"Well, what can I do? Is there some message that I can relay to her?"

He smiled wanly. "No…no. I just…no."

I linked my arm into his and walked him deeper into the wings, back where there were no people, where sound wouldn't drift to the stage.

The truth was, I knew what Oscar Brown wanted. He wanted a little love. Or, maybe a lot of love. I had overheard people talking, I had even heard Melissa, on the phone once, describe what she had had to give this man to get elected to the state senate.

Money…and something else.

And it was obvious, seeing the glint in his eyes, seeing the bulge in his pants, what he was here for.

"What do you want, Oscar?" I asked. "Melissa and I talk over everything. I know what she knows. So tell me what you want."

He stared at me then. "I think you know what I want."

I touched his pants then. I felt his cock, hard and throbbing.

I had never touched a man's cock before. But I had dreamt of it.

Oh, I wasn't a pervert, or anything like that, I was just emptied of the Y chromosome. I didn't have male inhibitions or impulses running my life. I was free to be me, and I was a woman.

"Perhaps I could stand in for Melissa."

His eyes were calculating. I had an allure to him. I was the first man to become a pure woman. Which meant that I was a virgin. Which made him drool and salivate all the harder.

"Perhaps you could."

I unzipped his trouser and pulled out the snake. It wasn't a bad size. I say that now, after having done a lot of fucking, and finding out that most politicians are usually pretty darned under-sized.

So he was adequate, and I stroked him. And I reached into his pants and fondled his testicles.

He gasped, and he moved forward.

He was shorter than me, but that was fine. I was the alpha dog here, no matter what he thought, and I took him in my arms and turned so that he bent back, and I kissed him.

On one hand, yuck. Mustaches. I made a note to avoid mustaches from here on out.

On the other hand, I could taste him. Women have better sensory apparatuses than men. They can define smells and colors and sounds better.

I could taste the odor of him. I could smell everything about him, from when he had last washed his clothes to what he had eaten for dinner last night. It was a delicious odor, and I marveled that Melissa had seemed not to like it.

What was not to like? He tasted like a man, like a Y chromosome, and I devoured that scent hungrily.

He grabbed my boobs. He wasn't a polished man, but that was okay. Hamburger can be every bit as delicious as steak.

But I wondered if he would ever take the pill himself.

"Oscar?"

"Mmmm," he was on his knees now. My dress was up and I was wearing no panties, so you can guess what he was nibbling.

"Would you ever consider taking the pill?"

He smiled up at me, and told me something that shocked me.

"What lose my Y chromosome? Not on your life."

"Why not?"

"Do you actually believe all that hooey about the Y chromosome being a bizarre mutation, a virus, a disease?"

"Well, I never actually thought about it."

"Hegemony represents the pharmaceutical companies. We know the truth.

"And the truth is?"

"The Y chromosome is entirely natural It is valid, and it makes men men."

"But why is it being touted as a disease?"

He shrugged, wanted to go back to eating me out.

I leaned down and grabbed his dick and lifted him to his feet.

"Yikes!" he yelped.

I leaned into his face. I said the one thing that women have said from time immemorial and which enables them to rule the world. "If you want to get off you're going to have to tell me why."

"Okay! Okay!" Then: "Money. If we make men into women that doubles the value of stock in cosmetics, in female clothes, in everything that a woman buys. More soap. More douche. More baby products."

"More baby products? Can I get pregnant?" I had never thought of such a thing.

He shrugged. "Don't know. Doesn't matter. When we have a war we sell more baby products. People make more babies. With so many men turning into women it will almost be like a war. There will be more people who make babies. That's just the way the human race rolls. Now, about my dick."

I was blasted. I had trouble thinking. Yet it all made so much sense.

I asked, "But what if too many men change into women? What'll happen then?"

He shrugged his shoulders. "We'll release the pill that makes women into men."

I was double blasted All capability for thought had left me.

He said, "Now, about my dick?"

So I stroked him, and decided to leave off fucking him and wait for somebody I really respected. As for him, when he started to cum I punched him in the face. And I had enough male musculature left, and he was such a wimpy asshole, I knocked him out and down.

He lay there in the gloom, his pecked stiff and rigid and squirting, even though he was unconscious.

I went back to the curtains where I had been standing before. I watched as Melissa ended her speech.

"When all men are women, then we will be finally be a truly equal society. Women will be free from the bizarre predations of men. No more rape, crime will become a thing of the past, and we will finally get along, like a true family should. Thank you."

Cheers followed her off stage. She came to me and hugged me, and she stepped back, held me at arms length, and examined me. Her eyes were shocked, and I knew what her superior sense of smell could detect.

I had a bit of cum on my hands from Oscar. It was pungent and aromatic, and a smell that she wasn't fond of.

I liked it. But then I had been a man, and I had fond memories of pleasant orgasms topped off with a heaping helping of sperm.

She didn't.

She associated sperm with being forced to do something with somebody who smelled bad.

My opinion? Tough luck, sister. Or wife. It was a changing world.

We went home, got undressed, and had a fight. Funny, I would have thought she would initiate a fight while she was dressed. Then, on later reflection, I realized that that was the way she worked. That was the way she had done me when I was a man. Get undressed, and while my lower head was doing all the thinking, have her way with me.

"How could you do that with somebody like Oscar Brown?" She snapped.

"You did. Why can't I?"

"That's different."

And I finally blew my top and laid down the law. "It is not different, furthermore, how dare you stand in my way."

"Your way?"

"My way. My way happens to be helping you achieve your goals. And if I have to suck a dick, or fuck some asshole, then so be it. And don't you ever try to ruin my life with your cheap, male standards."

"Male standards?" She was made dizzy trying to understand what I was saying. And it wasn't helping that I had stepped forward and grabbed her pussy. In fact, while I railed at her my hand grabbed her whole mons. My middle finger was in her hole, just the tip, but that was enough, and my hand squeezed her pudendum viciously.

She grew weak at the knees, grasped my wrist with her hands, but it was no use. I had her in my power.

"Please...please..." she gasped.

"Please Please what?"

But I was grinning. My finger was slowly sinking deeper as I squeezed harder. I was up to the second knuckle, and I manage to wiggle it a bit.

"Oh..."

Then I kissed her. I held her pud like a bowling ball and I mashed my lips into her. I kissed her ruthlessly, savagely, and I took her senses away from her.

She groaned, and I grabbed her tits. I dug my nails into them, and her knees gave out. She collapsed, and I went with her. She lay on the floor, gasping for breath, trying to free herself from my talons.

I kissed her some more, literally chewing on her mouth, sticking my tongue far in, occupying her mind with my mean-ness.

I let go of her genitalia and gripped her breasts with both hands. God, she was hot. She was now moaning, her pussy was so wet I could smell it. She pressed her hips up at me.

I put my hand down between her legs and shoved in three fingers.

"GAH!" she rolled her head back, not able to comprehend the terrific pleasure I was assaulting her with.

I began pushing my hand in and out. I could feel my knuckles moving against the ridge of muscles that surrounded her pussy.

I had lost a lot of male strength, but I still had a little, and I kept her down and kept jamming my fingers into her.

Not that she wanted to get up. She was in heaven. Gasping, drooling, thrusting her hips up against my fingers.

And then, she got so juicy, so moist, so desirous, my hand slipped inside her.

She froze, opened her eyes, and stared at me.

I made a fist inside her, I began ramming it in and out. She became like a rag doll, moaning and crying, holding onto my wrist with both hands, but trying to help me fuck her, not trying to stop me.

Then she started stuttering, talking almost as if in tongues. "Gaba daba wah wah." A chant, a moan, a prayer to some god of fuk from some lost age.

I used all my power, I rubbed my wrist against her clit, and she snapped her head back, her eyes rolled back, and she arched.

"AHHHHHHHHH!" Almost a scream.

Then she was hunching, trying to fold up like a fetus around my fist. She gave a few spasms, closed her eyes, and just lay there.

I undid my fist and slowly pulled it out.

She lay, her eyes half open now, and an expression of pure wonder in them.

I placed my hand to her nose. "Smell this?"

She did, and she nodded, too weak to do anything else.

"That's the smell of you, and guess who owns you?"

"You do," and she sighed, finally and totally happy.

This was what she had needed for our entire marriage, and I had had to become a woman to give it to her.

I licked her juices off my hand, then went into the bathroom. I needed a shower.

Melissa took the election by a narrow margin. She was the person who introduced the solution to the Y chromosome to the world. She was a US Senator, and she would spearhead programs to sell the 'Y pill,' as it came to be called, to all the countries of the world. She had truly changed the world.

And, I can say...I helped. In fact, my contribution was just as valuable as hers, if not more so.

The interesting thing is that people say she didn't win. They held that because she had used Hegemony software, and because Hegemony was rumored to cause votes to flip, she really hadn't won the election.

But she did. And it is a simple matter of mathematics to prove it. There are 161.1 million men in the United States. There are 166.7 million women.

And there you go.

END

Full Length Books from Gropper Press

Rick Boston and his beautiful wife, Jamey, move to Stepforth Valley, where Rick is offered a job at a high tech cosmetics company. The House of Chimera is planning on releasing a male cosmetics line, and Rick is their first test subject. Now Rick is changing. The House of Chimera has a deep, dark secret, and Rick is just one more step on the path to world domination!

This book has female domination, feminization, cross dressing, hormones, gender transformation, forced transgender and pegging.

The Stepforth Husband

The Sexual Matrix

PART ONE

"Hey, babe, you've got a choice.

She held out her hands. In the palms of those sexy, red tipped digits were two pills. One was red and one was blue.

We were sitting at the kitchen table at her home. She was facing me, and she was never more beautiful. Her long, dark hair spread over her bare shoulders. Her eyes smokey and mysterious. Her lips red, plump, and she licked them, her pink tongue sliding over them, moistening them, making them glisten.

And, I might add, we were naked. She had invited me over, gotten me naked, and told me she had a deal for me.

She sat there, facing me, and I could smell her arousal, and the glimpse I had had of her vagina indicated that it was wet.

I, of course, was totally erect.

God, I was in love.

Heather was the perfect woman for me. She was five and a half feet tall, massive mammaries, tiny waist, smarter than Einstein, and she had me. She knew she had me. From the very first day I set eyes on her, she had me.

"What's in them?" I asked.

"You've seen the matrix. You take the red pill things change, life goes crazy, you find out the truth and fight the evil forces of mental manipulation and sexual abuse."

Sexual abuse? Uh oh. That was the one thing about Heather, she liked to tease. A lot. I had gone home so many times with my pants bulging and my throat gulping and so turned on I couldn't stand it. My heart pounding, my penis throbbing, so full of lust that my eyeballs were steamed.

"You take the blue pill and you wake up in bed. Alone and horny, and we're done."

"D-done?" My heart dropped. Yes, she kept me horny, but on those few times when she did let me get off, usually by her hand, once by her mouth, and once, just rubbing the tip of my dick against her pussy....well, actually it was her rubbing her pussy lips against my dick. I was tied down at the time.

"Done, sweetheart. You either take the next step, the red pill, find out what evil lurks behind the curtain, or, see ya later alligator."

"See you..." my heart had dropped all the way into my sandals. I felt like the world was not just ending, but exploding into a cinder.

"But, we've had so many good times!"

Well, she had. Being demanding and pushing me around. Making me wait on her hand and foot. And I was teased, and stroked, and tied down for her pleasure, whatever that pleasure brought.

Which meant that I wasn't just having pleasure, I was in heaven.

"And we can have more, once you choose." She smiled. "Or we can call it quits."

"But what's really in the pills?"

"Your future. One way or the other. Your choice. And you better make it, because I'm not going to sit here, offering you your future, while you dither and dally."

"Can I have a drink while I think about it."

She shook her head, which, because we were leaning towards each other in kitchen chairs, was only a foot apart from mine. Her hands were in front of me, offering...what?

"You must make this choice with a clear mind. Your own mind." then she laughed. "For the last time."

The last time? what the heck was she plotting? What was in the pills? What would happen to me.

"Wait," I said, and I actually took my attention off her. My eyes glazed, and I actually had deep thoughts.

She was fine with that. In fact, I think she wanted that. She wanted me to do this of my own accord.

I thought of the movie The Matrix. Neo took a chance and found the love of his life. In a culture heavy with slavery and sweat and chains and mental machines that raped the mind, he found true love.

And, he learned Kung Fu.

I had watched the scene in the dojo a million times, Neo struggling, getting beat, Morpheus encouraging him to find the truth of himself, and then...he knew Kung Fu.

But it wasn't the kung fu that I kept thinking about, it was the love of my life.

I had already found the love of my life. My dick told me so. So why should I give her up? Oh, that's right. I had no choice, or rather, my choice was give her up, or take the next step. whatever that next step was.

"Okay," I said, my eyes focusing on her.

She smiled.

I took the red pill from her hand, I put it in my mouth.

Now she offered me a drink. Coke and bourbon, my favorite, and washed that little pellet down the old gullet.

She sat back, satisfied and watched me.

"What now?"

"We wait."

"What was in the pill."

She just laughed.

I sat back. I pushed my hair back. To one side of me was the window, and I turned and looked at myself. I was the same. I was Justin Brooks, suburban schmuck, just out of college. No prospects and a lifetime in front of me.

"I'm glad you took the pill, Justin."

I looked back at her. "Uh, so am I."

She giggled. "You sound so funny."

"What's supposed to happen now?"

Her lips pursed in a quirky curve. "I think this is where you see your reflection, you reach out and touch it."

I looked at my reflection in the window.

"Go ahead. Reach out."

So I did. Feeling foolish, but compelled by my fascination. I touched the tip of my finger to the window. Nothing happened. Mercury didn't run up my arms and into my mouth and turn me inside out.

I brought my hand back, feeling foolish.

I looked at her, she was laughing.

We sat there for 15 minutes, nothing happening, yet she just kept telling me to sit, to wait.

Then another 15 minutes,

Then I felt funny. My eyelids fluttered, and I gulped, and the world just sort of felt…skewed.

This was what Heather had been waiting for. She leaned forward, again licking her lips, and she motioned me to lean forward.

There we were a foot apart, staring into each others eyes, and she said. "Take off your clothes. Quickly. And don't stop looking at me while you do. You must keep your eyes on me, totally on me, nothing else, for the next five minutes.

I tell you, I shucked my clothes faster than a rubber band snaps. In 15 seconds I was sitting there, naked, my penis pointing towards her and throbbing uncontrollably.

She was fully clothed, her chest rising and falling in excitement. She reached forward with both hands and placed them around my penis.

"Uhhh," I groaned. She had made a point of telling me not to cum for a week. No masturbation. She had been insistent, and even grilled me every day. And I hadn't. I was hornier than a tuba.

"Justin. I have been waiting for this, but first I had to make sure you were right, that you were the one."

I closed my eyes, giving in to the feel of her hands stroking me, her warm palms sliding up my shaft. I could feel her breath on my face, gentle and sweet smelling.

"No. Open your eyes."

I opened them.

"No matter what happens, you must focus on me. I must become your world for the next few minutes, until you have an orgasm."

I nodded, licked my own lips, and felt her hands pulling me onward, stoking my lust, making my fires burn brighter. My testicles felt like they were swelling, everything getting tight down there.

She stroked, and she moved her face closer. Close enough to kiss. I stared at her lips.

"No. My eyes. And don't try to kiss me. Just do this."

I had no intention of doing anything else. I was about to cum. I lived for this. Sex with Heather. My world made whole.

She focused on me, and kept stroking.

I wanted her to fondle my balls, maybe slap them a bit. But she just stroked and stroked, and watched my eyes.

I wanted her to palm the head, maybe even to bend down and suck it a bit. But she just kept stroking, watching my eyes.

I didn't take long, maybe three minutes, then she slowed down, real slow. No premature ejaculators for her. She wanted us to look at each other for the full five minutes.

So I did, though I was gulping and sweating, and then the world started to turn over, to slant, and I felt like my stomach was turning inside my turning body, and my senses were all skewed, but I kept my eyes on her. No matter what bizarre acrobatics my senses were going through, I watched her eyes.

Her eyes, liquid pools of blue, never ending depths. The black hole in the center spreading out, overwhelming me, swallowing me. I felt like I was drowning, and I heard her voice… "Come on Justin, just a little more, you can do it."

She was far away, and I felt my core surge with love for her, and my penis, suddenly it felt like an old steam locomotive, chugging and chugging, steam spurting out of it. And I realized:

My dick was pulsing!

The steam was my spiritual energy, being shaped, being funneled, being drained into…her…her eyes…her…

I was cuming, my dick spurted, and suddenly everything started to go right side up.

I looked down, and she let me.

My dick hung there, a big, fat slug drooling semen. There were drops on the floor, but the major issue was in her hand.

I had been so messed up, so far out in some weird world, that I had hardly felt it, and I felt this massive sense of disappointment.

I watched, and she lifted her hand and tasted the sperm, then she smiled and sucked it into her mouth. Gobs and gobs of the sweet essence.

And I felt like I was falling down a drain pipe.

I reached out, grabbed the kitchen table with one hand, the other hand flailed around searching.

Heather laughed. Her teeth were so white and beautiful, so straight and powerful. I couldn't take my eyes off her lips stick, perfectly applied, red, giving her a lustful appearance. And I wanted her to lust for me. In fact, my whole being gravitated to the thought that I needed her to love me. I would do anything for her, if I could only get her to love me.

"How you doing, Justin?"

I blurted, "Please, I just need you to love me."

"If you want me to love you...get a hard on."

I blinked. I loved her, but there was a part of me that realized how non sequitur her command was.

I looked down. Without being touched. Without any stimulation, and after having just shot a massive load, my dick was erecting. I watched, stunned, as it rose to a turgid pounding.

"Wha...?" I said, confused.

She laughed and said, "Go sit in the living room. Wait for me. Do not say anything until I say you can."

I stood up and walked into the living room, and a part of me watched my body walking, and wondered...why am I doing this? She had told me what to do, and I didn't quibble, I didn't object, I didn't even ask why. I just did what she said.

I sat down, feeling a sense of amazement at myself. My submissive self.

A moment passed and Heather walked through the living room. She glanced at me, and I stared at her hungrily, my dick hard as a spaceship counting down. She just laughed and walked into the bedroom.

I waited. I listened to her shower. I just wanted her to come back to me; I just wanted to gaze at her!

Yet she was ignoring me. I could feel it. I knew it. She had done something to me, and she was enjoying her little joke.

I felt a little irritated. I wanted to go in and give her a piece of my mind. But when I told my body to stand up it just sat there. I was a useless appendage attached to a boner.

Fifteen minutes later she came out of her room. She tossed me a towel. "Dry me."

She took a position in front of me.

I stood up and began blotting the water off her. I put the towel to her body, pulling it around her, blotting and rubbing. I dried her breasts off, and my cock started to drip.

She felt a splatter of pre-cum and looked down. She laughed. "Don't get any of that on me or you'll be licking it off."

But I couldn't help it. I had been commanded to dry her off, and moving around her my hard dick swayed, and a bit of juice landed on her thigh.

"Lick that off."

Without a word, I knelt, placed my hands on her lovely legs, and lapped the pre-cum off her, which caused even more pre-cum to leak and fall on her foot.

"Lick that off, too."

I bent down, on all fours, and began to lick the pre-squirt off her toes.

"While you're down there, fuck my foot with your tongue."

She walked away, and I lurched after her, grabbing and missing and falling on the floor.

She laughed as she sat down and I scampered after her.

I took her foot, her beautiful, red toes, and I washed them with my tongue. I poked my tongue between her toes. I sucked on the toes. I kissed and licked the bottom of her foot. A piece of me was far away, dazed, protesting, but I couldn't stop.

Suddenly she raised a foot, placed it against my chest, and pushed.

I rolled back on my ass, scrambled to right myself and was ready to dive back to her feet, but she said, "No."

I stopped.

"Squat in front of me."

I hunkered down at her feet and stared up at her, awed by her incredible beauty.

She was giggling, having the time of her life. "Oh, Justin. Justin. I love you this way. I'm going to keep you like this for a long time. Would you like that?"

Like a dam bursting, I broke. I had been given leave to speak.

"No..."

"Say yes."

"Yes."

She smiled. "From here on out you will always reply appropriate to my wishes. If I ask, you may speak your mind, but you will always revert to doing what you think I would like you to do."

I opened my mouth and tried to speak, but I was going to say something inappropriate to her desires, and I was officially speechless.

"Okay. You may break rule one once."

"I don't...what is happening? Why am I doing...I don't..."

She held up her finger and I shut. Like a bear trap. Words died in me and I was bound by what I came to know as rule one: Do only what is appropriate to her needs.

"Now then, I really thought about this...should I leave you to wonder why you can't not follow my desires, but I figured you might eventually go insane, and we don't want that. At least, not until you have waited on me sufficient to be allowed to go insane."

She smiled.

I gulped and loved her forever.

"The blue pill was nothing. A placebo. Sugar. But we would have been done. I needed you to take the red pill, and if you wouldn't, then I would find somebody who would.

"What was in the red pill...wait, I should tell you where I got it from first, that will help you understand the significance of the red pill.

"My first name is Heather. But my last name isn't Johnson. It is Frankendick. You may remember reading about Dr. Frankendick in the newspapers last year? Nod if you do."

I nodded.

"Well, you remember that Dr. Frankendick and his wife were discovered in his home on an endless loop of slavery and sex. They were deemed to be insane and locked away.

"As a distant relative, their only relative, I took possession of their house, and this included samples of the chemicals that had reduced them to their bizarre state, and complete instructions for making other products.

"The drug that was used, that they invented and was actually used upon them, was a derivation of Rohypnol. The date rape drug.

"What I gave you was a pill of pure, undiluted essence of Rohypnol.

"The effect is to make you unable to do anything except what your master says. By making you stare into my eyes for five minutes, while the drug took effect, I became imprinted on you. I know, you loved me before, but you could always walk away, refuse me, and if you are going to be my boyfriend I can't have that.

"So you are officially my property, and you will always do what I say. And even though you will have thoughts, you will be unable to resist my commands. Do you understand what I have said? You may say what you will."

"I understand, but..."

"But what?"

"But what about my free will? What about my rights as a human being?"

She held up a finger and I slapped my jaw shut.

"You already exercised those rights when you made a choice and took the red pill. Now, enough chit chat. Chit chat makes me so wonderfully horny. Lick me to an orgasm."

I wanted to speak, to object, to say something, but all I could do was dive forward and bury my head between her thighs.

I licked, I gobbled, I ran my tongue up her slit and nibbled on the clitoris. All the time I was erect and dripping. My dick rubbed against the carpet and I groaned at the feeling of the head being roughly stimulated.

She lifted my head. "By the way. You will be erect and dripping at

all times, unless I say otherwise. And…you are not allowed to come."
I managed to stare at her incredulously.
She pushed my head back down. "Now come on. Do me right."
So I did.
"Use your fingers, use your nose," she moaned. She lay back and
began playing with her tits.
I could barely see her pulling on her nipples and her hips started to
move back and forth, fucking my face as I redoubled my efforts.
"Oh! Oh!" she cried, and then the spasms set in. Her pelvis jerked
and she held my face in place. I couldn't breath, but I couldn't back
away. I continued to eat her as her thighs tightened and squeezed my
face.
Finally, she pushed me away. I was weak from not breathing and fell
back on the rug.
She sighed, and I quickly came back to my haunches and stared at
her.
Far away, I was aghast, objecting, hating everything. But I couldn't
help but stare at her and love her.
She came to her elbows and said, "I need another shower. Go stand
in it and make the water the right temperature."
I ran for the bathroom, jumped in the shower and turned the spigots.
Fortunately, she had just taken a shower not long before, so I only
experienced lukewarm water, which quickly became hot. But I dreaded
the idea of doing this with cold water.
She came to the shower, "Get out and dry the floor. Next time close
the door so you won't get water on the floor."
I jumped out of the shower and ran for the towel I had previously
used to dry her off. I began scrubbing the floor. Meanwhile, Heather was
in the shower. She was humming, and I could see her soaping her
delicious breasts through the frosted glass. My hard on was, of course,
gigantic, and it brushed against the floor, stimulating me even further, but
there was no hope for relief. I was stuck in a place where everything
aroused me, but nothing released me.
She stepped out of the shower, "Dry me off."
I walked around her and rubbed her skin. It was so fine, so perfect,
and suddenly she grabbed my cock and began to stroke it.
My rubbing slowed down and I began to gasp. My cock was turning
red, pre-cum flowed out of the tip. I felt the surges beginning deep down,
churning my balls, driving the liquid up the shaft, but nothing came out
of the head.
Heather giggled. "This is so much fun. Is it fun for you?"
Appropriate, I answered. "I love it." And, truth, there was something
in me, underneath the protest and dismay, that did enjoy it.
She patted my cheek. She kissed me, and the world became white

65

and dizzy. Her mere touch was making me swoon, and she still stroked my cock. "Now, dear, I want you to dry the floor again, then you may sleep in the shower. You will awake at six o'clock, fully rested, and prepare breakfast. I want sausages and waffles and a mimosa. Bring them in and stand by my bed when everything is ready."

She walked away from me. As I knelt to the floor and began wiping up her water I heard her bed springs creak. A minute later the floor was dry. I turned off the light and stepped into the shower. Then commenced one of the most miserable nights I have ever experienced.

It was wet in the shower. It wasn't cold, but I was trying to sleep on wet tiles, and my flesh slipped on the tiles, and I bumped my elbows, and the tiles were hard to sleep on.

I kept waking up, wiping water off me, dozing, bumping a knee, existing in a sleepy state that couldn't get respite, and, to top it off, my erection wouldn't go away.

I didn't get any real sleep until probably five in the morning, and then it was just an hour, and I awoke, feeling freshly rested, and I stood up.

I tip toed past her bed. She slumbered peacefully, and in the glow of her clock I stared at her precious face. So beautiful, so perfect, and I loved her.

But I needed to hurry if I was going to get her breakfast.

Once out of the bedroom I ran for the kitchen. My dick bounced and liquid splatted on the floor. I knew I would have to clean up more mess later, but right now, I was being driven by my love for her. I had to do what she wanted.

I cooked the sausages and waffles, put everything on a tray, including butter and syrup and a glass half and half with orange juice and champagne, and I brought them back to her bedroom. I took a position where I could gaze lovingly at her. I stared down at her and felt my love swell, and my cock dripped endlessly.

A few minutes later she stirred. She turned over, stretched, opened her eyes, and looked at me.

"Justin! how wonderful of you. Place the tray right here." She patted the bed.

I put the tray down and she began eating. Little nibbles of sausage, lots of syrup. "Mmmm, you're a good cook."

I said nothing. I just watched her lips move and fell deeper in love.

She sighed. "You may talk, just…oh, hell, you can talk. I don't want you deaf and dumb or anything."

"Please," I said. "May I cum?"

She laughed, ate a little more, and said, "Now where is the fun in that? You give a big, old squirt, and then you are empty, no longer in lust. No, I prefer you to be horny, to be enslaved to me by the juices in your cock."

And I realized: *yes, I did love her, but that was just fueling my horniness, and...and I needed relief.*

"How long are you going to keep me like this?"

"A long time."

"What?"

"I have to tell you, I like you like this." She giggled. "I think, in the end, you won't want to escape. Your mind will just sort of snap, and you will realize that there are worse things than being my slave."

That was food for thought.

She finished eating. "Do the dishes, clean the kitchen, then come back and we will have a discussion. Answer me with 'yes, ma'am.'"

"Yes, ma'am." I took the tray and headed for the kitchen.

A short time later I was back, and she was ready for me. She was still in bed, but she had kicked the covers off and was playing with herself. She smiled up at me.

"Would you like to get in me?"

"Oh, please!" I blurted, actually lurching in place.

"Very well. You may fuck me until I cum, but don't you dare have an orgasm."

"Yes, ma'am." I was already on the bed, crawling up between her legs.

"Not so fast, bozo. Give me a good licking."

I stopped at her crotch and began tasting her. Oh, the torment. I could feel my cock erupting with pre-cum, my hips were lurching, and my cock felt like every throb was a spank.

"Oh, yeah. That's it, lover." She held my head and pushed her pussy into my face. "Now, come up and do me right."

I crawled up and placed my cock at her hole. Oh, God, my penis was massive! Redder than I had ever seen it, and the veins were pulsing with desire.

"Come on, shove it in."

Helpless to her commands, I moved my hips and pushed forward.

She gasped and held on to me. She pulled me tight, then bid me be still. "Don't move for a second. I just want to enjoy the feel of a good cock for a while."

I lay, motionless, my penis ensconced in her cunt, throbbing so hard I thought my heart would burst.

"Isn't this wonderful? Doesn't it feel good to just hold it?"

"No...no...I want to cum!"

She laughed merrily. "Oh, you silly goose. You aren't allowed to cum. Now start to move. Slide in and out, give it a twist or turn every now and then.

I fucked her, and my dick was controlling my mind. Well, she was controlling it, but my dick was second in line, and I was a far distant third. So part of me lusted and pumped and moaned and groaned. And my dick felt the goodness and was so enraptured, taking me down the path of compulsion and addiction. And a piece of me was screaming 'No! No!'

Heather knew what was happening. She watched the torment unfold on my face and she kept chuckling.

"Oh, yeah, baby. You're a good fuck."

She ground her hips upon me.

"Please," I managed to whisper. "Please, let me cum. Set me free!"

"Nonsense," she moaned. She reached own and felt my balls. Her eyes opened. "They're so hot! And they feel so full!"

"They are, and they need to let go. I need to be emptied!" I sounded so piteous, yet she just smiled.

"God, it makes me horny to see you like this."

And there was the catch 22. The hornier she made me, the hornier she got, and why should she ever let me squirt?

"Oh, God...God...Fu..." I drove my giant cock into her, and she began to shake and tremble.

"Oh, yes, here we go!" She held onto me then, and her pelvis shuddered and spasmed, and she squeezed me so tight I thought I might break. The orgasm went on and on, never ending, and then, suddenly, she lay back and gasped.

I lay in her, my heart pounding, my cock surging, and nothing happening.

She pushed me and I got off. I withdrew my cock and stared at it. It was glistening with her juices, the head was purple, and even as I watched white droplets formed and fell from the slit.

"Oh, God!" I moaned, and my hips thrust back and forth, fucking the air itself, trying to get some relief.

Heather lay back for a second, then she wheeled around and sat on the bed next to me. She looked at my poor, abused tool, and she giggled. She took it in her hand and started stroking.

"Now then, my dear. I've arranged for you to take a job. So I need you to lick me clean, ready the shower, dry me off, then clean yourself up. You may dress casual, and I will leave a slip of paper on the kitchen table with the address. They will be expecting you, so don't let me down."

"Yes, ma'am." I was sad, horny, excited. My dick was large, throbbing, and my balls felt super filled. I watched her hand work me, making me ever hornier and hornier.

"And, Justin?"

I looked at her. "Yes, ma'am?"

She smiled at me, squeezed my balls and pecked my cheek. "You're a good boy."

Then she lay back on the bed and waited for me to get on with my chores.

PART TWO

I reported to a sex store downtown. I walked in, looked at the walls of dildos, the butt plugs, the whips and glossy books, and I knew what my life was becoming.

Oddly, it didn't matter as much as it had. I was already getting acclimated to loving my hard on. I just wanted to work in the store, get done, and go home and gaze upon Heather, and...get off!

The driving motivation of my life. Getting off...with Heather.

I wanted to fuck her, suck her, bring her to frothy Os, in spite of the fact that she never let me get off. Or maybe because?

"You must be Justin." A girl wearing the shortest shorts I had ever seen, and possessing the juttingest tits in the world, sauntered up to me.

"Uh, yeah. Hea—"

She kissed me. She just walked up and splatted one on me. And it was a good one.

At first I was shocked, but it didn't take long to respond, and then I was giving as good as I got.

She broke it off. I wanted more, I leaned forward, tried to pull her to me, but she got a hand up and pushed on my chest.

"Oh, Heather wasn't kidding. You are a horny one!"

Well, yeah. I hadn't cum in a week, and now what Heather had done to me, I wanted to pop in the worst way.

But, of course. I couldn't.

So Ginger (that was her name) reached in my pants and grabbed me and led me back into the store.

Past the rows of toys and lubes and strap ons. Past fake asses and monster dildos. She kept glancing over her shoulder at me, laughing, tugging on my penis. "You're going to be our stock boy. You'll work in the back. Good thing it's summer, because Heather wants you nude all the time. Heather doesn't like clothes. And we're supposed to keep you hard, send you home all hot and bothered. Are you going to like that? Does Heather ever actually fuck you? Oh, that's Jill over there. Hi Jill! This is Justin. He's our new Peeny Boy."

My face was red, but there was nothing I could do, I was supposed to work for her, to follow directions as if they were given by Heather herself.

"There's the break room over there, and there's a forklift. You know how to drive a forklift? Good."

My cock was surging, my hips were jerking forward and I was gasping. I wanted to cum so badly.

Ginger didn't care. Well, she did care. She thought it was funny and she kept giggling and stroking me even harder.

When we finally stopped she looked at her hand and laughed. It was slimy with my pre-cum.

"Oh, you gusher." She wiped the goo off on my chest. "Now take your clothes off and get ready. I'll show you what to do."

I took off my clothes and now my boner, her handle, stood out for me to actually see.

"Oh, my. That is big! And it's so red! Does it hurt? I mean that must be painful."

I was naked but for shoes, and she came closer to me and began stroking me.

"Uh, yeah, can you…can you get me off?"

"Oh, I probably could, but where's the fun in that?"

"Yeah, but…"

She put a finger to my lips. "I love to hear you beg, and I want you to beg a lot, but right now, I have to show you how to fill orders.

"Now, before we start, I want you to stroke yourself. You may stop whenever you get too close, but as soon as the urge passes, it's back to stroking."

"Okay."

"Now."

I blinked, grabbed my cock, and began sliding my hand back and forth.

Oh, it felt heavenly. I was so close, and so horny.

She slapped me. Not hard, but enough to open my eyes. Keep stroking, but keep your attention on me, on the job.

"Oh…okay." I gulped. My balls felt like they were going to explode.

"Excellent."

Ding!

I looked to the side. On the end of a prep table was a printer. A sheet of paper shot out of it as I watched.

"Oh, goodie. Just in time. Hey! Justin…just in…it's a pun."

I stroked and nodded and gulped.

"Grab that paper and let's fill it."

I took the lone sheet of paper in hand, and she grabbed my cock and led me away.

"What's the order?"

I looked at the paper and focused my eyes, which was hard because my chest hurt with heat, my balls were tight, my dick kept pulsing against her grip.

"A strap on and a negligee."

"This is the strap on aisle," she pulled me down a wide aisle and we found the strap on item.

Then another aisle. Her pulling on me, me gasping and making moaning sounds. "And these are the negligees, look for number 302A.

I found the number. It was in a small packet.

"Okey dokey, back to the table."

At the table, while I kept stroking myself, she put the two things in a box, taped it, addressed it, and threw it in a big rolly cart. "That's for the mail man. Stop stroking."

I stopped. I was shivering. She was grinning. "I really don't know where Heather finds such wonderful boys.

"I...I need to cum." A long string of pre-cum was hanging to the floor.

"Catch that drool with your other hand."

I did.

Ginger came close to me. She put her fingers on my nipples and started flicking and circling them. "Now, eat it."

I felt the gag reflex try to kick in. My throat lurched and I wanted to puke. I lifted my hand and sucked the contents. Slightly salty but otherwise bland goo touched my lips, coated my tongue, slid down my throat.

I stopped wanting to gag. My eyes opened.

"Tastes pretty good, eh?"

"Not really."

"I think it does," and she looked at me pointedly.

"Oh," I blinked, and realized that it really was delicious. Just the right amount of bland. Yes, I liked it.

I nodded and she smiled.

"You see, pre-cum, and especially cum, is energy. And if it just falls on the floor it is wasted energy. And somebody comes along and mops up your wasted energy and squeezes out the mop and all your energy just goes down the drain.

"But if you eat it, it recycles, and you stay healthy, never skinny out, and you actually don't need as much food as you think. Isn't that great?"

"I, uh...I—"

She frowned and spoke in a warning voice, "I asked if that was great."

"Oh, uh, yeah. It's great. I love it. It's delicious." I was finding that just as I had fallen in love with Heather, following the directions of Ginger was making me fall in love with her. I did so want to please her. And I wanted to fuck her. And I wanted to cum. But we know the story on that.

"Okay. So you fill the next order, I'll watch."

As if on cue...Ding!

Stroking myself, I picked up the order form. High heels for a cross

MAD SCIENTISTS AND FEMINIZATION

dresser. I looked at the map which was posted above the table and located the aisle.

Heather followed me as I trotted, dick swaying and dripping, down the high heeled aisle.

I found the heels and climbed up a ladder for them.

Heather stood under me, one hand out to catch my drippings. "High heels. We're going to have to have you wear some. You'll find they're a lot of fun."

I descended to the floor and she held her hand out. I dutifully licked it. Yes, it tasted yummy.

"Good boy."

Then she followed me to the prepping table and watched as I boxed, addressed, put postage on, and threw the order into the mail cart.

"Excellent!" she laughed. "Now, in between orders you may sit on that barstool. You can face it in any direction. You should stroke yourself, keep yourself on edge, and wait for the next order. Go on, have a seat."

I got on the barstool and faced her. God, she was beautiful. Long, red hair, and those breasts... I asked, "May I touch your titties?"

She giggled. "Why Justin! You are so fresh!" And she gave me a light, almost loving slap on the cheek.

I touched my cheek in wonder. I wasn't fresh, I was compelled. I was in love. I just wanted to please her.

"Now you sit there and wait for orders, and we'll do stocking this afternoon. I'll call you when it's time for lunch."

She left and I sat on the barstool and looked towards the street. Out the big doors was a small parking lot, and then a driveway about fifty feet long. I watched cars whiz by on the street. I watched people walking along the sidewalk. They frequently looked up the drive, but I was at the back of the warehouse, in the shadows, and they couldn't see me.

Still, it was exciting to be sitting naked, knowing they could almost see me.

In fact everything was exciting. It was exciting to be in love with Heather, and now with Ginger. And there were other beautiful girls in the shop and I had no doubt I was going to be falling in love with them.

Ding!

I jumped off the stool and ran to fill the order.

"Justin, report to the lunchroom!" I was startled by the loudspeaker. I looked at the mail cart, it was full to overflowing. I had worked hard and I was happy. I was happy because Ginger would be happy, and Heather would be happy, and that made me happy.

I didn't realize that I was thinking less and stroking more.

I trotted towards the corridor leading to the shop. I held my balls with one hand so they wouldn't bounce, they were so full they were painful, and I pumped my cock with my other hand. I had to be careful, though. My cock was getting a little tender.

I entered the lunchroom and found that six other employees were already there. I saw Ginger, talking to another girl at the back of the room and I ran to her.

"Hi, Ginger."

"Hi, Justin. Did you have a good morning?"

"I did."

"And do you want to cum?"

"Oh, yes. Please, please."

The other girl giggled as I begged.

"Well, you can't cum, but we can relieve the pressure a little. Would you like that?"

"Oh, yes," I was all eagerness and cheer.

"Excellent, let's put you on the machine."

The machine was a weird set up of planks and bars, with a little motor and tubes in front of it.

She showed me how to lay on a big padded plank and put my head and hands on the edge of another plank that had half holes cut into it. She then lowered another plank, and I was laying in a sort of pillory.

"What does this do?"

"You'll find out. Now, let's put your dick in this suction cup thing, good, and you'll be expected to do all this the next time we milk you."

"Milk me?"

She attached a couple of clips to my nipples and I groaned.

She flicked a switch and the machine hummed and I felt suction on my dick, a pulsing suction. I grunted and would have thrust my hips forward, but she had put a strap around them, fastened me to the plank so I couldn't move.

"I...I..."

"Don't worry, you're not going to cum." She was behind me, and she pushed something up my rectum. I groaned and lurched against the straps holding me down.

"This will massage your prostate, and you will leak cum. You'll be all empty by the end of lunch."

She came to the front of the set up and smiled at me. I had to turn my head up to see her, and it hurt a little bit.

"Now you just relax and enjoy yourself, and I'll come get you at the end of lunch."

She walked away, and I stared at her round, sexy ass.

For a while it felt sort of awkward, just laying there and having my dick mechanically sucked. The other people in the lunch room, however, just ignored me.

I began grunting in a low tone. I wanted to cum, but the machine was designed not to let me have an orgasm. It just wanted my juice, it didn't want me to ruin the rhythm with a big O.

Then, a little later, probably halfway through lunch, I started to feel all loosy goosy. I just felt relaxed.

I could feel the suction on my penis, pulling, pulling, pulling.

I could feel the little motions inside my ass as the prostate massager rubbed and rubbed and rubbed.

And the clips on my nips felt painful, but in a good way.

So I slipped into some kind of subspace. I wallowed in enjoyment. I loved my horniness. And I was almost sorry when Ginger stopped the machine and set me free. She held up a glass and inspected it.

"Oh, you're a big cummer." She turned and put it in a refrigerator.

"What are you going to do with that?" I asked.

"We sell sperm to pharmaceutical houses, food research facilities, that sort of thing. Sperm is rich, and when you add it to foods the food overcomes any lack of nutrition caused by over used soil, too many chemicals, that sort of thing.

"They put sperm into food?"

"Of course they do. They've been doing that for decades."

"But...do people know?"

She laughed. "They don't care. When is the last time you looked at labels in the supermarket? Do you really know what all those chemicals are?"

"No."

"One of those chemicals is a scientific name for sperm. I tell you, if people knew what they were eating..." she tsked and shook her head. "Do you know how much nutrition is found in various kinds of mammal sperm? Even in animal feces."

"No!"

"Oh, yes. But what do you care as long as it tastes good, right?"

"Well, uh..."

"Say you love your processed food."

I found that my disgust was silly. I really did like yummy foods. And if sperm was the secret ingredient...that was fine with me.

"I guess I do. I really love food with sperm in it."

"Excellent, now here, put these on."

She handed me a pair of high heels. I stared at them like they might bite.

"But these are girl's shoes!"

"No, no. They're your shoes, and you really love them."

Gosh, I do, don't I?" I took the shoes, sat down and replaced my athletic shoes.

"Now, you can still run, but be careful. Better to walk fast, and do it like this."

She demonstrated, walking across the lunchroom. The few people still eating clapped. Her ass was swaying and she had one hand on her hip like a fashion model.

She came back. "Just place one one foot in front of the other and let your ass feel good."

So I tried it. It was awkward, but it felt good. There was a certain freedom in letting your butt sway back and forth. When I returned she said, "Just think. If you had tits they would sway, too."

I looked at her, but she just smiled. She didn't tell me that I wanted to have tits, and for some reason I thought this was curiouser and curiouser.

"However, that said, I have to say that your sway isn't enough."

"It's not?"

"Don't worry. I've got something in mind that might help. Here, put this in."

I stared at he hand. It was a butt plug."

"I can't—"

"You love the feeing of a good plug."

And, funny, I realized that I did. i had never used one before, but I knew that I loved the feeling of being filled.

I took the plug and, because the milking machine had reamed me a bit, I found it easy to insert the plug into my rectum. When I straighten up and tried to walk i found it awkward, but i could also feel that it would help me learn to swing my ass better.

The mailman had come while I was being milked, for the cart was empty. I went to the printer but Ginger stopped me.

We're going to do do stocking now. Go get the forklift.

The forklift was parked in a corner of the warehouse. I brought it out.

"There are a half dozen or so pallets outside. Go get them and line them up in the center of the floor.

"But that's outside!" I protested. "Somebody will see me."

"Do it," she snapped with a laugh.

So I drove outside, and saw what she already knew. Except for the drive to the street, the whole parking lot was surrounded by 12 foot fences lined with green material. There was no way anybody could see my nakedness.

I loved the feel of the sun and fresh air on me skin, and I quickly brought the pallets in.

"How's the cock doing?" Ginger asked when I stepped off the forklift.

I looked down. It was just half a chub. Long and slack, no juice dripping from it.

"Oh!" I panicked. I hadn't been stroking it. I started to grab it but Ginger put a hand on my forearm.

"Don't worry about it. You'll be drained a couple of times a week, and you'll feel fine and empty, no urge to masturbate for a few hours. But I tell you, about the time you go home tonight you are going to be one horny puppy. Now, you need to stock the products on the pallets. Here's what we do."

By the end of the day I was tired, but feeling good. I started to get back in my clothes, but Ginger said, "Just pick them up and go get in my car."

I did, and Ginger came out and started the car, as she drove down to the street she told me: "I'll give you a ride home today, but after this you'll be taking a bus." She told me the times and places for bus stops, then handed me a bus ticket. I stared at it. I wasn't much of a fan for buses.

"You're going to love taking the bus," she said.

"Oh, I forgot. Yeah." And I knew I really loved riding on buses.

We drove through the city, and it felt so odd to be sitting naked while a woman drove. Ginger seemed to know that, because she kept chuckling, and at stop lights she would pinch my nipples or grab my cock.

I started to get horny, and suddenly my dick was raging, like REALLY raging.

"Right on time," she quipped. Then she explained. We emptied you at lunch. About four hours later your dick gets hard, and you're going to be feeling super, super horny. You see, we got your body to let loose, but your mind still thinks it's got a full load."

I was processing that, trying to figure out what it all meant when we pulled through the gates and Ginger stopped. Heather came out of the house, and my heart leaped. Oh, God! I loved her!

"How'd it go?"

"Excellent. He's good worker, and we emptied him out for you."

Heather smiled, and my heart felt all warm and fuzzy. She opened the door for me. "Go in and clean the kitchen. Make sure you lick up any splatter."

"Yes, ma'am." I walked towards the house, feeling tall in my heels, my ass swaying and one hand on my hip and the other held up with the hand relaxed and palm down.

Click. Click. Click. went my heels. It sounded so sexy.

Ginger whistled and I turned around. They were smiling at me. I continued on into the house.

I cleaned the kitchen, and, sure enough, my dick started to leak, and it was so hard, and I felt so horny. I kept rubbing up against counters, and I stroked myself. When Heather came in I was down on the floor, pulling on my cock as I licked up pre-cum from the floor.

She laughed. "Very good, pretty boy. Now, there is a menu in the drawer over there, do your best and make it exactly right for my dinner. But before you do that…" she sat down in a chair and spread her legs.

I knew that I loved eating her pussy. I lived for it. I crawled across the floor as quickly as I could and I put my face to her snatch.

She groaned and pulled my head tight and clamped her thighs around my face. I took long, slow licks at her slit. Up and down, stopped every once in a while to suck on her clitoris.

"Oh, yeah. That's the way to do it!"

I knelt and focused all my efforts on her pussy. I wanted her to cum. I needed her to cum. I loved it when she came.

She began thrusting her pussy forward, tilting her hips and pushing my face down. At one point my nose was in her vagina, and she fucked it like a dick, moaning and groaning. She began pulling on her tits, then she gave a half shriek and pushed my head back.

Astounded, I watched as she came. She was sometimes a squirter, and this was one of those times. Golden liquid erupted into the air, two squirts, then she stopped. She pounded on her pussy with one palm and gave three more squirts, then she lay back and gasped.

"Oh, God! That was good." She sat up and looked at me. "I have a feeling you're going to be my favorite pussy licker of all time. What do you think about that?"

"Oh, yes!" I almost clapped my hands in glee. I did so love her. I wanted to be her most accomplished pussy licker of all time.

She smiled. "Good. Now lick the floor clean, then fix my dinner. Bring it into the computer room when it's ready.

"Yes, ma'am."

It took me a while to get the floor clean, but I did it. Then I worked on her dinner. She liked a lot of soups and salads, and just a little meat. She would cook a roast on the weekends, well, I would, and then she would have me cut little cubes to put in her salads through the week.

Interestingly, she had me mix some medicine into a nightly smoothie. I didn't recognize the ingredients, but she explained they were herbs that were designed to make her breasts fuller. They sure were working, her boobs really made my mouth water.

I finished fixing dinner, then served her.

She pushed back from the computer and had me place the dinner tray on a folding table next to her.

"Eat me while I eat," she commanded. Don't give me an orgasm, just keep gently licking. Be like a kitten cleaning its paws."

I went to work. I lapped and sucked and was very gentle.

Heather sighed and sat back. She held the bowl in one hand and used a spoon with the other. On the computer I could hear the sounds of fucking.

"I like to watch a little porn while I eat. It's so much better than the news."

"Yes, ma'am," my voice was muffled, being mouth being busy at the moment.

She finished her dinner, and she was getting hot. Her pussy was emitting more fluid, and she occasionally jerked her hips in a spasm.

She placed her dishes to the side.

"You may take this slop away. You can lick it clean for your own dinner, but make sure you run the dishes through the washing machine when you're done. When you're done I'll be in the bedroom."

I quickly took the tray away, and was conscious that my dick had returned to its perpetually erect state. And it was dripping. And I wanted to jam it in a pussy so bad I could hardly think.

Fortunately, she had left me some bits and pieces, she usually did, unless I didn't live up to her standards, so I had enough to eat. Barely. Then I did the dishes, and while the washing machine was cycling I ran to the bedroom.

She was laying in bed, reading a porn book and diddling her pussy.

"Ah, at last," she looked up as I entered the room. Then she said what I didn't expect. "Come fuck me. And you may cum if you wish."

I could cum? If I wanted? Boy, did I want! I was so hot and horny I almost literally dove through the air and into her snatch. I clamped my mouth on her pussy and sucked. I grabbed her tits with both hands. I was a wild man, totally out of control.

She giggled and didn't resist me.

I worked up her body then, lavished her beautiful boobs with glee. Working the nipples, massaging the mounds. Then I moved up and began kissing her.

She kissed back, and she had her arms around my neck as I reached down and inserted my penis into her sacred palace.

"Oh!" she groaned. "I love it when a man is hard and anxious!"

I ground into her, feeling her heavenly walls grip my cock and pull on it. I corkscrewed into her, feeling my shaft rub against the sides of her pussy. I tilted my hips and scooped my dick into her.

She began to moan with the savagery of my attack.

"Yeah, baby, fuck me." Then she kissed me as I desperately tried to cum.

And tried and tried and tried, and then it finally hit me, what Ginger had said. My body was empty of juice, but my mind was filled with the idea that I had lots of juice.

I could fuck all night and never squirt.

"Oh!" I blurted, when I realized the trap I was in.

Heather knew exactly what I was thinking. She laughed at the look on my face. She touched her palm to the side of my face in a caress. "Poor, poor Justin. And you thought you had a chance!"

"But...but..."

"Maybe you should just focus on giving me my orgasm. It'll be better that way."

So I did. I slowed my motions and focused on her pleasure, and, you know...it was better!

When she finally came I experienced a sense of accomplishment that I had never before experienced.

"Good boy," she said, pushing me away. Then she stopped and frowned. She looked up and said, "Have Ginger give you some proper fingernails tomorrow."

"Okay."

Good. Now go prepare my shower."

Eagerly, I jumped into the cold shower, my dick super throbbing but so denied.

Later, when she was ready to climb back into bed, she pointed to a small box in a corner of the room. "You may sleep in there from now on."

I entered what turned out to be a dog cage, pulled the door shut and curled my thin blanket around me.

Oh, I could have pushed the door open, but I wasn't supposed to. She wouldn't like that.

And I could have gotten up and gotten another blanket, but, again, that wasn't what she wanted. And what she didn't want...I didn't want.

All I wanted was for morning to come so I could rise, fresh and rested, and do everything all over again.

That was my life for a year. Working naked in a drafty warehouse.

Sometimes I would wear a butt plug.

Sometimes I would wear articles of female clothing. Corsets, garters, other things.

My fingernails were kept long and red.

My hair grew long and was styled in a very feminine fashion.

Preparing meals and cleaning Heather's house.

Being milked every Monday and Thursday.

Bringing Heather to daily orgasms.

A whole year of this bliss, and then, one day, a month into my second year, Heather told me to put on clothes.

This surprised me. I hadn't worn clothes, except of bus rides, or sporadic trips to a grocery store, for a year.

I put on the clothes I had arrived in.

"Come with me," and she strode out of the house.

I sat in the passenger seat as she drove across town. We stopped in front of an apartment house.

She walked up the walk, up the stairs, and to the last apartment in the complex. She opened the door and I followed her in.

It was one room, furnished. She showed me around the apartment. The refrigerator was full, there were towels in the closet and sheets on the bed. There was even tooth brush, tooth paste, and other items for keeping oneself clean.

She tossed the keys on the counter and turned to me. "This is your apartment. The lease is up in three months. By that time you will have a job and be self-supporting, or you will be out on the street."

"What? But what is happening?"

"I only keep boys for a year. Then they are on their own."

"But...but I don't want to be on my own! I don't know what to do! I just want to live with you and love you!"

She touched my face gently. "It's done, Justin. You're on your own."

Then, without another word, she left the room.

That night I was lost. I tried to lay on the bed, but I couldn't. I ended up sleeping in a corner of the bedroom, one sheet wrapped around my shivering body.

The next morning, I got up and didn't know what to do, so I took a bus to the store.

Ginger met me at the door. She placed a hand on my chest and kept me out. "You no longer work here. Please leave." The look on her face was sad, but somehow amused.

I went back to the apartment and tried to figure out what to do.

Nothing. I couldn't do anything. I tried eating, but even that simple act was fraught with difficulty.

The next day I went to Heather's house. The fence was too tall to climb, and I could only glimpse through the tall bushes surrounded the property. I didn't see any trace of Heather.

The first month passed slowly. I ate little and wasted away. I was weak, and I cried a lot.

I wanted Heather.

I wanted my life in the sex store.

I wanted to be naked, not have to buy clothes, or food, or anything. I just wanted to restock the shelves, fill orders, and get milked.

A couple of weeks into the second month I made my decision. I went to the open driveway that led to the warehouse. There was a naked man sitting on my barstool. I waited until lunch, then snuck into the warehouse. I climbed up a rack and slid into the crawlspace above the store. It wasn't my doghouse, but it would do. I lay in a corner and sniffled, and, when the store closed that night, everything locked up tight. I cried myself to sleep.

This went on for several days.

I grew hungry. I knew I was starving. So one night I climbed down, entered the kitchen and looked through the refrigerator. It didn't hold my beloved scraps, but there were a few leftover lunches. I ate them, then crawled back up into the crawlspace.

The next day I heard voices in the lunch room. And I heard voices in the store. I sat, shivered in fright, and wondered what had happened.

At the end of the crawlspace, above the store, there was a small office. It was Heather's office at work, and there was a small door that opened on the crawlspace. Suddenly it opened. A shaft of light pierced the gloom, and Heather stood in her office, looking into my gloom and doom.

"Justin. Come here."

I expected her to be outraged, but her voice was gentle, even kind.

I crawled through the crawlspace and emerged into her office. She sat behind her desk, waiting. Ginger was standing to one side. On her computer monitor was a picture of me scavenging into the refrigerator. I had been caught on the security cams.

"Justin. Justin." She smiled ruefully and shook her head at the sight of me. She turned to Ginger. Feed him, clean him up, and bring him back here."

"Yes, ma'am."

Ginger took me down stairs. I was wearing clothes, shabby and dirty, and she gave me others to carry with me. She drove me to Heather's house. She had me stand on the front lawn, and she gave me a bar of soap and hosed me down. I was commanded to scrub. Afterwards i put on the clothes she had given me.

We went to a restaurant. I ate, voraciously, as she had told me that Heather wanted me to eat, and she watched me, an amused smile on her face.

"The crawlspace. I never would have…" and she shook her head.

She took me to a beauty salon and had my hair washed and styled.

She had my fingernails repaired. Bright and beautiful.

Then she took me back to the sex store, spritzed me with a squirt of perfume, and pushed me up the stairs.

I climbed the narrow steps to Heather's office. This was what I dreaded. She was going to kick me out again. I wouldn't be allowed to love her.

I entered the office and she looked up. She pointed to a chair. "Sit."

I sat.

She finished some work, then stood up and stretched, then she came around the desk and pulled a chair up to face me. We were now sitting in chairs, face to face, like we had been when this had all started, when she had first offered me a choice of pills.

"Justin. You are so sad."

Yet she smiled, and her happiness was my happiness.

"I'm sorry." And I started crying.

She lifted my face with one hand and told me to stop crying.

I tried, the tears stopped, but I couldn't stop sniffling.

"I'm sorry."

"For what? For loving me? Why be sorry about that?"

"But...I..." I truly couldn't think.

"Justin. Almost 14 months ago I gave you a pill. It made you love me. It was your choice. Whether you knew what you were doing or not, you made the choice."

I nodded, a burble of sobs caught in my throat.

"That pill was only good for a year."

I blinked and stare at her.

"That's right. You haven't been on my super Rohypnol for a couple of months. You haven't been compelled to serve me, to love me, to give your life to me...you just wanted to."

"But...that can't be!"

"Oh, it is. 14 Months ago you made a choice. That choice expired, and for the last few weeks you have been living another one."

"I have?"

"Yes, Justin, and I'm about to ask you to make another choice."

"You are?"

"Yes, I am."

She turned to her desk and picked up something with each hand. What she picked up was small and I couldn't see what her hands were curled around.

"You can't claim ignorance. Now you are making a choice with full knowledge."

She turned her hands over and opened them.

In one palm was a pink pill. In the other was a blue one.

I stared at them. I stared at her.

"If you take the blue one it's all over. You will go back to your apartment, find a job, live your life, do what you want. Your choice."

"And the pink one?"

"The pink one is super concentrated hormones. No Rohypnol, this has got to be a choice of your own accord."

"What will it do?"

"It will change you into a girl. You will work at my store. You can live with one of the other girls. I will set up a small fund for you to eventually retire on. You won't see me much, but I'm sure you will learn to love one of the other girls. Ginger, perhaps. She's like you."

"Like me?"

"She was a warehouseman for a year, and she made her choice."

I blinked.

She grinned. "You can't tell from looking at her, can you?"

"Does she…does she still have…"

"Her package? That's for you to find out. That's always everybody's individual choice. And speaking of choices,"

We were perched, leaning towards each other. Close enough to breath each other's breath. Close enough to kiss, but those days were over. I had choice now, I had other lips to kiss…or not.

Pink or blue.

I picked up the pink pill and tossed it down my gullet.

Heather sat back with a smile. She had a glass on her desk, and it was filled with Coke and bourbon. She handed it to me and said, "Welcome to the real world."

END

Full Length Books from Gropper Press

MY HUSBAND'S FUNNY BREASTS

It's not so funny when
it's happening to you!

GRACE MANSFIELD

Tom Dickson was a happy camper. He lived a good life, had a beautiful wife, then he started to grow breasts, his hair grew long, and his body reshaped. Now Tom is on the way to being a woman, and he doesn't know why.

This book has forced feminization, cross dressing, hormones, gender transformation, pegging and breast growth.

My Husband's Funny Breasts

Feminized by Neuralink!
A simple medical procedure goes haywire!

PART ONE

Sylvia kissed me. "Just think, you won't be a fathead anymore."

"Har de har har," I responded wryly.

I smiled at my wife from the hospital gurney. They were about to take me into the operating room. The doctors had already talked to me, the nurses had given me a sedative, and my brain was about to be fixed.

What was wrong with my brain? A little too much cholesterol causing a slight swelling. Yeah, if you read that right then you can make the joke: I was a fathead. And that was the point of my wife's little quip.

But, joking aside, I was going to be outfitted with a Neuralink. You know, those little gizmos invented by Elon Musk? Just a simple, little chip with awesome powers. It could actually interface with my brain, increase blood flow to certain areas, and, voila, I could be adjusted into good health.

Not that I wasn't already in good health. Heck, I was young and strong and, except for a little fat in my brain, healthy as a horse. A healthy horse.

But Neuralinks were the latest thing, my doctor recommended it, so…why not?

I could like a life free of cancer, diabetes, heart problems, everything.

"Are you ready, Mr. Lacey?"

"Ready as I'll ever be."

I gave a little wave of my hand to Sylvia, my wife, as the nurse rolled me down the corridor. Five minutes later I was slumbering peacefully. Ten minutes later the doctor made a small incision in the side of my head, just below the bone of the skull, and slid a little, teeny, weeny chip into my head.

The little thing, it was actually about as big as a fly's testicles, was guided up through the brain. It would work off my body's electricity, last 100 years, and I might actually live that long, and…and I had the strangest dream.

"Put that on!" My wife was wearing black leather and snapping a whip.

"What? What?"

"I said," she snapped the whip and struck my rump and I felt a sharp pain, "Put that on!"

"Put what on!"

"You know what!" Then she was cracking the whip, and I was running, and she was chasing me, and I yelled…

"Did the monkey pee?"

Nurses chuckled.

"What?" I opened my eyes.

"How you doing Mr. Lacey?"

I stared at the nurse.

"The operation is over. How do you feel?"

"What did I just say?" I was a little groggy and trying to figure things out.

"You asked if the monkey peed."

She chuckled, and behind her my wife giggled.

The nurse held a glass of ice chips and water to me. "Take a sip. And don't worry about the monkeys. People often say strange things when they come out of anesthetic."

"Did the monkey pee," Sylvia laughed.

"Har de har," I murmured, holding back a grin. "What time is it?"

At that moment the doctor walked in. "Hey, Mr. Lacey, high fives and flowers. You are a raving success."

He then showed me pictures of my brain, showed where the chip was lodged.

"And I don't have to do anything? The chip is all programmed?"

"Not a thing. Except maybe have a glass of champagne. The Neuralink is self-contained. You're good to go. In fact, are you still here?"

We all laughed, the nurse had me get into a wheel chair and they rolled me right out of the hospital.

"Oh, good to be home," I said, entering the kitchen from the garage.

"You've only been gone a couple of hours."

"Yes, but in that time I cured the world of dread diseases."

"Wow! You're quite the stud. Want to see if that chip will increase blood flow to your penis?"

I laughed and opened the fridg. "First a celebratorial bit of bubbly, then I will attend to your wicked desires."

I took out a bottle of chilled champagne, worked the tinfoil, and popped the cork.

While I performed such a delicate task Sylvia hugged me, and he rarms went around my body and fondled my not inconsequential manhood.

"Mmm. I can feel that blood flow already."

"So can I," I said as I poured two flutes full.

And I could. My penis was fully engorged, pressing my pants out, and throbbing with the pulsing of rich, red blood.

I handed Sylvia a flute and we toasted, and I smiled inside. Just think, I Ron Lacey will never have a dread disease. I will live to a happy, old age.

"Next year is my turn."

Sylvia was healthier than me, she didn't have any fat on the brain, so I had gotten my implant first. Next year we would have the money and she would get one. We were looking forward to a healthy, blessed life.

She reached a hand into my pants and found my snake. "Hmm. Yes. Blood flow is starting up. Patient is expected to rise to the occasion."

"He has risen."

She pulled me, by the penis, out of the kitchen, through the house, and into the bedroom.

In the bedroom she unzipped my pants and pulled them, and my underwear, off. My turgid member did a dance of happiness.

She took my balls in her hands and massaged them as she sucked on the head of my cock.

Sylvia is a beautiful woman. About my height, maybe twenty pounds lighter, and those twenty pounds are in her tits.

Yep. She is top heavy. And atop that hourglass figure is perched the most beautiful face. Full lips, blue eyes, blonde hair. Man, I won the lottery when I won her hand.

She rose up, my cock still in her hand, stroking, stroking, and whispered, "Are you going to make me wait?"

I pushed her back on the bed and she yelped happily.

I spread her legs and did the gobble. That's what we call it, 'The Gobble,' when I lick her slit, slid my tongue over her labia, suck on her clitoris and give her the finger. Or two.

"Oh, yes!" she moaned, as she arched her hips up unto my face.

I slithered up her body and began kissing her tits, one after the other, as my hand worked her pussy.

"Mmm....mmmm!" her voice was soft and velvety, husky and filled with desire.

I pushed her up further on the bed and knelt between her thighs.

She reached for me, but I pushed her hands away and slapped her pussy with my dick.

"Hey!" she giggled.

"That's what I dreamed, when I was waking up. That you were whipping me, trying to get me to put something on."

I held my dick and used it like a soft club, slapping her thighs, her pussy, and she laughed and protested, then I placed the head into her vagina.

"Oh," her eyes grew wide.

"You've had the rest, now try the best," I spouted the old ad slogan.

"I prefer the best," her eyes were half closed as pleasure inundated her and warmed her core.

"Then you shall have it. I moved my hips forward and my penis inexorably entered her.

She gasped and grabbed my arms with her hands. She held on as I filled her up.

"Oh, yeah. Yes." She breathed. Her eyes were open, but she wasn't seeing much. The pleasure was swarming her.

"Uh oh," I froze.

She looked up at me, "What?"

"Brain alert! Brain alert! Too much blood to penis, must handle." I began to fuck her jerky style, just plunging an inch and jerking back.

"Oh, fuck!" She yelped. "I love it when you do that!"

"Uh oh!"

"Oh, no!" she moaned, when I froze again.

"Pussy alert. Bweep! Bweep!" I began to circle my cock in her, rimming her and feeling the head, deep inside her, move in circles.

"Oh...FUCK!"

"Uh oh!"

"NO!"

"Squirt alert. Prepare for incoming!"

"Oh, Heysoos Xristo!"

I began lurching, pouring my seed into her.

"Oh, you fuck!" she groaned. "I'm not there, yet."

But it was too late. I pulled back and my already limp dick flopped out of her.

"Sorry, babe. But you're just too hot."

"Well, you're going to have to finish me the other way."

"No!"

"Yes! I don't care if it's messy, get down there and use your tongue!"

She pushed on my shoulders, then my head, and squirmed around. Then she was pulling my head into her crotch.

Funny, I was usually strong enough to resist. But I guess undergoing the operation had made me temporarily weak.

"Hey...MMMPH!"

I didn't like eating her out after I squirted in her, but she loved it. She said there was something about a man praying at the alter after the offering had been given turned her on and made for special orgasms.

Well, whatever, I was in for it now.

I tasted my sperm, and it was sort of bland, a little salty, a little musky. Okay, I could handle that.

I licked and sucked her hole, and she began to discharge more and more. Heck, I had never cum that much, and I ended up swallowing a couple of tablespoons of my own gizm.

"Oh, yes! That's the way!" She kept my head tight and bucked, and began to cum. For a long minute I was subjected to the wild gyrations and gymnastics of her hips, then she relaxed.

I slowly raised my head. She looked at me and laughed. "You're a mess."

"Bweep," I said sadly. "Mess alert."

I stood up and headed for the shower. Sylvia relaxed for a minute, then joined me.

Happily, we soaped each other. I soaped her tits and she soaped my dick, and...okay, we're sex fiends. Can you blame us?

Then we dried each other off and returned to the bedroom. She was in her closet, picking out underwear and clothes, and I picked up her bra and put it around my waist. I remembered how she did it, fastened it in front and then slid it around. I snaked my arms under the straps and pulled them over my shoulders, then I bent to pick her panties. As I was stepping into them—

"What are you doing?"

I looked at my wife. She had the most puzzled expression on her face.

"What?"

"What are you doing putting on my bra? And...and my panties."

I looked at myself and was supremely confused. I didn't understand what she was objecting to. I mean didn't I always...didn't I... "Huh?"

Bra, goes on woman, slowly percolated through my cranium.

"I don't know." I just stood there trying to figure things out.

"Well take it off!"

"Oh...okay."

She watched as I moved, as if in a dream, and took off her bra. I took the bra and her panties to her hamper and stood over it, looking at them. I wanted to put them on. What was going on? I wasn't a cross dresser. I needed to—

"What's wrong with you?" Sylvia took the bra and panties out of my hands and put them in the hamper. "Bweep! Bweep! Stupid alert!"

She shook me and I snapped out of it.

"What the fuck," I had a twisted expression on my face. "Why the hell did I do that?"

"I don't know, but don't do it again. It's freaking me out."

"Bweep?" I asked.

"You got that right. Now get dressed, in your own clothes, and let's head out for some yard sales."

So I did, and we did, and things just got worse.

We stopped at a corner house, big yard, and blankets and tables were spread out and filled with goodies.

Usually, I go looking for things like tools, manly toys, things like that. Sylvia examines art nick nacks and ponders whether they will fit into our house.

Today, however, I fond myself standing in front of a table, fingering lingerie. And I must have creeped people out, just standing so quietly and feeling the material. As if from far away I heard whispers, and people moved away from me. But I was fascinated by the soft texture of the filmy underthings. They felt so delicious, and I could imagine the softness sliding over my body. And my dick would be so hard. And they should make men's under things of this material. Why, I'd be hard all the time. I'd be—

"What are you doing?" Sylvia hissed into my ear. She tugged my shirt and pulled me around.

"What? I…I'm just looking…" Again, I was terribly confused. I had been doing the right thing, looking at clothes, and the clothes felt right, and I just wanted to…

"Come on," she whispered harshly. She pulled me from the yard and I suddenly noticed everybody staring at me.

"Why are they looking at me?"

"Because you're creeping them out. Obsessing over women's underwear and…and your pants!"

"What about my pants?" I looked down. I had worn sweat pants, and they were bulged out. The shape of my dick could be seen tenting the material. "Oh!"

What the hell had I been doing? That was why those people…I was so embarrassed.

Sylvia pushed me into the passenger seat, and went to the driver's seat. I was moving too slowly, so she just took over. As we started up from the curb she groaned, "Last time I'll ever take you to a yard sale. What the hell were you thinking?"

"I don't know. It just felt right. I…thought I was supposed to be there."

"Feeling women's underwear and rubbing your cock?"

"I was rubbing my…"

"Didn't you get enough nookie this morning?"

"Honey, I'm sorry, I don't know what happened."

But she wasn't placated. She drove with a stoney face, and when we arrived at home she stomped into the house.

I watched her storm into the kitchen. I didn't know what was wrong with me. I felt like something had gone sideways in my head, but I didn't know what. I mean, I was happy, everything was cool, but…then I got excited by female clothes.

And I do mean excited.

Sylvia and I had made love this morning, yet an hour later I was erect and throbbing, and I think my legs were even trembling a bit, as I stood at the yard sale and examined woman's underwear.

What the heck?

I got out of the car and started walked towards the kitchen, and stopped. My head turned. My body was facing the kitchen, but my face was looking at the laundry. The washing machine. The drier. The pile of dirty clothes.

My wife's clothes on top, with her brassiere sticking out from under a dress. A purple dress. With little white flowers. Such a pretty pattern.

My body turned away from the kitchen, faced the big basket full of clothes. I took a step. Another step, and something inside me gently reminded me, 'No.'

But that little voice was nothing in the wind of my desire.

I found myself standing over the laundry. I reached down and picked up the bra. I sniffed it. I felt it. I admired it. Sylvia had such wonderful taste when it came to clothes.

I took off my shirt.

My dick was poking out in my sweats, a tent pole of massive proportion. A tent pole for the Ringling Brothers and Barnum and Bailey circus.

I ignored my crotch, well, not completely. I enjoyed it, but I had to put on the bra.

I did, and it felt good…but empty. I wished I could fill the bra. And then I realized I could.

Aunt Jane had had a mastectomy last year. She had worn breast forms for a while. When she went back home she had left them with us. I had tossed them into a box in the corner of the garage. All I had to do was go get them.

Breast forms. In a box.

That little voice was whispering to me…'that's wrong…don't do it…take off that bra!'

I told the little voice to shut up and get out. I walked back to the far corner of the garage, lifted the box down from a shelf, and there they were. Ds. The same size as my wife. A perfect size to fit my bra.

Not my wife's bra…but my bra.

I pulled a cup out and managed to slide a boob into the cup. I did the other one.

I just stood there, feelings of pleasure washing through me. I felt so sexy. My hard on was like a gun barrel. Long and pointing and ready to shoot.

I walked back to the laundry, feeling so sexy, feeling myself bounce inside the bra. If only I had real boobs. That was what I really needed.

I bent down and picked up a pair of panties. I could see a bit of dried discharge in the crotch. I lifted the panties to my nose. I smelled the dark spot. Mmm. I put the panties on.

I stood there in the gloom of the garage, knowing something was wrong, but helpless to do anything but look at the purple dress.

Purple. A royal color. A rich color. I picked it up and shimmied into it. I had to pull it over my breasts, and it felt so good. It felt like when I rolled a ribber over my cock, but for my whole body. My whole body felt like a penis in the dress. The material slithered over me, sexually charged my skin.

I felt so good, so right, so…the door opened and Sylvia looked out.

"Oh, My God!"

I turned and stared at her. She slammed the door. Locked it.

I started sobbing. I knew something was wrong, but I didn't know what. I went to the step by the kitchen door and sat down. I could feel the cold cement on my butt. My cock was poking the dress out, my tits were so big and beautiful…and all I could do was cry. I knew Sylvia was in the kitchen. I knew she was listening.

"I'm sorry," I said, as my tears fell on the floor. "I don't know why I'm doing this."

Nothing from the house.

My back was lurching with the sobs now. I was happy, I really was, but something was wrong and I couldn't figure it out.

"I can't stop myself. I'm sorry."

For five minutes I sobbed, my heart pouring out, my tits jiggling in my bra. Then I heard the door unlock.

The door opened, just a crack. I didn't look. I couldn't stop myself from crying.

It opened all the way.

"Ron?"

"I'm sorry," I wailed.

She stepped out on the step. I kept crying.

She sat down and I leaned my head towards her, big splatters of tears falling on the floor.

Then I was hugging her, crying, happy, but miserable, and nothing made sense.

"There, there," she said. "It's okay."

For long minutes I sobbed, then, because she was there, because she was now holding me, an arm around my shoulder, comforting me, I began to dry up.

"I'm sorry." I snuffled and wiped my eyes.

She said: "I think it's the Neuralink."

"You…you think so?" I rubbed my eyes with my forearm, and

wished I didn't have hair on it, on them. Or on my legs.

"I'm going to call the hospital."

"What do you want me to do?"

"Just sit and wait."

"Can I have a drink?"

"Pour me one, too."

"Okay."

She stood up and went back into the house.

I managed to stand up and I walked into the kitchen. As I mixed the drink I heard her talking on the phone.

"What do you mean I signed release forms! If course I did! We both did, but that's neither..."

I took a sip. A long sip. I listened some more.

"But he just had the operation today, and now he thinks he's a woman!"

No, I didn't. I didn't think I was a woman. I *was* a woman.

"Why the hell would I want to talk to your lawyer? I want you to look at my husband and make this stop happening..."

I drank some more. A lot more. Then, because Sylvia was taking so long, I drank her drink.

Mmm.

And I admired my breasts in the kitchen window. Big ones. Hefty. Auntie had a rack, and so did my wife, and now so did I.

"I am going to sue your ass off!"

She stomped back into the kitchen, and I admired how her boobs shook with every step. I had boobs that would shake with every step, I just had to make them real.

She looked at me, sitting there with a simpering look on my face. She whispered, "Fuck!" Then she looked at the empty glasses, said another dirty word, and began fixing herself a drink.

"What'd they say?" I asked.

"We signed release papers, there's nothing they can do, the phenomena isn't connected with the operation, call the lawyers."

"Wow," I said, feeling one of my boons. "Do you think I can get implants?"

Sylvia was putting the bottle back in the cupboard and she froze, then she began to cry. Long, wracking sobs that shook the frame. Sort of like the sobs I had done.

I went to her and hugged her, and she froze for a moment, then melted into me. "It's all right," I whispered. "Everything is going to be fine."

For a long minute she cried, then she toughened up. She backed away from me and said, "I'm going to call our lawyer."

"What do you want me to do?"

She looked at me, and she had the most curious expression on her face. A twist of disgust and fascination. She said, "I don't know. Go find some high heels, and some nylons."

"Really?"

She shook her head. "Knock yourself out." Then she picked up the phone and went down her contacts.

I went down the hall and into our bedroom. I went into our closet. Her high heels were in a row at the back of the closet. I picked a pair with straps. I figured if my foot went past the platform the straps would keep them on me.

I grabbed a pair of pantyhose and went back out to the bedroom. I could hear Sylvia droning from the living room.

"Look, Charles, it happened right after the operation...uh huh. But what's the big deal about this Corporate Shield thing? Oh...but..."

I took the time to trim my toenails, then I pulled the panty hose up my legs. It took some work, I remembered something about Sylvia rolling them, but I couldn't figure out what that was. Eventually I did get them on, and I pulled them up tight, making my balls scrunch into my crotch a bit, which felt really good.

Funny. I didn't want a pussy. I liked having a cock. I especially liked having a big cock. For a small and slender man I had a pretty good sized ding dong.

I stepped into the heels.

I stood in front of the mirror and admired myself. I was lithe and slender, except for the big boobs. My lips were full and...my lips.

I walked to my wife's make up table. I looked at all the creams and potions and thing. I didn't understand much. There was some mascara, I could do that, and I had seen Sylvia use those weird scissors things on her eyelashes, but I was interested I...oh, there it was. I picked up a gold tube. Except it wasn't lipstick, it was a weird applicator, a little brush thingie, but the color was red, and I had seen Sylvia use it, so I used it.

I heard Sylvia hang up the phone. I heard her walk into the kitchen. She must be making another drink.

I painted my lips thoroughly. Two coats. Got every nook and crevice, and I smacked my lips. My mouth was red, and sexy, and if I was a man I would have kissed me.

But my hair...yuck!

I picked up her brush and tried to comb it, but though I made it neat, it just sort of lay there. It wasn't long enough. I didn't have enough body. I wished I had seen this coming. I would have grown my hair out long ago.

Then it hit me. Sylvia had a wig. Once she had gotten a short hair cut, and hated it. So she had worn a wig for a couple of months...and it was still in the closet!

I ran, well, walked and almost fell, into the closet. On the top shelf, way in the rear, I found the box with the wig. It was long and blonde, gentle curls that would drape over my shoulders. I took it out of the box and slipped it onto my head. I tried to slide the clips into my own hair, and I think I did pretty good, then I turned around and closed the closet door. There was a mirror on the back of the door, and I stared at myself.

I was beautiful. I hadn't been a big man, narrow shoulders, and I fit perfectly into the dress. I did have angular hips, but the shape of my bosom gave me enough curve to make up for the hips. What was interesting was that my running legs were so shapely, and I was glad I wasn't a hairy fellow. Though I did need to shave this and that...

"Ron?"

"In here," I called. I brushed my hair back a bit, and was about to open the door when Sylvia opened it. She stood there, frozen, and stared at me.

I stared at her. I heard that little voice telling me things were wrong, but I didn't understand what could be wrong. I just felt so right and beautiful...what could be wrong?

"Oh...oh..." she stuttered.

"Are you all right?"

She gulped and nodded.

"What did the lawyer say?"

"He, uh, he said we wouldn't be able to sue the, uh, manufacturer of the Neuralink. Not unless we sue the doctor first, but we can't sue the doctor because...oh, my God."

"What?"

She shook her head. Then she said, "Come out to the kitchen. I need another drink."

I followed her through the house. I admired her ass. It was rounder than mine, quite sexy. But I thought my ass was pretty good. I tried to duplicate the way her butt swayed. I felt awkward in the heels, but I think I managed to get my butt to look sexy.

"Sit there," she said, pointing to a chair.

I sat, and she got down the bottle and placed it on the table. She filled our glasses with ice and poured them half full with Wild Turkey. Then she opened the fridg and took out a can of Coke. She poured half the can into one glass, and the other half into the other glass. Then she shoved a glass at me, sat down, and took a big glug.

I giggled. "We're going to be alcoholics."

"Today it's okay," she returned soberly. She kept staring at me.

"What? Did I get it wrong? Did I do something wrong?"

"No. No."

"Then what?"

"It's just that...why did you use lip stain?"

I just saw it."

"You know it lasts longer than lipstick?"

"Oh. Is that bad?"

"It is if you want to be seen as a man in the next few days."

"Oh." I frowned. Then, brightly, "I don't."

She shook her head, took a big swallow, then went back to staring at me.

"So what do we do now?" I asked.

"Tell me, why did you start putting my clothes on?"

"They just look so good, and they feel so right."

"But you realize you're a man?"

"Oh, of course," my disappointment must have showed because she took another big gulp.

I sipped. And I looked at the slight trace of lipstick…lipstain…on the rim of the glass. Sexy.

"So are you going to continue this?"

"This being…being a woman?"

"Yes."

"Well, I guess I am a woman. At least I have a woman's breasts, but my dick is so big and hard."

I noticed," she spoke drily.

"So I guess I am a woman."

"Okay." She finished her liquor and got up to make another one. As she waited for the refrigerator ice to fill her glass she said, "I was freaked out. You really freaked me out. But I guess it was just the shock. I mean, you've always been so manly."

"I'm sorry." I didn't know what I was sorry for, but it felt appropriate to say that.

She turned to me, leaned her butt against the sink and spoke almost contemplatively. "Now that the shock is over…I have to say you make a good looking woman. If it wasn't for the hips you'd be a better woman than me. What are you going to do about work?"

"I don't know. Should I do something?" I think I realized there was a disconnect in my mind, but I couldn't imagine what it could be.

"Tell them you're transitioning."

I frowned.

"What?"

"Government contracts."

That made us think. Would the government keep giving my company contracts if I was…feminized?

"Come on," she grabbed my hand and led me to the computer room.

We sat down and she opened a browser and went looking. She typed in, 'government contracts and sexual transitioning.' Right away we hit pay dirt. There were a whole host of sites advising of transgender rights.

"But am I a transgender? Or a crossdresser? Or what?"
Sylvia regarded me. "I don't know. Let's ask Quora."
She pulled up Quora and typed in a question: 'My husband got a Neuralink, then started dressing like a woman…is he a crossdresser or transgender?'
She started to close the computer, but I stopped her. "What else does it say about cross dressers?"
She turned back to the computer and started surfing. We found a massive community of cross dressers, and transgenders, and just about everything else under the sun.
Fascinated, we learned about drugs for transitioning, ways to keep a pecker solid under hormones, the benefits of surgery vs hormone therapy and on and on.
The most fascinating thing for me, however, was Noogleberry. Noogleberry was a company that made breast pumps. Not for milk, but to make the breasts larger simply through a pair of cones and a pumping device. The cups are placed over the pectorals, the air is pumped out, and over months the breast tissue forms into tits.
"I can have tits! Real tits!" I exclaimed.
Sylvia looked at me. "Do you want me to buy this thing?"
"Oh, yes!"
So she ordered their deluxe kit, and I dreamed about having a nice, big set of knockers. No more breast forms. Just real tissue. Real tits!
After that we kept surfing, looking at educational sites, perusing porn sites, and growing hornier and hornier.
Finally, Sylvia turned off the computer and pushed her chair around. She looked at me with lust filled eyes. "Fuck. I just came this morning, but I'm ready again. Could I actually prefer you as a woman?"
"Maybe, but I'm a little concerned with my dick. It feels so big and large in this dress. How will I ever hide my bulge?"
She dismissed that, "First, we fuck a lot. Second, we can get you special underwear, a gaffe, I think it's called. Female impersonators wear them. Third, if that doesn't work we can put your cock in one of those chastity tubes and tied it back between your legs."
"Ouch."
"What a woman will do to be beautiful, eh?"
"Whatever it takes, I guess." Then: "Would you like to go to the bedroom?"
She sat and didn't move, and her eyes were far away. Then: "I need something more. I'm still a little freaked out by everything."
"A little more alcohol? Maybe a little making out?"
She nodded. "That might do it."
We returned to the kitchen and filled our glasses up again. Funny, we had done a lot of drinking, and we were high, but we weren't getting

drunk. I think we were too wired for the alcohol to really hit us. So we sat and sipped and talked, and halfway through the night Sylvia went and got her make up kit. We talked for hours about make up, about shades and hues and how to blend everything just right. Then she made me up. God, it felt good. I felt my face come alive, and I was astounded at how different, and brilliant, my eyes started to look. She glossed my lips and I felt magnetic. We even tried on some jewelry, and decided to get my ears pierced.

After a couple of hours Sylvia leaned across the table and pressed her lips to mine. Oh, it was wonderful, soft, caring. We had open eyes, and I know I was trembling. Then we sat back and kept talking, and giggled every once in a while.

And we kissed again. And again. And my lip gloss got on her lips, so she had to make herself up.

Finally, near midnight, drunk, but still not too drunk, we adjourned to the bedroom.

Arms around each others waists, we made it into the bedroom.

"You still have a hell of a bulge," Sylvia observed, taking her dress off. I stared with lust at her large breasts.

"I've been hard all night," I admitted.

"Not for long," she laughed.

She took off her bra and panties, then she came to me.

"Maybe we should leave my dress on, just pull my panties down."

She nodded. "This is so weird," she kissed me, "I'm kissing a girl. I feel like I should be accused of Lesbianism, but it's not…you're still a man down there. Where it counts.

"The best of both worlds," I said.

We sat on the bed and began really making out. She felt my fake boobs, and I felt her real ones. She pulled my dress up and scooted my panties off and stroked my cock.

"Geez," she blurted, "it feels bigger!"

"The better to fuck you with, Little Red Riding Hood."

We laughed, then I moved down to her nipples and gave them a lip stained sucking.

"Oh, God," Sylvia moaned. "It's weird, knowing your lips are so red, it makes my nipples harder.'

I reached into her cavity with a couple of fingers and began massaging her rim. She moaned and circled her hips, trying to fuck my fingers.

Then I pulled my dress up and knelt between her thighs. My dick was fully engorged, and it did feel bigger. I put it at her portal and we paused for a long second.

Staring at each other, glorying in our eyes and lips, our hips and tits. Then I began to push the head gently into her.

She grunted, and her hole opened a bit and allowed me in. Just the head sat in her hole, big and dripping, lubricating her.

She reached down and grabbed my balls. She pulled me gently, and I began to slide into her hole. Inch after excruciating inch, she swallowed my cock with her pussy. Our eyes were locked. I pressed on her tits with my hands, and she gave a mournful groan. "Ah....God! It's never felt this way!"

Then I was all the way in, my pubes pressed against her pubes, and we just stopped and waited. We watched each other, and gloried in the feel of my big dick stretching her out, filling her up, connecting us in every which way but loose.

"Oh, Heysoos, I'm almost afraid to move. This feels so good. I don't want to risk losing it."

But we could only hold still for so long, then I twitched, and she turned her hip a bit, and we were off to the races. Out of control. Filled with love and lust. I fucked her deep, and she held on, and touched my face, my lips, and watched me with soulful eyes.

I was penetrating her, I was grinding and groaning and pushing my penis into her snatch.

I had cum too soon this morning, but I managed to hold off this evening.

She began to lurch, to cry out, and her hips made little, slamming motions into me.

I felt her muscles twisting me, rippling along my cock, and just as she began to relax I let go,

"Oh....oh!" Semen shot out of my dick and coated her insides. She lay under me and enjoyed the feeling of my pulsing, vibrating cock, then we were done.

"Oh, God," she murmured. "I never knew...fucking a woman...I should have tried it before."

"But what about the cock?"

"Keep the cock, lover. And keep it hard." She kissed me then, and we lay there, entangled, and drifted off to sleep.

KNOCK KNOCK KNOCK!

I sat up in bed. I felt wonderful, but a little bleary. "What's that?"

Sylvia rolled out of bed and said, "I'll get it."

She padded through the house, and I listened, then she came back. "Honey, come out here."

Puzzled, I followed her into the living room. She held the curtains open a slit and I peeked out.

News vans. Four of them. And a gaggle of reporters standing around on our lawn, cameras at the ready, news gals fixing their make up.

"What the hell?" I asked.

Sylvia went to the door and called out, "What do you want?"

"Mrs. Lacy, is it true Neuralink turned your husband into a woman?"

"Mrs. Lacy, are you going to sue Neuralink and..."

"Mrs. Lacy. We're FOX news and would like a statement regarding..."

"We'll be out in five minutes!"

"We will?" I asked, a bit scared.

"Absolutely. We can't sue, but we can make life miserable for those assholes at Neuralink."

She led me back to the bedroom, but first, we need to fix you up."

Quickly she dressed me. Put me in one of her good dresses. Fixed my make up, brushed out my wig.

"I need a shower."

"Later. This is more important."

"You're really going to have me step out there like this?"

"Hey, you wanted to be a woman..."

I did, but this was so...sudden!

It was closer to ten minutes, but we were pretty good looking for a rush job. Sylvia opened the front door and stepped out.

An explosion of questions, but Sylvia merely held her hands up and waited.

When everybody had calmed down she said, 'One person at a time!" And she pointed at channel 5.

"Mrs. Lacy, did Neuralink change your husband into a woman?"

"Neuralink did effect my husband. He had the operation and immediately became fascinated with being a woman. How far this change is going we don't know. Yes...CNN."

"Can we see your husband?"

"In a minute. She's shy, as you can understand, so give her a moment to get ready. I'll answer questions, and when we're done she'll come outside. I'll tell you right now, this is a shock, and she won't be answering any questions. And if you bozos get too obnoxious we'll just go back in the house. And, oh, yes, we will be turning the sprinkler system on immediately after we finish this little shindig."

I listened from behind the door. My heart was pounding and I was actually having trouble breathing.

"You, Channel 6..."

"You refer to your husband as 'she," Does this mean that..." the questions went on.

And, finally, Sylvia opened the door. "Come on out."

"I was fully femme. I had huge breast forms. I was made up and had long, blonde hair. My legs were sexy, and my dick, thank God, was limp.

I stepped into the sunshine.

Pictures. Click, click, click.

And I suddenly felt good. Confident. Like a good looking woman should. I held my head up, and this improved my posture, and my breasts stood out.

And I started to get a boner. Oh, shit.

Fortunately, Sylvia noticed, and quickly pushed me into the house.

Reporters banged on the door, people were shouting questions, and it was obvious that reporters had about as much manners as a coyote eating a rabbit.

Sylvia smiled and stepped out onto the porch. She picked up the metal rod that turned the sprinkler system on. She placed it on the little cross thing that controls the water, and said, "Five…four…"

The reporters scattered. They tripped and fell and scampered off our property.

Sylvia turned the water on at two, and a couple of reporters screeched and jumped.

Sylvia came back into the house and we laughed. Our eyes were bright, and everything was looking good.

In an hour things were going to look better than good.

An hour later we had finished eating, and were talking and laughing about the news people, and…KNOCK KNOCK!

Sylvia frowned. She went to the door, prepared to blast whatever stupid reporter had decided to not follow the ground rules. I followed along.

"Mrs. Lacey? My name is Herman Denkers. I represent Neuralink."

Sylvia cocked her head and pursed her lips. It was curiosity mixed with defiance.

"May I come in?"

"Wipe your feet."

He did, she opened the door, and he entered.

And looked at me. And breathed, "Oh, my!"

"So what do you want?" asked Sylvia.

He turned to her and assumed a businesslike attitude.

"Neuralink finds itself in a strange position. The company doesn't wish to admit any kind of guilt, after all, no tests have been done, but we feel it would be best…" blah, blah, blah. Lawyerspeak. About as significant and boring as speech can get. But, in the end…

"We are prepared to offer you one million dollars. We would like your husband to enter into a comprehensive study of his condition. You won't be required to…" Blah, blah, blah.

My eyes opened wide. A million dollars. We would be millionaires! We could travel the world! Own a big house. Never work again! OMG!

103

When Herman was done it was Sylvia's turn.

She looked at me, and I shrugged. I was thinking more about make up than million dollar deals. I was too dazed to think coherently.

"Mr. Denkers. I am a regular person, I don't understand a lot of what you said. But I will tell you what I think you said, in plain English, and you might not want to say anything, but you're going to have to nod your head, or shake it, and then write us a check. Right now."

"Yes?" he spoke tentatively.

"What you said is that you don't want us speaking on Facebutt anymore. It's bad publicity. And while you are not willing to cop to what you did to my husband, you are willing to pay us to cancel our Facebutt account and never speak of what has happened to Ron. Is that a fair summarization?"

Carefully, he nodded.

"Then we want ten million dollars. We will be part of your study, though we reserve the right not to take any medicines or have any procedures done without our full consent. We will cancel Facebutt, and do you need a pen?"

Herman Denkers paused. Then he pulled out his cell phone and texted somebody. I caught a glimpse of the text.

10 mil?

The answer came back less than 15 seconds later.

Do it.

"I've got a pen…"

The door closed and we stared at each other. In less than ten minutes we had made ten million dollars.

"I could have gotten more," whispered Sylvia. She put her arms around me.

"Oh, you push over," I wrapped my arms around her.

We giggled, then we laughed, and we couldn't stop laughing.

No more newspapers. We could buy a country estate and live in comfort. Travel. And no more of that stupid Facebutt shit. I really hated that big tech company.

Six months later…

I sat down on the side of the bed and took my Noogleberry out of it's case. The cups were shiny and padded perfectly. I wore them for a couple of hours at a time, and my boobs were getting quite large.

Silvia entered the bedroom. "You need any help?"

"If you could hold this one in place I can hold the other one."

She held the cup over my tit and I placed the other one, then started pressing the handle. Air began to leave the cups, and my breasts began to grow larger.

"How large are you going to make them?" asked Sylvia.

"Not sure. I'm a C right now, and I'd like to be as big as you."

"Sounds good. Look at how the nipples are standing up."

As the breasts grew so did the nips, and they were like little half inch rockets, standing up and waiting to blast off.

"And they feel so good. Whenever I do this I get hornier and hornier."

"I didn't notice," said Sylvia drily.

I laughed. "Sorry, you can always say no, if you want."

"And miss out on the big dick?"

We chuckled.

"Why do you think it's getting so big?"

"Well, the tits I understand. I'm causing my boobs to get bigger, and that calls for more blood flow, and the Neuralink can't tell the difference between my brain and my tits."

Sylvia nodded.

"As to my dick, I just think that the more we use it, the more blood it pumps, the more blood the Neuralink thinks it needs."

"Well, whatever, it sure is making me a happy camper. It must be near ten inches now, and it really fills me up."

"Fill me up, buttercup," I sang to the old tune.

"So what do you want to do about me?"

We sat and stared at each other. My boobs were getting bigger, more blood was flowing, I was getting hornier.

"Well, we can get you a Neuralink if we travel out of country, but we risk brand X, and I don't think we'll score ten million dollars if something goes wrong."

"What do you think could go wrong?"

"I don't know. Probably nothing. but...we could always force Neuralink to do you. We do own a lot of the company now. And they are the most reliable."

She smiled. "That was pretty smart of you to invest five million in them."

"I knew there would be a demand. Heck, it wasn't just the good health, it was the fact that every person who wanted to transition would want to get the implant. And statistics have proven that almost half the men in the United States want to be women, and half the women want to be men.

"Would you still love me if I turned into a man?"

"More than ever."

"But…"

"Look, honey, the worst that could happen is that we would have two swinging dicks in the family, and we'd have to start doing it anal. Are you ready for something like that?

"Wow, to have a dick. I don't know. I mean, I sure do like yours, but…" she shrugged.

"Or we can just keep thinking about it, keep it on the back burner."

"But what if I don't turn into a man? Not everybody changes sex, and they're getting better at predicting."

"Then there are the benefits of being super healthy, never getting sick, and living twice as long…" she said.

It was my turn to shrug. Thinking about it, I said, "Man, woman, it doesn't matter what we are…all that matters is that we love each other. And I'm pretty sure that I know the answer to that one."

She nodded. "Okay, then. I think I've made up my mind."

"You know what you want to do?"

"I do. I've considered all the pros and cons."

"So tell me! I can't wait to find out!"

She did, and I was so happy for her.

END

The
Feminization
Games

GRACE MANSFIELD

Jim Camden was a manly man, until the day he crossed his wife. Now he's in for a battle of the sexes, and if he loses...he has to dress like a woman for a week. But what he doesn't know is the depths of manipulation his wife will go to. Lois Camden, you see, is a woman about to break free, and if she has to step on her husband to do it...so be it. And Jim is about to learn that a woman unleashed is a man consumed.

This story has female domination, forced feminization, cross dressing, chastity belts, pegging, shrunken manhood and orgasm denial.

The Feminization Games

Boob Maximizer

He wanted biguns…he got 'em!

PART ONE

"I guarantee it will work."

Lance Smith snorted. "It will make tits bigger?"

"Guaranteed."

"And how do you know?"

"Come here..." Doc Brown led Lance into a back room. In the room were several tables laden with bottles, bunsen burners, and exotic machines.

Lance was actually impressed. He had known Doc Brown since college, and while the guy was a little over the top, it was obvious that he was sincere.

"See...see!"

Doc Brown pointed at a cage on a table in a corner. Lance leaned down and peered closely. Mice. Little white mice that were a little plump on...Lance peered even closer.

"Oh, my God!"

"That's right," Doc Brown folded his arms and took on a smug expression. "They have tits."

"Can I see one?"

"Sure."

The Doc opened the cage and took out one of the two mice. He held it up so Lance could examine it.

Sure enough, the mouse was...stacked. it had big tits. For a mouse.

"Can I touch it?"

"What are titties for?" giggled Doc Brown. Truth was, he was a virgin, and the idea of sex embarrassed him.

Lance reached forward and touched the tiny boob. Sure enough, it was a tit, almost looked human, except that it was miniature and on a mouse.

"OhmyGod!"

Doc put the mouse back in the cage and closed the door. "There's your proof. What do you say now?"

"I say I want it."

"It's expensive. A thousand dollars a bottle."

"I don't care! I'd take a dozen bottles if you have them."

The Doc frowned. "This is a very concentrated formula. One dab should increase bust size by a full, uh, cup, or whatever they measure boobs by.

"That's okay. I understand. Can I have a dozen bottles?"

"Okay," and in the Doc's mind he was thinking, 'It's your funeral.'

A short time later Lance was writing a check for $12,000. It was his whole savings, but…but he was so excited.

He chortled, "Man, when Mazie sees this…she's going to love it!"

"Remember, only a single dab massaged into the skin."

"Sue, yeah. I got it," Lance said, not giving it much thought, then he was out the door.

Behind him, Doc Brown looked at the check and smiled. Then he frowned. If he was any judge of character, he'd better start working on an antidote, or a 'shrinker formula,' or something.

"Honey, I'm home!" Lance called out cheerfully.

No answer. Good. Mazie was still at work. Boy, was she going to be surprised.

He went into the bedroom, opened the paper sack and took out the twelve bottles of Boob Maximizer. The bottles were small, and they weren't labeled. He put them in the drawer of the little table next to his bed. Then he frowned.

Truth was, Mazie hadn't been receptive to the idea of getting implants. And he had tried creams and potions before, and she had just laughed.

"I'm a comfortable C cup. I don't want to carry big, old behemoths around and get a sore back. You want big boobs then you better think about getting your own implants."

Huh. Short-sighted woman didn't know what was good for her. But he'd get her there. Once she had a massive set of mammaries she'd be thanking him.

He took one bottle and went to his wife's make up table. Hmm. Eye shadow wouldn't work, nor lipstick, although the idea of Mazie with big, puffy lips was somewhat appealing to him. Ah, he picked up a blue and white bottle. Cerave. Just the thing. A skin moisturizer his wife always used.

He took the squeeze bottle into the bathroom and squirted the whole thing down the toilet. Then he opened the bottle of 'Boob Maximizer' and started putting the stuff into the empty tube.

Oh, man, it was difficult. The old saying, 'it's like putting tooth paste back in the tube,' came to mind.

Still, he put the bottle and tube nozzle to nozzle, and the stuff went in eventually. Huh. Even smelled similar. But not the same. He frowned. He still had a little space in the tube of Cerave, so he went to the kitchen. Hmm. smell and texture, they had to match. Good thing most things were white. He spurted a bit of mayo into the tube, then held it up. Felt the same. Yeah. This would work.

He heard the sound of his wife's car enter the driveway.

Cripes! He ran back into the bedroom and placed the tube back in its position, then went out to greet his wife.

"Hi, babe." He gave her a big kiss.

"Whoa..." she said breathlessly. "You must have done something bad to be that horny!"

He laughed. "I've been a good boy." In his mind he was chuckling at how bad he had been, and how happy she would be when she had some truly bodacious boobs.

"Well, Mr. Good Boy, help bring in the groceries and we'll get some dinner started."

So he did. And all the time he kept sneaking glances at his wife's form.

She was five foot five, good figure, but, like so many women, she needed some help up top. And she was going to get it. He mentally rubbed his hands together in satisfaction.

Dinner. A little TV. Time for bed.

All the while Lance kept glancing at Mazie.

"You sure you didn't do something bad?" she joked. "You've been staring at me all night long.

"How could I not stare at such a beautiful woman?"

"Wow. Flattery, too. What it is you've done, I give you permission to do it again."

They laughed, and he made a mental note to 'do it again.' Heh. Right!

They went to bed, and made he couldn't control himself. The idea of her having mountainous mounds made him so horny. He rolled over and grabbed her breast.

"Wow, you don't waste time, do you?" She kissed him. A gentle, loving kiss.

He managed to turn it into a tongue poking, slobbery thing, and they were off and running.

"Oh, baby," he moaned, running his hands over her body. His chest felt warm and tight with desire, and his penis was hard a rock. An extra hard rock.

"Boy, something's got you all hot and bothered. Babe, your dick is like a steel rod. And...my gosh, you're dripping all over the place."

"Just my love for you," he mouthed her breasts, sucking on the nipples gently. *And my love for your big breasts about to be,* he thought.

She laid back and helped guide him into her. He was shaking with desire as he pushed forward and...

"Oh...fuck!" he blurted.

"Oh, no! You didn't cum already, did you?"

The feel of his squirtem coating her inner thighs was the answer.
"I'm sorry, I'm sorry."
She hugged him. "It's okay. I should have realized you were a little too excited."
"I'm sorry."
"You could always get down there and do a little mouth work..." she said, hopefully.
Lance was silent. He wasn't fond of oral sex, and especially if he had just squirted all over. One thing he really didn't want was a mouthful of his own cum.
Mazie sighed and pushed him off her. "All right."
Lance rolled onto his back and lay there. His balls were empty, and it felt good, but he really wanted her to have big boobs. If only she would rub that Cerave into her chest.
Mazie lay on her back and waited for Lance to go to sleep. She needed a little private time with Vinnie the Vibrator.
But Lance was restless. He was fantasizing about her chest and couldn't sleep.
Finally, Mazie got up. She had a wet spot under her and she wanted a towel, and it would be nice to take a quick shower and wash his squirt off.
She took a luxurious, hot shower, even washed her hair, and then came out of the shower. She would have to dry her hair, but that was okay. She picked up her hair dryer and went into the next room.
She needn't have bothered. Lance was quite awake.
She came back into the room and got into bed.
Lance's eyes burned in the night.
Mazie rolled over, closed her eyes, and went to sleep.

And so the week went. Every night Mazie came home to the very energized Lance. The evening passed and Lance seemed extra horny.
And, truth, Mazie was getting extra horny. Lance kept squirting before she could get close, and then he lay awake and watched her with big eyes. She wasn't able to get out her vibrator, and she ended up taking late showers. Now cold showers, to calm herself down.
Funny. People always thought it was the guys who had to take cold showers, but, not so. In fact, if Mazie got much hornier she was going to pop!
"Geez, honey, what's got into you?" she asked on Friday night.
"I'm just a little extra in love with you," he quipped.
"Well, that's great." Inside she was sort of tired of the extra attention. She just wanted an orgasm and not all this endless slobbering and quick on the trigger ejaculations.
For his part, Lance was going crazy. He wanted her to put Doc

Brown's formula on her tits. He wanted her to grow, and grow, and... GROW!

He wanted her to have massive triple Ds. He wanted to bury himself in sucking and fuck her boobs and...and she just took her showers and never used the stuff.

Finally, Saturday afternoon, they were getting ready to go out and she was sitting at her table. She picked up the tube of Cerave and squeezed a small glob into her hand.

Lance grinned and watched.

Suddenly Mazie frowned, and sniffed at her hand. "Huh," she grunted. "Smells bad."

She took the tube into the bathroom and squeezed it down the toilet. "I hate it when stuff goes bad."

Lance stared, open mouthed, and watched a thousand dollars go down the drain. Fuck! What the fuck! Shit! A thousand dollars.

"Well, no loss," Mazie said, re-entering the bedroom. "I can just pick up some more."

Lance almost cried. But he still shot early that night.

Sunday afternoon, and Mazie went out with a couple of her girl friends. While they late lunched Lance took the empty tube of Cerave out of the trash. He smushed another bottle of Boob Maximizer into the empty container. He used more mayo, and a bit of ranch dressing. When he thought the smell was perfect he wiped the tube clean and put it aside. When Mazie got another bottle he would compare the odors and texture, make sure everything was perfect, and replace the new with his special stuff.

Heh. This was going to work out, after all.

The week passed. Lance squirting all over the place, usually before he could even get inside her.

Mazie was actually getting used to this, and she did manage to get together with Vinnie the Viber, so it was okay. A little frustrating, but not too bad.

But, by Thursday, Lance was going crazy. She hadn't replaced the Cerave, and he was desperate.

"Are you going to get a new bottle of that Cerave stuff?" he finally asked on Thursday night.

"Not yet."

"Well, I'm going by the store tomorrow. I'll pick one up for you. 'Cerave,' that was the name, right?"

"Oh, you're a honey. Thanks, babe."

She kissed him lightly.

And he immediately kissed her sloppily, grunted and groaned and palmed her boobs.

She giggled. "I don't know what you've been putting in your tea, but..."

And they had an almost marathon sex session. Almost, except for the fact that Lance came too soon. But at least she got him to use his fingers.

"Honey, you've been leaving me high and dry. It's time to help me out."

So he risked getting his hands all gooey and finger banged her. Yuck.

The next day he picked up a bottle of Cerave, and before she got home from work he sniffed it, made sure his concoction was just the same, then put his tube in the box and threw out the new tube.

"Thank you, honey." She took it into the bedroom and put the box on her table.

The next night it was still there. And the next night, and the next.

Lance was almost out of his skull. He wanted her to use the stuff. He wanted her to have big boobs.

Finally, unable to stand it any longer, he asked, "How's that new cream I bought you?"

"Oh, it's fine," she said without thinking.

But she hadn't opened it.

Lance could almost cry.

A week later he saw that the box was gone and the tube was...where was the tube?

He found it in the trash. Empty.

Trying to sound nonchalant he asked Mazie, "I noticed the Cerave in the trash. Didn't it work out?"

"No. Something stinky about it."

Another thousand dollars down the drain! And her boobs were still the same size!

"Well, I'll pick up another one for you."

"Don't bother. I'm growing discouraged with the product. I'll find something else."

The next week she brought home some Vanicream.

By that night Lance had managed to throw out her original cream and replace with a cream of his own making. He spent hours trying to get the smell and texture just right. At least this time it was a jar and not a tube. Made it much easier to get the stuff into the container.

And, a day later, he found it in the trash.

FUCK!

A month later he knocked on Doc Brown's door. The Doc opened the door. He was as seedy and wild-eyed as ever.

MAD SCIENTISTS AND FEMINIZATION

"Yes? Oh...yes... the Lance fellow. How's that cream working out?"

Lance followed the Doc through the house and into the laboratory. "Not good, Doc," and he explained how he couldn't duplicate the texture and smell and his wife kept throwing everything out. "And I only have a few bottles left!"

Doc frowned. "What kind of cream is your wife using?"

"She just got a jar of something called 'Neutrogena.'"

"Hmm." Doc sat at a computer and found Neutrogena. "Yes, these chemicals...uh huh...I can do that."

"What?"

Doc turned away from his computer. "I can duplicate their formula so your wife detect the difference."

"Really?"

"Child's play."

"Really? I don't know how to thank you!"

"Of course it will cost..."

"But, Doc, I'm sorry, I have no more money!"

The Doc quickly figured the math out in his head. The cost of the chemicals, the time, about $10 total, but he was entitled to a little profit. "Well, normally it would be about $10,000 for something this complex..."

"But Doc!"

"Since you're a valued customer, however, five thousand dollars."

Oh, crap! Lance thought. He didn't have five thousand dollars.

"Check or money order is fine," Doc mentioned.

Lance's mind raced. "How about a credit card?"

"Nope."

Lance's mind raced some more. He could get the cash with the card, then... "Okay."

An hour later Lance showed up with the cash, and a bottle of Boob Maximizer.

Doc took the money and bottle and promised he'd have something in a couple of days.

Lance replaced the bottle of Neutrogena with his special bottle. Perfect. Perfect. And he went to greet his wife, who had just driven into the driveway.

And, extra blessing, his wife didn't make him wait a week or two before applying the goop to her skin. That very night she sat at her table and rubbed the sweet smelling ointment into her breasts.

He stared at her massaging her breasts, and he gulped, and he felt faint.

Mazie stood up and sauntered towards him with a grin. "What do you say, sailor, want to show a girl a good time?"

He nodded, hardly able to breath, but when she pulled the blankets up they both stared at his cock. He had already cum.

And, the next morning..."EEEEK!" Mazie sat up and stared at her chest. Lance was instantly awake. He had been so horny and frustrated that he hadn't slept well, anyway.

Mazie's chest was near doubled in size! From a comfortable size C she was now a double D, maybe even a G!

Lance stared in shock. He had expected some growth, but not this much...and certainly not this fast!

"Oh, my God!" he burbled.

"What...what has happened?" Mazie got out of bed and almost fell over. Her boobs were so heavy she was going to have to find a whole new sense of balance. She staggered across the room and stared at herself in the mirror.

Her breasts were enormous! They were so big she had to hold them with her hands. And she knew she was going to need to get stronger just to heft them like this. And a bra! My God! She was going to have to see Omar the tent maker to get a bra to fit these...these...massive...

"Oh, my God!" Lance was next to her staring, and licking his lips. He had never seen so much flesh, so much pulchritude, such delicious... even her nipples had grown! They were the size of thimbles, and he had never wanted to suck anything so badly in his life.

"Oh, baby," he whispered, drooling, and he bent his head.

Mazie pushed him away. "What happened? What is going on? How can this be...?"

"Don't worry about it, honey, your boobs are just fine. Just the way I like 'em."

She suddenly got it. She stared at him. "You did this."

"No...no, I—"

"You've been horny for months, and getting me all that skin moisturizer which kept going bad...what did you do?"

"I didn't do anything," he moved forward, reaching for her massive chest. He needed to feel them, to suck them.

"Tell me the truth! What's in the moisturizer you kept getting for me?"

"Nothing, honey. I just—"

She slapped him a hard one. Right across the face. Suddenly he realized that she was actually mad.

"Ow!" He stared at her.

She stood, frightened and angry at the same time, holding her huge boobs up with one forearm. the boobs overflowing and looking so delicious that Lance was in danger of cumming right then. Just looking at them and he was going to—"

"What do you do to me," she hissed.

And, finally, mentally cornered, Lance said, "It's just a little boob maximizer. It's good for you."

She slapped him again, but this time with a fist.

"Fu—!" he was knocked back.

Then she kicked him. Hard. Right in the you know where.

Lance doubled up and fell to the floor.

"You stupid son of a..." then Mazie was sobbing.

Lance groaned and tried to figure out what the big deal was.

"I can't believe you did this to me," Mazie said for the hundredth time that afternoon. They had spent all morning with her screaming at him, and it didn't look like she was done. Not by a long shot.

"I'm sorry, honey. I thought you'd like a little extra, uh, femininity."

"That's what you call it? Extra? You made me into a freak!"

"But...but..."

Lance stared at her chest. He was so damned horny. He had never seen such magnificent boobs in his life, but her anger...wow!

Mazie picked up the car keys.

"Where are you going?"

"To get a bra," she snarled. "And I'm using your credit card." then she was out the door.

And back two hours later, and in an even worse mood. "You son of a bitch! You maxed out your card...I had to use my own."

Her tits now poked out in front of her. And they were really poking. They were like road cones, big ones.

Licking his lips, Lance said, "Well, but...I'm sorry. I had to pay for the last jar of...of..."

She gripped him by the shirt front and twisted her fist. He found himself staring into her baby blues, which weren't looking so babyish right then. "What else did you spend money on?"

"No! nothing! I didn't—"

"How much did you spend on that stupid cream in the first place?"

"Nothing! It was free! I didn't spend—"

Mazie went to the computer, pulled up their bank account, and stared in astonishment. "Twelve thousand dollars!" She turned to him. "You spent $12000 on some stuff to make my boobs bigger?"

"Well, I didn't mean to. I just...he, uh...I couldn't..."

"You stupid, fucking, son of a...come with me!"

She grabbed his shirt front again and pulled him towards the bedroom.

"Honey! Please...you're taking this all out of propor—"

She stopped in front of her make up table. Lance could see her monstrous boobs in the full length mirror, and the mirror wasn't even wide enough to accommodate her new boobs.

She grabbed the cream and unscrewed it. She scooped a huge glob of the stuff out and slapped it on his chest.

"You want big boobs? You got 'em! See how you like living with these...these...these FREAKS on your chest!

She scooped the rest of the ointment out and slapped it on his chest. She put her hands on his chest and started smushing it through his shirt and onto his skin. He tried to back up, but she went with him, pushing her hands onto his pecs, squooshing the cream into his skin, his pores.

"See how you like it you son of a bitch!"

Then he was falling back on the bed, and she was on top of him, pounding on his chest with her fists and crying.

"You fucking...fucking..."

Then she was in the bathroom, slamming the door, and sobbing like her heart had been broken. Which it had.

Lance sat up, now he was crying. He was stunned, dismayed, and finally figured out he had done something bad.

Yes, his wife finally had the tits he had dreamed of, but he was pretty sure he was never going to get to touch them.

Dismally, he wiped the goop off his chest, then took off his tee shirt and put it in the hamper.

The day, as days are wont to do, passed.

Mazie came out of the bathroom. She wouldn't look at Lance except to glare, and she was mumbling curses under her breath.

Lance tried to talk, but her withering stare, her icy demeanor, he wound up saying nothing.

Dinner...without dinner.

Her drinking straight from a bottle, saying things like... 'If I had a knife...somebody give me a gun...son of a fucking bitch!'

Him trying to keep a low profile, and gulping frantically as he caught glimpses of his wife's huge profile.

Her slamming the bedroom door so hard it shook the house.

Him sleeping on the couch. Sad, miserable, and scratching at his chest, which had suddenly started to itch.

Slowly, time ticked.

Midnight, scratching and rubbing at his chest. He was truly miserable, because the itch seemed to be deeper than skin, no way to get surcease from the growing itchiness.

One o'clock. He felt like clawing at his chest. The itch was worse than anything he had ever felt.

118

Two o'clock. Even his nipples hurt. He felt like grabbing them and ripping them off his fevered body.

Three o'clock. Rubbing his chest so hard, his pecs felt inflamed he had rubbed them so hard. They were starting to feel not just itchy, but pained.

Four o'clock. The itching had grown into a pain so terrific, and his head hurt, and he tossed and turned, and...finally, went to sleep. Or, more like passed out from the pain.

Seven o'clock. He rolled over and felt something hit him in the chest. Blearily, he opened his eyes, looked down at his chest, and...

"EEEE!"

He had HUGE tits! BIG tits! MASSIVE boobs. He sat up and placed his hands under them. They overflowed his hands and he just sat and stared.

The bedroom door opening, and Mazie was suddenly standing over him, staring at him.

He looked up, opened his mouth, tried to speak, couldn't say anything.

Mazie started laughing. She laughed and laughed and laughed. "Hah hah! Sauce for the goose is sauce for the gander you stupid idiot!"

"But...but...but..."

He was crying now, and big drops fell on the huge expanse of flesh swelling from his chest.

Mazie, laughing hysterically, returned to the bedroom. Ten minutes later she exited the bedroom. Her chest was big and high, and she didn't look at Lance.

"Honey...please...can't you..."

She merely laughed at him and walked out of the house.

For an hour Lance sat and held his new tits. He cried, he snuffled, he wondered what he was going to do.

Finally, he stood up, and nearly fell over. The weight on his chest made him want to do nothing but walk forward.

He went into the bedroom and put on a tee shirt. His boobs sagged and he looked ridiculous. He realized that he needed a bra.

But where does a man get a bra? And especially for boobs as big as his?

He headed out to the garage and grabbed some duc tape. The next half hour was an education in frustration and enlightenment. How does a bra work? How much of a load do the straps take? How does a strip of tape duplicate the cups of a bra?

Finally, feeling very awkward and silly, he was able to put on his shirt. In the mirror he found that he had not made a bra so much as just bound his chest. The result was a big puffy chest, and boobs that hurt.

Hurt or not, he had to do something about them.

"Doc! You've got to do something!"

Doc Brown's eyes opened wide at the site of his customer with a bulging chest.

"What the heck is…"

Lance pulled off the strips of tape, and nearly died when his nipples felt like they were being ripped off.

Doc Brown goggled, then he grinned. "My stuff really works, doesn't it?" Then: "But why did you put it on yourself?"

"I didn't. My wife put it on me.

"Well, wow. You're really stuck now."

"But don't you have an antidote?"

"Sure. $10,000."

"WHAT!"

Doc thought about all the household ingredients he had used. And in the proper proportion. "Well, for you, $9,000."

"Okay. You have a deal. Where is it."

"Not so fast. Money first."

"But, I don't…Okay."

He took out his wife's credit card.

"Cash only."

"But…I can't…Can't you trust me? I've been a long time customer!"

"I trust you to get the money first."

Lance sighed and nodded. Head hanging, he walked out the front door.

At the bank he tried to get a loan. No dice.

Then he tried to open another credit card. Less dice.

Finally, he tried to take out a loan on his house.

Nope.

"But why not?" he beseeched the banker.

"You've already got a loan out."

"I do not! I inherited that house! It's free and clear."

The banker reached into a drawer and pulled out a contract.

"I lent the money this morning personally."

"Let me see that!"

The banker held the contract so Lance couldn't reach it, but so that he could read it.

"But…that's impossible! Why would my wife borrow all that money!"

"I don't know. You'll have to talk to her."

Feeling lower than a basement in a parking garage, Lance left the bank. He drove through the streets unaware, his mind trying to come to grips with his dilemma. He was entirely aware of his big tits getting in the way of the steering wheel.

What to do? What to do?

Finally, he realized he was going to have to go beg Doc Brown. Maybe the scientist could be convinced. And, if he couldn't, Lance began thinking of more drastic measures.

He pulled up to Doc Brown's house, went up the walk and knocked on the door.

"Yes?" Doc called through the door.

Lance frowned. "Doc, I've got to talk to you."

"I'm busy right now. Come back later."

Lance pounded on the door. "Doc! Let me in!"

"Go way!"

Sounds behind the door. Low voices.

Lance pounded on the door so hard the latch gave way. The door swung inward, and Lance goggled.

Doc Brown was...his wife...they were hugging....they had been kissing...what...what...

Doc Brown was irritated. "I said I was busy!"

"But that's my wife!"

Doc turned to Mazie, "But you said you weren't married."

"I won't be. I'm going to see a lawyer right now."

Doc turned back to Lance. "You see? Everything is on the up and up."

Mazie walked out the door, as she passed Lance he noticed that her chest was normal. "Hey! Wait! Wait!" He ran after her, tugged her arm and she turned. Yep, her tits were back to being a nice size C.

"What do you want?"

"Your tits! How did you get rid of them?"

She smirked. "Doc Brown gave me the antidote. I didn't know you had bought the Boob Maximizer from him. Good thing he was my first stop."

"But...but, honey..."

Mazie advanced on Lance. "What?"

Helpless, he backed up and blurted, "The bank...you took out a loan!"

She smiled. "Yep. And I signed your name. Good luck on paying it off."

"But...you can't sign my name."

"Sure I could. I've been signing it for years. My signature is now more accepted as yours than yours is."

"But...but why?"

"To pay for the antidote, stupid."

"But...that's $20,000!"

"It's not my money so I don't care."

"But...but..."

Mazie ended the conversation by stomping off. Lance watched her car disappear down the street, then turned back to Doc Brown.

Doc was looking at the latching mechanism and scratching his head.

"Doc! you gotta help me!"

"You really busted this door."

"The hell with the door. You gotta give me the antidote for these... these...

"Oh, I don't have any more of that."

"But...you don't..."

"Your wife just bought all of my stock. She got a good deal, too."

"But you have to make me some more."

"Oh, no. No can do. Your wife took the recipe, and I simply don't have the time to recreate the formula."

"But, Doc!"

"Sorry."

"But...why were you kissing her?"

Doc Brown looked puzzled. "I don't know. She just saw your car pull up and started kissing me."

Lance didn't know what to think of that, so he snarled, "Ahh!"

Lance drove around for a while, but soon realized that he was going to do nothing but run out of gas. He finally headed for home. When he got there his wife's car was in the driveway. Struggling to keep his breasts up, his arms were getting tired, he walked into the house.

His wife was sitting on the sofa, smirking at him.

"Well, my stacked husband is home. How's it going, Mr. Big Boobs?"

He trudged past her and entered the bedroom. Then he came back out. "Uh, Mazie?"

"Yes, dear?" she drawled sarcastically.

"Do you really have the antidote for...for these?"

"Hmm. I do recall having a couple of bottles of Boob Maximizer antidote. Now what did I do with those silly, old bottles?"

Lance went down his knees, and almost fell over, and began begging. "Please, honey. Please! Can't you let me have some?"

"Not until you've learned your lesson."

"Believe me, I've learned it."

"No. You haven't. You haven't until you have fully experienced what it is like to be a woman. And especially to be a woman with big breasts."

"But...but...but what can I do to convince you to give me the antidote?"

"Well, for starters, you look silly standing there and trying to hold your boobs up. The specially made bra I used is on the bed. Go put it on."

Lance went into the bedroom, found the bra, took off his shirt and put it on. He felt instant relief for his sore arms. The straps were heavy on his shoulders, but he could stand the weight.

Marveling at this fact of woman's architecture, he went back to the living room.

Mazie started laughing. "You look ridiculous."

He stood, red-faced, and hung his head.

"You look like a man wearing a bra. Do I look like the kind of woman who would be married to a man who wore woman's clothing?"

"Uh...but there's nothing else...I..."

"I guess we're going to have to make you look like a woman."

"WHAT?"

She stood up and went into the bedroom. He followed helplessly.

She handed him a bottle of Nair. "Take the bra off, put this on, wait fifteen minutes then shower."

He took the bottle, stared at her, but had no choice. He gave a nod and began taking off the bra.

15 minutes later he stepped into the shower. He watched dismally as his body hair swirled into the drain. He stepped out to find Mazie waiting for him. She snickered.

"Can I have the antidote now?"

"Are you kidding? We've just gotten started. Put your bra on and sit at my make up table."

He did, and Mazie was right there waiting. "Now, this is moisturizer. A simple bath won't get you clean enough." She cleansed his face with a little pad. "Now, this is primer. This will..." and she led him through the steps of make up.

Fifteen minutes later he stared at his face in the mirror. His eyebrows had been plucked, his eyelids were shaded, his lips were red... he didn't look like a man at all. But he also didn't look like a woman. His face might be pretty, but his haircut was a man's, and he still had the muscles of a man.

Mazie was biting her lip, trying to keep from laughing.

"Please," he begged.

She stepped into her closet and brought out a dress. It was skimpy and stretchy and low cut. She tossed it to him. "Get dressed."

"But..." but there was nothing to say. He pulled the dress on. Mazie pulled him in front of a mirror.

He wasn't a big built man, and his big tits gave him more than enough curves. The most amazing thing, however, was the decollete. His big boobs stretched out the dress and he had about a mile of skin showing. It was so stretched that his nipples were visible.

"Oh, my God," Mazie muttered.

"What?"

"Look!"

She pointed at his crotch and he looked down. His dick was erect and quite prominent.

"What, but, what do…" he was confused.

"You like it! You like having big boobs and wearing a dress."

"Honey," he cried. "I don't! Please, give me the antidote!"

"Not until you've learned your lesson."

"Believe me, I've learned my lesson."

"It appears you've learned something else, too." She rubbed up against him, and his cock grew even harder.

He pushed her away.

"What? You don't want to get it on? I've got to tell you…you're sort of turning me on. How many times have I gotten dressed up for you, just to go out and have some fun. Now you know what it feels like. Kinky and horny."

Lance just shook his head.

But, if there was any good news, it looked like Mazie was getting over being angry. At least, she was grinning.

"Now then, try on my wig…yes, oh, that does wonders."

He looked in the mirror at himself. His face was so red it shown through the make up, but he actually did look like a woman now. Except for the big bump in his groin.

She rummaged the dresser and pulled out a corset. "Put this on."

He held the thing and was aghast. It was so small, and the fabric felt so…tight!"

"Come on, we haven't got all day."

Shamed, but still erect, he lifted up his dress and pulled the corset over his torso.

He didn't have much of a belly, and now he had less. And the bump in his dress was less.

Mazie stood thoughtfully and studied him. She shook her head.

"What?"

"Not enough. I know. Your dick is pointed up. Put it down."

It was difficult, the material was so tight, but he managed to push his dick so it was pointing downward. It hurt.

Mazie laughed. "There we go. And, look, you're trying to bend a little bit. Trying to relieve the pressure?"

He nodded.

"Well, good. It makes your butt pooch out."

"Honey, can't we—"

"Nylons," she tossed him a pair. "You've…no wait. Let's paint your nails, first."

He tried to sit down, and it was a struggle, but he finally made it. He could hardly breath, and he felt like he was going to suddenly snap straight and slide out of the chair.

Mazie bent down and painted his toenails a bright red. Then, while he was waiting for them to dry, she put fake fingernails on his fingers and painted them a bright red.

"Blow on your fingernails. I'll help you with the nylons."

He blew, and she unrolled stockings up his legs and fastened them to the straps hanging from the corset.

Finally, she went to her closet once again, this time bringing out some high heels. His favorite...when they were on her. High, so her calves would shape up. Open toed so he could see her nails poking out so sexy. Sling back.

But they were on him, not her. His toes, his calves.

Of course he overflowed slightly, and they were tight on him, but... they were still sexy. He could feel his dick trying to get harder and he bent over and groaned.

"Oh, I think he likes it," Maxie laughed.

"Please, honey...I've had enough."

"Nonsense. Now stand up and let's get a picture."

She pulled him to his feet, which made his feet truly ache in the tight shoes, and pushed him in front of a mirror. She stood next to him and snapped picture after picture. She even held the camera with one hand and felt his big tits with the other.

"Hey!"

"Hey, what?" she snapped. "You're always groping me. How do you like it."

And, the funny thing, he did like it. He liked the feel of his flesh being squeezed. He liked the stimulation to his nipples. He was glad the corset was hiding his excitement, because he knew Mazie would just laugh harder.

"Okay, you've dressed me up. Can we undress me and give me the antidote?"

"What? All dressed up and nowhere to go? Not a chance. We're going to Charlie Coyote's."

"NO!"

"Yes. And we're going to get drunk and look for men to fuck."

"Mazie! I can't! You can't make me do this! Give me the antidote!"

"Not until you've had the full experience."

"But I've had the full experience."

She suddenly grew tired of his whining. She put her face right up to his and snarled. "You emptied our savings, and then I had to take out a loan on the house. We're broke, in debt, and all because you wanted a bigger set of tits. Well, buster, you've got them now, and you're going to find out what it feels like to have every man staring at you, looking for a feel, wanting to fuck your little, round butt. Now go get in the car. I'll be out in two minutes."

His mouth opened and closed.

"And don't start crying. I don't want you to ruin your make up."

Totally defeated, but still with that betrayer hard on, he staggered out of the house.

Ten minutes later Mazie came out of the house. what had taken her an hour to accomplish with him she had done for herself in minutes. She was fully made up, wearing a green dress, a little more modest in the cleavage, and strutting.

Well, she was a good looking woman.

Lance stared at her.

"Get out," she said, opening the driver's door.

"We're not going?" Lance said hopefully.

"Oh, we're going, but you aren't driving with your first set of heels."

Lance got out and went around to the passenger side. He saw neighbors staring and he wished he could shrink into a ball and roll away.

Mazie laughed. "You don't like the neighbors staring at your sexy legs and big boobs?"

He didn't say anything.

"Here, we forgot to put earrings on you."

She had a little bottle of alcohol and she dabbed his lobe, then shoved a needle through it.

"OW!"

"Baby." She put an earring on him. it was long and dangly. Then she did his other ear.

"And don't forget this." She handed him a choker. It was black with little diamonds on it. This will emphasize your tits, and you want the men to notice that you've got a big pair, right?"

He shook his head, and was aware of the danglies brushing against his neck.

"Okay, sport. Let's go have some fun."

Charlie Coyote's was an eatery during the day, and a night club at night. Every night beautiful women and handsome men slid across the small parquet floor to a five man combo.

"Oh, things are rocking tonight, aren't they?"

Mazie locked the car and came around to link her arms with Lance's.

"Mazie. Please don't do this to me."

"Heck, I didn't do anything to you. I believe it was you who bought the Boob Maximizer."

"Yeah...but, I'm sorry."

"No you're not. Not yet. Now, come on."

She walked him across the parking lot, and it was good that he did because he was finding it very difficult to walk in high heels.

Inside the bar the place was jumping. Men and woman danced, couples and small partiers talked at the tables, and the bar was three people deep.

Mazie found a table and pointed Lance towards a bar. "A couple of drinks. You know what I like. Here's my purse, and it might help if you tried to speak in a higher voice."

Lance found himself standing alone, looking back at the table where Mazie waited with a grin, looking towards the bar.

It was only twenty feet away, but it felt like a mile.

Lance walked slowly, and measured his steps carefully. He was unsteady, but he managed to make it.

He stood and waited, and slowly moved through the crush.

And a hand cupped his bun!

"Hey!" He squealed, and a couple of fellows smiled at him. One fellow, a swarthy fellow with a sly look, merely grinned.

"What you want, ma'am."

He turned to the bartender. He opened his mouth, but nothing came out.

"Order?"

Finally, he managed to blurt. "Pina Coloda and a Coke and bourbon."

"What?"

He had to say it again, and he tried to raise the pitch of his voice.

The bartender started mixing, and he opened Mazie's purse and searched for money. No money. But there was a credit card. Maybe there was a bit left on it. But maybe not. What to do...what to do.

The barman put the drinks down and asked, "You want me to run a tab?"

He nodded.

He picked up the drinks and turned around and his boobs slapped into the guy behind him.

"Whoa," the guy gulped and stared at his chest.

"Sorry," whispered Lance, and he staggered through the crowd.

Now he was so embarrassed that he was in a hurry. He almost fell, but managed to make it back to the table. He gave Mazie her drink and sat down next to her.

She sipped appreciatively, and he gulped his whole drink down in a gulp.

"Whoa," she quipped. "You might want to make things last."

"Okay. Okay. You've had your fun."

"No…no. I haven't. Now the game is simple. You've got to get a man to come on to you."

"I've got to fuck a man?"

"Oh, maybe. You could give a blow job, or if you can find a man that likes trannies, your butthole is definitely for sale. No charge." She giggled and sipped some more. "So, you're all dressed up, and you've got to trap a man."

"But why?"

"Because that's what women do, silly. Why do you think I get dressed up before I go out?"

"I…because…"

"Because I want you to fuck me. I want you to suck my boobs and show me how much you love me. And now that's what you have to do."

"To…to have sex…"

"Like I said. A blow job is fine. Extra points for taking it up the heinie, but that's the price of the antidote to those big pillows you're toting on your chest. Now, watch me, and I'll show you how it's done."

She gulped her drink, grinned, then stood up and headed out.

She stood in the back of the crush around the bar, and he watched as she shifted her weight and rubbed her thigh against a guy's thigh. A look, a smile, and a conversation was started.

for a moment he felt a sharp rise of jealousy, and he could only imagine what that conversation was. 'You come here often?' 'Yeah.' 'Want to fuck?"

He looked away and tried not to imagine his wife with another man.

For a long minutes Lance sat there and wished he had another drink. Well, he had to get one, and he had to get out there and…and press his thigh against some guy's. So he—"

"Want to dance beautiful?"

The fellow was big, athletic looking, and towered over Lance.

Lance's mind went in seven directions, but he nodded.

The man held out his hand and Lance stood up. They stepped onto the dance floor.

Lance wasn't much of a dancer, but he did know how to lead. Problem was, he wasn't expected to. The fellow took him in his arms and swirled him through the pack of dancers.

Which was good. Lance found himself holding on, and being supported he didn't trip and fall over on his heels.

They danced, and Lance actually found the sensation of being controlled and guided over the floor exhilarating. Time and again he thought they were going to collide with another couple, and the fellow picked him up and swung him this way and that, and his heart was thudding in his chest.

His over-sized chest. The fellow was staring down at it whenever he could, seemed almost mesmerized, and Lance began to feel a strange sense of power, of control over another human being.

Finally, after two quick dances, the fellow guided him to a quiet spot to the side of the bar. "I'm Johnny."

Fuck! He hadn't thought of a name. "Betty," he blurted, momentarily losing control of his voice. It was the name of his cousin, and it would do.

Johnny tilted his head slightly and smiled. "So you come here often?"

Lance shook his head.

"Would you like a drink? Maybe unwind a bit? You seem awfully nervous."

Lance nodded and whispered, "Bourbon and Coke."

Johnny waved to the bartender and called out an order. The barkeep nodded and went about preparing the order.

Johnny moved Lance back, and suddenly Lance found himself with his back to a wall. Men and women streamed past them into the corridor with the bathrooms off it. Johnny braced one arm on the wall next to Lance and Lance found himself effectively corralled.

"You know, you really are a beauty."

Lance stared wide-eyed. Johnny was leaning closer, talking intimately. "You haven't been dressing up long, have you?"

"Dressing up?"

"As a woman?"

"I...I..."

Johnny laughed, showing some white teeth. "There, you're all nervous again."

The barman appeared and handed them drinks.

"Two more, Todd," Johnny said.

Todd nodded and went back behind the bar.

They sipped, and this time Lance forced himself to actually drink slowly.

Johnny said, "What amazes me is your chest. I mean, those are real. Yet you don't look like you've been taking hormones. How'd you do it?"

Lance's voice sounded like it was from another planet to him as he answered, "Good genes."

Johnny chuckled. "I guess so."

The drink helped. Lance began to relax.

Johnny helped by holding up the conversation, smiling, and treating Lance respectfully.

A second drink, and Lance started to get dizzy.

"You okay?" Johnny asked, suddenly concerned.

"I don't know. It's gotten really hot. Do you feel hot?"

"We should go outside, get a little fresh air."

"Oh."

"Come on, we can go out the back."

That was the point that Lance figured something was wrong. A couple of drinks never made him feel this dizzy, and it was so damned hot.

Johnny supported him and walked him down the corridor. They stepped through the back door and into a parking lot.

"What's happening?" Lance asked. His voice was slurred.

"Come on over here. You can sit down in my van."

"What? Don't wanna. I need to go…"

He tried to move away from Johnnie, but the bigger man effortlessly kept him walking towards a far corner of the parking lot.

"Don't wanna…lemme go…"

The van door slid open and another man was in the door. He grabbed Lance by the arm and pulled him.

"Wow! Nice boobs!"

Then Lance was in the van and the door was sliding shut. He felt hands on his body, grabbing his buns, feeling his tits. What had been sexy and gave him a hard on was no longer sexy.

The driver's door opened and closed, and the motor roared to life.

"Let's go…"

Lance tried to struggle, but he was thrown back by the sudden motion of the van. He fell and was pushed onto a mattress. He tried to move, but he was held down and hands lifted his dress.

"Fuck, this bitch is built!"

Voices laughing, then his panties were pulled down and…and thumb was pushed into his rear!

Lance tried to move his butt away, but his butt was drunk, too, and, it did sort of feel good, even though everything was wrong and…

WOOOOOO!

Red lights flashed and the inside of the van was lit up.

"Shit!" Somebody yelled.

"Go around!" Johnny screamed.

"I can't!

CRASH!

Lance sat on the back of an ambulance and cried. He had been drugged. Rohypnol the cop had called it. The 'date rape' drug.

A few feet away a cop was talking to Mazie.

"Yeah, they get some poor tranny, drug her, take her out and rape her and beat her up. Your husband is lucky."

"So you were waiting for them to make a move?"

"We've been watching them for a week. Just sorry it had to be your husband."

A few more sentences, then Mazie thanked the cop, came over and sat down next to Lance.

Lance sobbed. Fuck his ruined make up. He couldn't stop.

"You ready to go home?"

Lance nodded.

"Come on." Mazie took his hand and led him to their car. Lance was aware of people staring, but he didn't care.

Mazie put him in the passenger seat, then got in the driver's seat and started the car up.

They drove through town silently, except for Lance's snuffles and gulps. They arrived at their house and Mazie got out and came around to Lance. She got him out and walked him into the house.

She guided him into the bedroom and sat him down in the make up table. She began repairing his make up.

"What...what are you doing?" a frightened part of him was scared she'd make him go out again.

"Lance, you're an asshole. But you're my asshole."

He listened as she educated him.

"Women have to watch out for men. We are weaker, we don't know how to fight, so all we can do is pick the people we want to be with. But when the man you want to be with is a bully...that's bad."

He nodded, knowing exactly what she was saying.

"To be betrayed by my own husband...heck, I know you like big boobs, but I don't want them. What you did...it was wrong."

"I know," he cried. The tears coming again.

She waited for him to dry up.

"Now you know. Now you've been helpless while some asshole has his way with you. Did you like it?"

He shook his head. He had stopped crying so she finished repairing his make up.

"So what are we doing?"

"Your lesson is almost done. But there's something else you have to learn." She rolled lipstick on his lips. He tasted the wax and found himself pressing his lips together instinctively.

"You have to learn the good side. The side I was experiencing before you had your momentary lapse of sanity. It would be a shame if you came out of this knowing only the bad. Are you ready?"

"Ready for what?"

"Come with me."

She led him into the kitchen. She mixed him a drink, but with only the bare touch of bourbon. She had him drink it while she turned on the music. Then she took him in her arms.

They danced, and he felt her hips sliding against his. For the first time since the Rohypnol he felt an erection. It felt good.

131

They danced, swaying, not moving around much, but moving. She began kissing him. Holding him and pressing her lips to his. He felt the buzzing begin in his mind. He felt the heat in his chest. She felt his boobs, gently, hefting them, holding them, palpating them.

"You can feel mine, if you want."

He did. He touched them carefully, aware of what an asshole he had been, and he found a sweet joy, no matter that they were small, in fondling a part of the woman he loved.

They danced into the bedroom.

"Would you like to experience love as a woman?" she asked.

He found himself nodding. Gulping, but nodding.

Mazie lifted his dress and pulled his panties down.

He lay there, hardly able to breath. The corset was so tight, so restrictive, but that gave him other sensations, good sensations.

She stroked his cock, then she arranged a couple of pillows and turned him over. She went into the bathroom and returned quickly. She had a jar of Vaseline.

"This is what it feels like." She slathered lube on his hole and he marveled. It didn't hurt. It felt so good, and he felt himself giving minute jerks to her gentle fingers.

She inserted a finger into him and he gasped and arched.

"It's good, isn't it."

"Yes," he mumbled.

She put two fingers into him and began reaming his butthole. He couldn't help but groan.

Then three fingers.

"Would you like me to get out my vibrator?"

He nodded.

So she did. She touched it to his brown star and slid it gently in. He was relaxed now, and it slid easily, filling him, making him open his legs and moan.

"I'm going to turn it on now."

She did, and he began to cum. Not an explosive cum, but a sneaky ocean that swelled up and overwhelmed him.

"Oh...oh..."

She worked him, swirled the vibrator inside him, and she stroked him, and the semen left him.

Finally, she pulled the vibrator out and turned it off.

"Oh, God!" he breathed.

"Want more, don't you?"

"Yes," he said into the pillow he had been biting.

"We can do it again. We can do it all you want. But you're going to have to do something for me."

"Anything." He turned over and looked at her with eyes of love.

"Keep those tits for a while."

"What?"

She pulled his neckline down and began suckling his breasts. The sensation was out of this world, and though he had just cum he couldn't deny the heat going from his chest to his chest.

"You see," she finally said, "I realized something. I realized that I like you with tits. I like you all made up. But I also like you with a dick. Do you know how wet I got making you look like a woman?"

For the first time that night, in fact since this whole thing had started, Lance found himself giving a strangled sort of chuckle.

"So I will give you the antidote, but not for a while. And I am going to dress you up and make sweet love to you. Is that okay with you?"

Lance nodded.

"Good. Now, I've been doing all the work. Would you mind freshening up your lipstick, then coming to bed and eating me to a frothy squirt?"

"I'd love to," Lance answered.

And they hugged, and then he did as he was told.

END

Sam thought he was a tough guy. He was cock of the walk, a real, live, do or die Mr. Tough Guy.

Then he made a mistake. He took on the wrong … woman.

This is the story of what happened when Sam finally met his match and learned who the really tough people were.

This book contains female domination, male submission, forced feminization, male to female transformation, cross dressing, chastity, pegging, and much more.

Too Tough to Feminize

National Lipstick Day

then the men started growing breasts…

GRACE MANSFIELD & ALYCE THORNDYKE

PART ONE

"I can't believe it!" I snarled as I walked into my girl's club meeting.

I'm Janice Keskin, I'm five foot six, 130 pounds, heavy on the top, blonde and blue eyed.

The other three girls, members of our little 'Girl's Club' looked at me.

Sherri snorted. "Sounds like man trouble." She's a ginger. Good tits, but nowhere near as big as mine. Her own blue eyes crackled with humor.

Annie Boscone laughed. "Don't pick on little Prissy Tits. She's a brunette and she might even be tittier than I am. She likes to make up her green eyes very smokey. Very sexy.

"Come on, girls, let's find out what the problem is before we slap her tits." Felicia Gandsill sat back and gave me a friendly but jaded look.

Sherri and Annie giggled.

I plopped down at our table on the patio of Charlie Coyote. Coyote is the best Mex eatery in LA, and we met there once a week and sipped a drink. Or two. Or three or four.

I waved to Jose and he waved back. My drink was on the way. The other girls were already started.

"Okay, what did Ronnie the Bozo Brain do now?"

I stewed until a drink arrived, then gulped half in one sip—I had to catch up, right?—then put my elbows on the table and started talking.

"Look, it's national breast awareness month next month, right?"

The girls nodded.

"Well Ronnie, Mr. Bozo Brain, knows we all get involved in that, and he said...he actually said..."

"Come on, out with it girlfriend," Felicia said, checking her lipstick in a compact. She didn't have to check, she was always flawless.

"He said that a woman without boobs is not really a woman."

The other girls blinked. Felicia looked up from her compact, Annie and Sherri both opened their mouths.

Felicia was the first to speak: "What a rude fuck."

"Man," I muttered. "I'd like to teach that knucklehead a lesson."

"You and me, sister," grunted Annie.

Sherri said, "I know he said it, but you also know he gives LOTS of money to our charities, and last year he really made us proud."

"Are you sure he wasn't thinking about a character in one of his movies?"

"No. No character. We had it out. I called him a lot worse than Bozo Brain, and he backed off, even looked sheepish, claimed it was just a bad joke, but he still said it. And I can't believe it."

We were all silent then, and Jose appeared, fresh drinks, disappeared.

"We should teach him a lesson," offered Felicia.

How do you teach a movie mogul a lesson?" asked Annie of all of us, of no one.

We sat and thought then, and just because we looked like Bimbos didn't mean we didn't have some serious brain power among us.

Annie gnawed on a thumb. Sherri stared into her drink. Felicia...she always the dangerous one...Felicia was tapping her tube of lipstick on the table, her eyes a million miles away.

"It's too bad..."

"What's too bad, Fee?" asked Annie.

"It's too bad we can't teach him what it feels like to be a woman."

Chuckles.

"Fat chance," I snorted. "That manly man? He injects testosterone directly into his dick."

Smiles. Talking about men's dicks always makes us smile.

"So what if we took away his dick for a while?"

We all looked at Felecia. "What?"

"Not forever...but what if we could just make him limp?"

Annie laughed. "Short change him?"

Sherri: "The Incredible Mr. Limp It."

I giggled. "That man wants sex every day, sometimes multiple times a day. If he didn't have his dick he wouldn't know what to do."

"No...no. I'm serious. Look, let's set him up with Cancer Awareness Day. We can have him do something ludicrous, then we can slip him something to make his dick totally limp, and then..." she grinned.

"And then we convince him that something about cancer..."

"We don't want him to think he has cancer."

"Side effects...it's got to be side effects..."

The ideas were flowing now, and the girls were bubbling with excitement.

"Of course, it can't be permanent..."

"But he's got to think it's permanent..."

"But what would make a man limp for a few weeks?"

Felicia tilted her head slightly and grinned, "Do you remember that fellow I sponsored last year? The convict? For re-entry into society?"

"How could we forget," Annie spoke ruefully. "You were bragging about the size of his dick for months."

We giggled, but Felicia leaned forward and grew intent.

"He told me that the prison system is experimenting with drugs to make convicts limp. Well, sex offenders, specifically, but—

"But if we could apply such a drug to a sex fiend..."

"Can you see it? Ronnie, Bozo Brain, Mr. Big Hollywood Stud... limp."

We all laughed.

Jose brought more drinks.

"So what's the name of this drug?"

We looked blank, but Annie reached into her purse and brought out an iPad. Sherri was right on her heels.

Felicia and I made limp dick jokes while they surfed the net, then Annie looked up.

"Heysoos used a pogo stick for a crutch."

"What?" I asked.

"It's pretty common. And it's easy to get a hold of."

"Spill it, sister."

"Depo Provera. It reduces testosterone. That simple."

"Where do we get it?"

"It's in our birth control pills."

"What?" We all blinked.

"So we just give Ronnie our birth control pills and he goes..." I held my pinkie up and made it droop.

We all started laughing then. The idea...the ease...it could be done.

"But we have to do something so he doesn't equate us giving him pills with his puny peter."

Silence. Jose with the drinks, bless that boy.

"I've got it," blurted Felicia.

"Herpes?" asked Annie.

"STD?" wondered Sherri.

"Very funny, my fat and stupid friends."

Annie and Sherri giggled.

"No, we need him to do something that can be suspicious of a side effect."

"Your English is atrocious," I observed.

"Fuck that," she took a big gulp and faced us. "One year everybody shaved their heads."

"I hated that," I said.

"And we've worn ribbons and vagina hats and..."

"Get to the point."

"Lipstick."

We were blank, but Felicia was on a roll.

"Look, we have a big meeting, we all put on lipstick...even the men..."

"Oh my God!" I saw it.

Annie: "You could get Ronnie to give the main speech, capped off with him putting on lipstick. Everybody cheers…"

"That night he takes you to bed and…can't satisfy you."

Now we were all hysterical, holding our guts and laughing loudly. Jose brought us drinks to quiet us down.

"But, I don't want him to go limp forever."

"Nah. Just a little Depo."

"And he becomes a 'little' man."

More laughter.

"You know," mused Sherri, "I'll bet we could put the stuff right into the lipstick. Not have to even give him a pill."

And so the plan was born.

"Hey, Honey!"

"Ronnie looked out from his closet. He is a handsome dog. Got an Errol Flynn grin, wears his hair long and wavy, and has a big penis.

Oh, Lord…do I love that big penis.

"Yeah, babe?"

"You need to let me give you a blow job!"

"You sure? We're almost late as it is."

"Oh, I'm sure." I giggled on the inside. All aboard for the last train to Funsville.

He came out of the closet and crossed the room to me. I was sitting on the bed and I unzipped his fly and extracted that wonderful hunk of man meat.

"Oh, that feels good," he sighed as I slurped on his hog.

I gripped the shaft and began stroking. My hands barely went around the thing, and he shuddered with pleasure.

He began to rock gently, sliding the big tube between my painted lips. "Oh, yeah…" he crooned.

I slapped his balls lightly. He jerked, and I knew that turned him on. I could feel his balls tighten up, it wasn't going to be long now.

I reached round his buns and felt for his asshole.

"Oh, fuck," he blurted as I slipped a finger into him.

There we stood, me sucking and poking, him thrusting and lurching, and I felt ignition. His dick jerked, I could feel the muscles of his asshole tighten, and the jism began to course up his cock.

"Mmm,!" I moaned as I gulped and gobbled.

"FUUUU…!"

Squirt after squirt. Big squirts. His last squirts for a month.

Finally, no more spurts of semen, I backed away. His cock was drooping.

Smiling, he tucked Mr. Happy into his pants and zipped up. "Thank you, baby."

"My fun," I smiled and stood up, and we continued getting ready.

"We would like to welcome our main speaker, our own movie mogul, Ronnie Kreskin.

I was in the front row, waiting. The girls were with me. Their husbands were on the stage, behind Ronnie.

A young man was handing out lipsticks to the men in the crowd, and there were a lot of men.

"Ladies and gents! Thanks for the welcome! I'm here today because we have an enemy. Breast cancer is a deadly disease that must be eradicated. This year we are going to...

He droned on. He was a good speaker, and everybody was hanging on his words, but I, and the girls, were nervous. This was a pretty damned big joke, and we weren't drunk now.

Of course, we had thought about it all month, and we thought we had all the angles figured out. Still, to take away a man's boner...now that the time was here we were suddenly appreciating the seriousness of it all, and perhaps even that we might have gone overboard.

On stage, Ronnie was finishing up.

"In past years we have worn ribbons and wrist bands. We all shaved our heads..." a few people in the audience groaned at that memory. Shaving heads wasn't all that popular amongst the Hollywood crowd. Actors, especially, rely on their looks.

"This year we have decided that the men will show solidarity with the victims of this terrible disease by the simple act of wearing lipstick." He held up his specially prepared tube of lipstick.

"Furthermore, we are going to wear lipstick not just for a day, but... for a while. I will wear this paint until there is no more left in the tube... and I invite my brothers to join me in common cause."

Cheers.

Oh, fuck...until the lipstick was gone? We had planned on one application, one dose of Depo, then we throw out the culprits and...and lipstick could last up to 300 applications.

He was going to get three hundred doses of Depo? Oh, crap. I had to get ahold of that lipstick and get rid of it!

On stage my big-dicked husband swiped lipstick across his lips, and began the descent into 'small dick-ism.'

The very next day the 'Girl's Club' held an ad hoc meeting. We ordered drinks, but didn't do much more than twiddle the swizzle sticks.

"Shit," murmured Annie.

"Double shit," agreed Sherri.

"Are your guys applying the lipstick regularly?"

"Yep."

"Like clockwork."

"Fuck," I said.

"Not any more," Felicia sighed.

"Okay, we have to get that lipstick away from them."

"Are you kidding? Jim keeps it on him all the time. He gets off on putting it on."

"Men!" grunted Sherri. Give them a pair of panties and they turn into crossdressers.

I took a drink. Made myself take a drink, and stated: "We got into this by being drunk, so the solution is going to be found by getting drunk. Bottoms up, bitches."

We all hoisted and, now that the ice was broken, gulped.

I waved to Jose.

So we sat in Charlie Coyote's and sips turned into gulps, and gulps turned into glasses, and...what's that old Japanese saying? 'A man takes the first drink, the first drink drinks the second drink, the third drink drinks the man.'

Huh.

Of course we were all women, but I think it would apply to us.

Shortly we were giggling.

"Let's see, 300 swipes in a tube, five swipes a day, 60 days or two months of them castrating themselves."

"God," muttered Annie, "That's a lot of Depo."

"Oh, hell, we didn't even know if it would work. "

300 times as much as we planned, it's going to work."

"And that's not the bad news."

We all turned to Felicia.

"You know I had that company mix the Depo into the lipstick and then remold it all?"

We nodded.

"Well, efficient company, they didn't do it just for four tubes of lipstick. They didn't just do it for the tubes we gave our men."

We looked at her blankly.

"I just got the bill. They put Depo in all of the lipsticks."

"All of them?" I was blinking...something was coming through, Earth to Janice....

"You mean..."

"They all?"

Felicia nodded. "Five hundred men applied, and will likely be applying Depo colored lipstick to their lips for the next 60 days."

It was too much. We just kept looking at each other, then we were giggling, then we were roaring. 500 men. The movers and shakers of Hollywood...limp.

"Limp!" I laughed.

"Chemically castrated," Annie was laughing so hard she was having trouble breathing.

"No more cheating!" Felicia pounded on the table.

Then Sherri sat up straight. "Oh, no!"

We looked at her.

"I need a new dildo!"

And we were off again, pounding the table, slapping each other on the back, laughing fit to bust a gut.

But, for all our laughter, we were now too scared to try and get our husband's lipsticks.

Heck, they would notice and wonder.

And, to complicate matters, what if we did get ahold of the Depo Lipstick? When it became common knowledge that the men in Hollywood were limp, it would focus attention on our men if they weren't. And we couldn't afford any questions after this. As great as our joke was, we could never let anybody in on it.

The men didn't notice anything for a week. They were horny, randy, and fully charged Maybe even a little extra charged.

Annie wondered if maybe the Depo didn't work.

But on the eighth day...

"Crap!"

"Come on, honey," I soothed Ronnie. "It happens."

"Not to me! I have never failed to rise to the occasion. Never. N... E...V...E...R!"

"First time for everything. Now, come here. Let's make out and get horny and I can play with your rectum."

He smiled. "Rectum. R...E...—

"Shut up." I climbed on top of him. I felt his limpness under my pussy. Heysoos, now that the moment of. truth was here I missed it. Now that I couldn't have it, I wanted it more.

We rubbed our bodies against each other, we kissed, and I tasted his waxy lipness, and I rubbed his prostate for a while.

Funny thing about anal sex. Ronnie wasn't big on it, but he did like an occasional poke. But now that he couldn't get it up he was liking it more. Well, heck, if it was all he could get...you know?

So I poked and prodded and he groaned and moaned, and his desire for sex slowly waned. That's the thing about doing it anal. You don't get orgasms, at least Ronnie didn't, but poke him enough and he became satisfied, as if he really had cum.

Huh.

He couldn't have sex, so he was accepting the next best sex, and... this could prove to be interesting.

So the eighth day came and went, and the first whispers circulated through Hollywood. They came, interestingly enough, from that bastion of privacy, the doctor's office. Many of the movers and shakers go to the same doctors, and for all the men to suddenly become limp...to complain of ED...to say that erectile dysfunction never happened to them... somebody was obviously going to make a conclusion.

And the nurses, not so bound by convention, would be the first to giggle and whisper and spread the rumors.

On the 15th day Ronnie heard the rumors.

"Heysoos!" he grumbled as he entered the kitchen, went straight for the liquor cabinet, and poured himself a giant bourbon and Coke.

"What's the matter?" I asked.

He gulped a big one, started to make another drink.

"Honey?" I touched his arm.

He turned to me, and the look in his eyes...it was terrible.

"There's a new disease."

"What?"

"Some kind of specialized STD or something."

"What are you talking about?"

"The men in Hollywood are all...we're all..."

"For fuck's sake...what?" I actually shook him.

"We're impotent."

"Can't have babies?" I knew what he was talking about, but I had to carry out a show of obtuseness.

"Christ!" He drank again, put down the glass and said, "Can't get erect."

"Come on," I joshed. "Stop joking."

"I mean it. That's why I haven't been able to get it up for a week."

I stilled my face. God, I was putting on a good acting job. But it had to be good. My man, of all the men in the world, would recognize a bad acting job.

"Are you serious."

He actually pulled down his pants, just slipped them down over his hips, and held his dick. "Does this look serious enough?"

"But, honey!" I grabbed his dick and worked it. It was like trying to jack off a wet towel. "This can't be!"

He was actually close to tears. "Well, it is. I've got a doctor's appointment tomorrow."

"This is terrible!"

"Tell me about it," he moaned, and he reached into his pocket for his tube of lipstick.

I watched while he painted his lips, and here is the funny thing: At first I felt like shit. I felt guilty. It was supposed to be a joke, but it got out of hand...and now...now I felt a little tiny shiver of excitement inside.

It was just a spark, but it warmed me, and I suddenly had a feeling, a thought, a...sense of power.

Heck, I've heard the old saw that sex is power, but to see it in this fashion, to take away somebody's sex and have it result in...in a sense of...power...it was too much.

Ronnie made another drink, poured it down his throat, and I had to stifle a bit of laughter.

Was I sick? Could I be enjoying my husband's tragedy?

Apparently, I could.

So Ronnie went to the doctor's and found out that testosterone had mysteriously disappeared from his body. He wanted to take extra testosterone, but the doctor said they had to take tests, they didn't want to mess with the body if it was in a mysterious state of change, so he didn't. And the Girls Club met.

The next day we sat at our table at Charlie Coyote's, and on the surface we were a dour bunch.

"So we've castrated Hollywood," mentioned Felicia.

We all looked at her. She was solemn, but there was a tinge of...of some unexpressed emotion.

And that unexpressed emotion was hidden under the psyches of all of us.

We were sad. Distraught. Miserable. And felt like laughing.

"Has anybody managed to get the lipstick away from their husbands?"

We all shook our heads.

Annie said, "I gave up. I don't want him to recover before everybody else."

"In it to win it," I misapplied the quote. "They all have to reach the finish line at the same time."

Nods, and gulps.

Sherri blurted. "I'd like to get him some more lipstick."

We all blinked, and didn't say anything for a long minute. She had said something that was true for all of us, whether we admitted it or not.

Felicia said, "I bought another dildo. I broke the other one. This new one is bigger, and it vibrates. Want to know something funny?"

We stared at her. she was borderline hysteric, but then we all were.

"Jim feels guilty because he can't pork me, so he begs to be allowed to use the dildo on me." Then her voice faded. "He's desperate...like a slave."

That was the moment...that long, drawn out space of silence while we grokked what Felicia was saying.

I broke first. I giggled.

Then Sherri chuckled.

Annie grinned.

Felicia looked at us. "I know…"

We didn't break out in huge belly laughs, but we were changed. Somehow we had suddenly accepted what had happened, what we had done, and seen it not as a tragedy, but as an opportunity.

"I put his lipstick on Frank yesterday. Then again this morning," admitted Sherri. I rolled it on, watched the color transform his lips, congratulated him on being such a manly man and standing up for us like that…and I kissed him. Just a peck. I don't want that stuff getting in me."

"Can you get more of that lipstick?" I asked Felicia. "Or maybe just lip balm or something?"

Then Annie surprised us. "Lipstick. And for them to be willing to keep putting lipstick on, it's going to change them."

I asked, "Change them how?"

"Ted is growing breasts."

Now that was something to think about.

"They aren't big, just little mounds, but they are real. They are titties, like what we had in puberty."

"Wow," I breathed out, and my eyes were shining.

"But we'd have to give up getting porked," said Annie.

"Would we?" mused Felicia. "There's other men. And Jim feels so damned guilty…it would be easy for me to convince him to let me have a surrogate."

"I like the dildo. A good vibrator rocks my world I think I like it better than the soft, bendable cum oozing and messy peter," Sherri observed.

"Strap ons."

"Anal sex for them."

"We could milk them."

"Is this a crime?" I rained on the parade.

"Is it?" asked Felicia.

"We're doing things to them without their permission. Body changes that could be considered…I don't know…maiming?"

"Transition is maiming?"

"I think Frank has always wanted to transition."

And so the ideas flew around our circle. And we drank, and the whole thing stopped being a joke and became a project. A serious project.

After a month I noticed that Ronnie was getting boobs.

"Honey? Is your chest swollen?"

He was just out of the shower and he looked down at his chest. Sadly, like he had been defeated, he said, "Yeah. And the nipples are

145

bigger. And they itch."

"Ronnie? Are you telling me that you...are you going through... puberty?"

He began to cry then. I went to him and hugged him, and that was the moment I felt the most guilty. Yet, the feeling of power was growing in me.

Watching him show girly emotions, seeing the physical changes in him, the way his muscles were getting smaller and softer...it was... exciting.

I know. I'm evil. I'm bad. But I also felt like somebody was charging my whole body with electricity.

I was in charge. And I wondered...if I could keep him going...could I...would it be possible...could I get him to agree to transition?

"There, there. Let me feel your chest."

He stood while I cupped his flesh, squeezed it, and felt his boobs.

"I feel..."

"What?"

"That turns me on."

"Oh..." I grinned.

"But I can't..."

"It's okay."

"But I could still do you."

"Oh, honey, you would do that for me? In your condition?"

"Getting you off is the only enjoyment I get these days."

"Then let's let you have some fun."

He smiled.

"I'll get the strap on out."

"And put on some more lipstick."

He did.

"Man, that Depo works fast!"

We were having our weekly Girl's Club.

"I'll say. Jim is already ready for a bra. I think he's going to get a big set of ta tas."

"Ted looks like he's going to be small," Annie sighed. "I did so want a man with big boobs."

"It's funny," I said. "Now I know why men want women with big tits. The shoe is on the other foot now, and I want a man with big tits."

"Is Ronnie going to be big?" asked Felicia.

"I think so. He's ready for a bra, too, and the mounds are large. wide."

"There's some sniping in the mags."

We all looked at each other.

"Crap," said Felicia. "All we need is some investigative reporter uncovering...stuff."

"I don't think we're in any danger," I noted. "As long as we keep our traps shut."

"Will it be...will people look at us funny as we feminize our men?"

"Other women are doing it. I saw Lannie Ginsberg the other day, her husband was wearing culottes and Mary Janes."

"It might look funny if we didn't."

Heysoos," I whispered. "What have we done?"

Yet there was no remorse among us. If anything, we were more determined.

"I bought you a bra."

Ronnie stared at me. "I don't...it...it's just Mastectomy. "

Mastectomy. The use of the word showed that he had been researching on the net, and I had a feeling that he was looking into more than just men with boobs.

"Are you thinking of hiding your...your tits?" There. I said it.

"I'm thinking of having them removed."

"Oh, no. I don't want you to."

"But, honey...I feel funny!"

"A good bra will help that."

He frowned.

"Listen, baby, do you know how much fun it is to have tits?"

"Well, I like to suck on them."

"Oh, good. Come here." I took his hand and led him into the bedroom. He followed along docilely. I realized that the Depo was making him more submissive, and that actually made me a little wet.

I pushed him back on the bed and stood between his legs and undid his buttons.

He watched my hands, watched my red fingernails, push the buttons through the holes. He was breathing hard.

"You have beautiful hands."

"Thank you." And I knew he was talking about my nails. His eyes weren't just on my hands, they were on my long nails.

I pushed his shirt back and looked at his mounds. Heysoos, they were almost A cups.

"You definitely need a bra."

I bent my head and took a nipple into my mouth. He gasped, and it grew stiff, and I sucked.

"Oh..." he moaned.

"Doesn't that feel good?"

"Oh, God. It feels like electricity shooting through my body. It just doesn't reach my...my groin."

"That's okay." I pulled on his pants. He raised his hips and legs and

I slid them off him. "Let me suck it anyway."

I had tried to suck his cock the first couple of weeks, and it was... cool. It wasn't hard, I could deep throat it, and it felt like I was in charge.

Now it was even better. It had shrunken a little bit, and it fit into my mouth easily. I rolled it around my tongue as I played with his nipples.

"Oh, God!" he moaned.

I pushed him back on his back and sucked on his balls. They fit into my mouth easily.

"Honey? Janice?"

"Yeah?"

"Could you...put a finger in me?"

"Oh, honey," I was feeling this sense of power overwhelming me. "I'll put two fingers in you."

He groaned and spread his legs.

I sucked his dick, I felt his tits, and with one hand I began to massage his little, brown button.

"Ah...oh yeah!"

I slipped a finger into his anus. He twitched and jerked, but nothing happened in his dick.

I reamed him, and he began to moan rhythmically and twist his hips. I put two fingers in him.

"Fuck," he said, freezing for a second, then happily absorbing my digits.

I finger banged him for a while, and he was breathing and tilting his hips up and trying to get ore, so I gave him more.

Three fingers. He was near going wild now. His hips were writhing, he was pushing back against my fingers.

I couldn't believe how powerful I felt. I had my fingers in him. I was causing him to twist and lurch and groan. His eyes were closed and his face concentrated on feeling the powerful sensations running through him.

I began to jackhammer him, in and out, powerful strokes that let him know who was in charge.

"Fuck me! Fuck me!" he said, hardly able to say the words for his excitement.

I fucked him hard, and thought about putting my whole fist in him. I thought that maybe with a little extra push, maybe a little more lubricant, and it would slip right inside him.

Got, what a heady feeling. To have a man yelling for more, it gave me so much pleasure.

I had heard the term 'power exchange' before, but now I knew what it meant.

Finally, exhausted, and my arm feeling a bit tired, he nodded and stopped moving. He hadn't cum, in fact, he was hornier, but he was satisfied.

And I had the strange feeling that he had been close, that with a little more work he was going to have an orgasm. wouldn't that be fun? Wouldn't that be the ultimate?

Back at Coyote...

"The reporter for the gazette has figured out that all the men who are impotent were at the cancer event."

Annie, Sherrie and I watched Felicia.

"But I don't think it matters. We just have to keep it quiet."

"The chemist said he can create more lipstick. How's everybody doing with their men?"

"Jim is actually eager. I think he likes this transitioning stuff."

We all smiled.

"Ronnie is getting there. I'm buying him lingerie this afternoon. His boobs are B cup."

"Frank is getting weird, but what choice does he have?"

We all nodded.

"What about Ted?"

Annie glanced at me. "He's a full time crossdresser now. I brought up transitioning, and I think he's going to go for it."

"Excellent," I complimented them all. "I'll put in the order for more lipstick. I don't think we need chapstick, and lipstick is more fun."

We high fived.

"This feels weird."

Ronny sat on the bed in front of me. He was wearing a bra, panties, and a garter. I rolled the nylons up his legs.

"Nonsense," I rejoined. "Don't you love the feeling? All shaved and electric and everything?"

"Well, yeah. But...it's...I feel like a girl!"

"Well, I hate to say it, man of mine, but your body is looking more and more girlish."

It was true. His boobs were definitely girl boobs. And his face was changing. The fat was being redistributed and his face was rounder, softer.

The most interesting change, however, was to his whole body.

He weighed less, and his limbs were becoming softer and smaller. His arms looked like girl arms, and his legs were girly. He did have a bit of a bony ridge around his hips, but that seemed to be reducing, too.

"I'm going to look into nails and hair for you."

"What?"

"Honey. Right now you look like a girl trying to look like a man." That was a clever way of getting to him. "You might just as well relax and go with it."

He grumped, but he didn't look all that unhappy.

I sat down next to him. "Ronnie, you wear lipstick all the time, your body is changing. It's time we thought about what we're going to do with you."

"What?" he asked suspiciously.

"I know you didn't choose all this, what's happening to you, but maybe it's time you embraced it."

"You mean transitioning."

I nodded.

Actually, the way I was pushing him, he didn't have much choice, but he frowned.

"Will you at least think about it?"

"I will."

"By the way, I got you some new lipstick. A couple of new colors. Here, let's try a bright pink on you."

I pulled him to my make up table and sat him down. I rolled a bright pink lipstick, heavy laced with Depo, of course, on his mouth.

He made an O of his mouth and studied himself.

"Oh, my God. You are so-o-o sexy!"

"I am?"

I picked up a brush and began teasing his hair into a feminine do. It reshaped the appearance of his face, and he turned his head slightly this way and that.

"Isn't that pretty?"

"Uh, yeah. I guess."

"And could you practice speaking in a higher tone of voice?"

"Sure," he tried.

I giggled. He was like a younger sister to me.

"I think we should invite them to one of our meetings," Felicia put forth.

Three frowns met her statement, then I thought about it.

"It might help them accept their situation," I mused.

"Exactly. We need to get them out, let the world see them, let them accept how the world sees them."

"I had a reporter call me and ask for an interview," I stated.

The other girls looked at me.

"Nothing suspicious, just wanted to ask some questions about the Awareness Event."

"It's all suspicious," observed Felicia. "There were 500 women at that event. Why just you?"

Truth, I was a little worried. Not a lot, just a little, but...what was I supposed to do about it?

"I told her no, so it's no big deal."

"What was her name?"

"Linda Shwartzenberg, or something like that."

Felicia frowned. "She's a real reporter. Not one of those snowflakes that report on the weather or fashion. You need to be careful."

"I told her that I didn't want to discuss anything and asked her not to call on me."

"Gently?"

"Very gentle. She didn't suspect a thing."

"Those reporters, they suspect everything."

It was a glum moment, but glum moments always pass, and shortly we were discussing the progress our men were making.

"He'll be in a dress by Friday."

"He actually likes having perfume on."

"I think this latest batch of Depo is stronger. Frank is actually mincing and speaking like a woman."

"If you make him wear a gaffe it will hide better."

We talked and sipped our drinks and had a gay, old time, and we didn't know that the dam was about to bust.

We decided on a Friday afternoon for the girls 'coming out' party.

Girls, that was how we were speaking of our husbands.

All of them had reduced height and weight, all of them had round hips and boobs. All of them had long hair or wigs. All of them were drop dead gorgeous when they were fixed up.

"I don't see why I have to have painted toenails if my feet are going to be in shoes."

"Stop thinking like a male," I spoke testily. He was very submissive these days, and he responded better to a firm command.

"Yeah, but nobody can see them."

I smiled. I had a surprise for him.

"Yes, but you know, and it helps you feel sexy."

"I don't want to feel sexy," he lied.

"Then you're a silly girl," I chastised him. "And there's only one cure for that."

"What?"

"Tonight, after our little soiree, I'm going to deflower you."

He caught his breath and looked at me.

"What?" I asked. "You're not ready?"

"I...I guess I am."

We had talked about this extensively. Being taken like a woman would be the final nail in his coffin. Oh, bad comparison. Let's just say it would be the last straw in his acceptance of womanhood.

"Then what?"

"I don't know."

I smiled and pinched his cheek. "Little Miss Virgin has got the willies."

"I guess."

"Don't worry, honey. I'll be gentle. It will be wonderful."

He nodded, but wan't convinced.

"Okay. Tootsies are all done. Let's paint those claws."

He looked at his hands. I took one and spread it out.

"I'm giving you hard gel nails. They are tough, and be careful when you pee. You don't want to be stabbing your dick."

He laughed ruefully, then he got a far away look in his eyes.

"What?"

"This all started because my dick stopped working."

"So?"

"I don't know...I just...I just wished it would work again."

"And give up all this fun?"

"Well, yeah. I know..."

"Honey," I patted his cheek, "When I get done with you tonight you're going to know what real fun is."

I finished his hands and began working on his face.

He had been wearing lipstick for three months now, but only a smattering of make up. It was time to complete the transition of his appearance.

I cleaned and moistened his face, then began applying concealer, foundation, blush...and it was working. I realized that even his facial color had changed. As I worked I realized that he was going to make a beautiful woman.

I painted his lids a grey, smokey color. It made his eyes mysterious, like they were beasts in a cave...loving beasts.

Then I put on his lipstick. Red. Power red.

When I sat back and inspected my work I was blown away. He was absolutely stunning.

"Here you go," I handed him his surprise.

New heels. With open toes so his pretty nails would show.

"Oh, my gosh!" He took the shoes and looked at me.

I smiled.

Excited, he put on the shoes and tried standing up.

Oh, he was laughable, tottering and stumbling, but it was good, and we laughed together.

He practiced walking for a while, then we put him in a skirt and blouse.

"How the heck do you button buttons when they're the wrong way?"

"It's you that have them on the wrong way."

"Bull."

"Women did the sewing. Why would they make their own buttons backwards."

We laughed at that one.

Finally, fully dressed and made up and looking like a million dollars, he...she...was ready to go.

I quickly stepped into a suit, put on some severe make up that looked a bit masculine, and put on my own heels.

Interestingly, I was taller than him.

He was originally five foot eight, and I was five foot six, but now, both of us in heels, I was an inch taller. Man, did that make me feel good. I felt big and powerful and ready to rock.

So we walked out the door and headed for Charlie Coyote's. It was a beautiful LA day. No clouds, warm, but not too much. Even the traffic was light.

I pulled up to the restaurant, I was driving because Ronnie couldn't handle high heels and the gas pedal, and the valet stole the car.

We walked into the restaurant and I kept telling him how gorgeous he was, and he even made his heels go click, click, click. Jose greeted us like two ladies, even leering a bit at Ronnie. Embarrassed the crap out of Ronnie, but I loved it. And he would grow to love it.

We crossed the patio and the others were already there.

There was a very awkward moment as our guys checked each other out and came to grips with their situation. None of them had elected to feminize, but they had all been guided into it, so...here we were.

Then one of the guys, Ted, mocked himself. "Hello, dahling, you look absolutely mahvelous."

The giggles and laughter started, and once started, it didn't stop. Jose, starting to be a little confused by the mix of feminine/masculine mannerisms, brought drinks, lots of drinks, and the party started in earnest.

We girls had talked about this a lot, how we should act, what the best way of bringing the boys along would be, and we had decided we would have to contain ourselves and just pay lots of compliments.

And, for Heysoos sake...don't talk about the thing we had done with the lipstick.

Inspecting our guys, it was obvious we had done a good job. They wore clothes and looked quite natural. Their make up was impeccable, and they were even good at some of the feminine mannerisms.

Once I caught a glance of Ted putting on lipstick and I nudged Annie, who nudged back and giggled.

We ordered a light dinner. We had all schooled our boys on how to eat like ladies, and they handled it like champs.

Finally, done with dinner, we began to imbibe purposefully.

"I've got to tinkle," said Ronnie.
Annie said, "If ya gotta go…"
"Uh, which bathroom should we use?"
Uh oh. In all our skullduggery we had never thought of that.
"Use the lady's room," Felicia suggested.
"But, uh…"
"Nobody will know," I said. "Second, if somebody does figure it out, tell 'em you identify with being female."
We all laughed at that one.
Sherri quipped, "Frank, go hold her hand."
"I'm not—"
"Yes, you are. Ladies always tinkle in pairs."
He looked around at everybody and there were solemn nods.
Frank and Ronnie got up and headed for the Little Girl's room.
Everybody else went back to drinking, and nobody thought anything of the two men, then they came back. With a woman.
Oh, you could hear the antenna go up.
Ears pivoted on the sides of heads and eyeballs focused.
She looked to be about 30. Dressed right, but a bit utilitarian. Pencil skirt and jacket. Short bubble cut. And we could feel her—Women's intuition—we could feel that there was something off about her.
"Hi guys," said Frank, and he wasn't trying to disguise his voice. "This is Linda."
Linda. Oh, fuck. Could she be…was it…?
Felicia jumped right in.
"Hi, Linda. What do you do?"
Annie and Sherri were already grabbing for their purses.
I was holding a palm down to Ronnie, hoping he hadn't said anything.
He said, "It's okay. She knows about us."
Fu-u-uck! Knows what?
"I'm a reporter."
I reached for my purse, and Ronnie's and tried to get up, but Linda had positioned herself so we couldn't slide out from the table without moving her, and she wasn't moving.
"That's wonderful. We're all leaving now."
The guys were sitting and looking around stupid, except for Frank and Ronnie, who were standing next to her looking stupid.
"I did wonder, however—"
"Got to go. If you could get out of the way?"
Ronnie was blinking. He didn't understand. None of the guys did. And how could they?"
Linda not only didn't get out of the way, she passed out sheets of paper.

"This item right here…"

I knew what it was I recognized it. Felicia had shown it to me.

"…an order for lipstick for the recent Awareness Event…"

"Get out of the way," I hissed.

That's the problem with women. They haven't been trained to punch somebody in the nose. To be precise, I hadn't been trained to punch a reporter in the nose. I was trapped, and everybody was trapped behind me.

"This item here, Depo, it's used to castrate criminals. It seems that it was included in the list of ingredients…"

"What?" asked Ronnie. Frank and Ted looked at the reporter. Jim looked at Felicia.

"Do the guys here know that you've castrated them? Chemically?"

We girls were starting to talk now, to raise our voices. We shoved, and slowly Linda gave way…and turned to Ronnie. "How do you feel about being chemically castrated? Losing all your testosterone? How do you feel knowing that your wife deliberately stole your manhood and—"

I pushed her over. I grabbed Ronnie, and, suddenly, he didn't budge.

"Wait," he said. He looked down at the sheet of paper. He looked down the list of ingredients and I saw him mouth, 'depo provera…'

He looked at me.

"Honey, we have to go."

He looked at the paper again. He looked at Ted and Frank and Jim. All their faces were showing various stages of shock and dismay and… betrayal.

"Honey," I tried, "It's not what you think…"

A cameraman appeared from somewhere and began taking close ups, capturing conversations. Linda kept talking and talking… "Technically, this is an act of terrorism. After all, there were 500 people at that event. And from all accounts all the men have been suffering Depo effects.

"Mr. Keskin," she singled Ronnie out. "Are you okay with your wife taking away your penile function?"

"I…who…" he was answering her, but his attention wasn't on her. His attention was on me.

"Ronnie, we've got to go!" I was pleading now. Begging. All my power gone. All that wonderful feeling of being in charge evaporating.

He made up his mind. He turned to Linda and said, "Your invasion of privacy will not go unrewarded. We will sue you. Now get out of my way or I will punch you and your cameraman and walk on your face."

He was so intent she blinked and backed up, and Ronnie led the way out of the restaurant.

We split up and headed for our separate cars, and now I was following Ronnie. At the car Ronnie stopped. I stepped up and opened my mouth and he cut me off by saying, "You drive."

He got into the passenger seat. I scurried around and got into the driver's seat and started the car up.

"Honey, I'm sorry. It all started as a practical joke. The effects are supposed to wear off. We didn't mean to..." I blathered and blithered all the way home. Ronnie just sat there. He didn't say anything. He didn't look at me. He just sat and...and sat.

We pulled up to the house. I clicked the remote and gate closed behind us. If I saw any reporters on my property I was going to get Ronnie's Dirty Harry gun and shoot them a hole in the belly.

We got out, me still talking a mile a minute and not really saying anything, and I followed Ronnie into the house.

Through the house.

Into the bedroom.

Me still talking.

Ronnie got undressed. He put on a negligee, very sexy, my favorite, and went back to the kitchen.

I followed him, and finally he said something.

"Have a seat." He indicated the kitchen table.

I sat down. I had never been more miserable in my life. I could see my marriage going up in flames. Yes, I had broken laws, but that wasn't what concerned me. All I could think about was losing Ronnie.

He poured a couple of drinks. Bourbon and Coke. He placed one before me and sat down opposite me.

"You'll forgive the need for alcohol. but recent events require it."

I started to talk some more and he just shook his head. "A little silence would go a long way right about now."

So I sat. Silent. Tears began to pour from my eyes.

Ronnie watched me.

There had been times in my life when I had cried, and those tears had melted Ronnie like he was a snowman in the Sahara.

Not now. Now he just contemplated me.

After a couple of hours of just sitting there, he spoke. "So it's...this Depo stuff is going to wear off."

"Well, yes, but..." and I explained about the chemical error and how they had upped the dose.

He had the lipstick on him. Habit, he had carried it out and placed it on the counter. He reached over and picked it up. He opened it. He sniffed it.

"So this is the culprit." He sounded almost whimsical.

He twisted the bottom and the lipstick came out of the tube. He carefully painted his lips.

"Did you laugh every time I did this?" He smacked his lips.

"Oh, God. Ronnie...what can I do to make it right?"

"Not much," he shrugged. Then he sighed. "You know, this has been the most amazing adventure of my life. I learned things, I'm so fucking horny I can't stand it, and now, even right now, I want nothing so much as for you to take me. Like you promised."

Oddly, there was a bit of hope in my soul.

"Will I lose these tits?" he hefted his globes. "Will I get my man muscles back?"

"I don't know. There was a lot of the Depo...we didn't plan..."

He held up his hand. "No excuses now. What's done is done. And, I have to tell you, there is only one thing that confuses me."

"What?"

"That I still love you."

"You do?" I sniffled.

"Oh, with all of my heart. My female heart. I've loved this...what you did to me. I wouldn't have chosen it on my own, but...maybe that's just as well."

"It is?"

"Oh, don't look for forgiveness. There are things going on in my mind that would scare the crap out of you."

I said nothing. He was so calm, and I realized he was just masking his rage.

He sighed again, poured more drinks, guzzled one fast, made another one, and he looked so pensive.

He was like a locomotive that had been wound up and sent down the track and was just looking for a town to run into.

Yet...yet there was something more.

Finally, he said, "Well, there's only one thing left to do."

"What's that?"

"Fuck me. Take me into the bedroom. Let me find out if this journey was worth it."

"Oh..."

He held up his palm. "I'm going to go get on the bed. How would you like me...face up or face down?"

"On all fours."

"Okay. That's what I'm going to do, and it's up to you to convince me not to take a club to your hide. Your one chance."

I nodded.

He finished his drink, didn't look at me, put the drink down, walked out of the kitchen.

Now I was breathing hard. One chance, to make him love me. One chance out of the mess I had created.

I stood up, finished my drink, and followed him into the bedroom.

He was naked, his limp balls hanging down, his butt facing me. Between his legs I could see his udders hanging from his chest.

He was quiet, waiting, breathing shallowly.

I took off my clothes and opened up a dresser drawer. I took out the strap on.

"Would you like the big cock or the small one?"

And I felt it. Seeing his ass, all submissive, waiting. Smelling his perfume. His asshole looked...ripe. I felt it.

I felt that little dribble of power.

I was going to fuck him.

I was going to be on top.

And the sensation of sexiness suddenly overwhelmed me.

I had betrayed him, yes, but I had this chance to convert him. To convince him. But to do that I couldn't go in like a whining, snively bitch. I had to go in like a conquering hero. I had to fuck him, to lay him out and spread him open. I had to take charge, show him who was boss.

I had to treat him like he was a woman and fuck him like I was a man.

He had answered me, told me which cock, but I hadn't heard him. I screwed the big dick into the harness and snapped. "Doesn't matter what you want, I'm going to give you what I want."

I could feel his sudden alertness, electricity surging through him, sexuality trying to make his worthless dick hard.

I grabbed a tube of lube and began smearing it on his ass. I filled his crack and squirted it directly into his hole.

He moaned. It wasn't much, but I knew I had him.

"What's that? Bitch?"

"Nothing."

He was shivering now. Shaking. I touched his white flesh, felt his female skin. Oh, this was going to be good. And I was going to feel it just as if I had a real dick.

I placed the head of my big eight inch dildo up against his brown button.

"Honey, I'd like to say this is going to hurt me more than it does you, but it won't."

I pushed forward. I didn't slam it, or jerk it, but I was inexorable, a force of nature unleashed.

He yelped, then he gave way. He fell forward and I rode him to the mattress. I fell his ass ring resist, then, because of my weight, it gave way, opened up, and I slid smoothly into him.

I fucked him. Not gently. Maybe later we could do the gentle bit, but right now I had to take over, take control, rule my man.

"You lousy fuck," I blurted. "You know you want this, and you act all hurt and everything..."

I sawed into him, my hands were on his ass, spreading his cheeks.

"But you really just want it. You like it. You like being a woman.

You like feeling the frilly, sexy clothes. You like the make up. You love that fucking lipstick which gives you a limp dick.

I pulled out and shoved in. I reached under him and grabbed his balls. I used them for leverage.

"AIIIEE!" he screamed. Not loud, but it was a real scream.

I shoved it in. "Every time you put on that lipstick it made you soft inside. It made you female soft, and you loved it. You loved feeling the emotions. You loved the way I told you what to do. Admit it."

I pulled out and rammed in.

He groaned. Whatever bruising I had imparted, it was being replaced by exquisite pleasure.

"Admit it. I'm going to fuck you until you admit it. You love being a woman!"

"I love it," her cried, and I knew he was leaking tears. But tears of joy.

"And you like my dick in you, and you like being all soft and cuddly, and you're sorry for acting like you were upset."

"I'm sorry...I'm sorry!" He was crying loudly now, and his hips were pushing back, his butt was trying to swallow my dick.

"And you're sorry and you love me forever!"

"I'm sorry and I love you forever!"

"And you'll always be my bitch!"

"I will...I will..."

Suddenly his whole back tightened up, spasmed, it almost threw me out of his asshole. For a second I was confused, then I understood.

"OH...OH...FUCK!"

He was having a prostate orgasm.

His whole body was twisting, writhing, jerking, ripples of pleasure began wringing him out. I reached under and grabbed his cock. It was spurting. Long dribbles of white hot semen.

I fucked him some more. I drove my big cock into his backside again and again, and the sperm kept oozing out, and his back rippled and writhed.

Then, finally, he slowed down. He began to collapse. He was exhausted, and he was empty, and he was stupid. I had literally fucked him stupid.

I slowed down, then I pulled out of him. I wiped the end of my cock on his ass, slapped his ass, then went in to take a shower.

On the bed Ronnie just groaned, not sure where he was, but sure of one thing, I had delivered on my promise...I had made it all worthwhile.

EPILOGUE

The next few months were wild. The story hit the news outlets and I and the girls quickly became the latest craze.

We were guilty, and men reviled us.

We were innocent and women celebrated us.

Not a day passed without a crowd in front of our houses. People with signs, marching, demanding the death penalty, asking us to run for office.

Then came the trial. Oh, the sordid details that oozed out, even though none of us said much. We all pled the Fifth, but somehow newspapers made things up and...and the uproar roared up even louder.

Our husbands stuck by us, stood by our sides, and if it was just them we would have gotten off. But it wasn't just them.

It was 500 other men. Men who brought their tits to court and demanded justice.

Those same men were often caught on camera out on the town, often wearing sexy, female clothes, sometimes even showing their tits to an admiring public.

The jury was split on the serious counts six women found us innocent, six men found us guilty, of committing acts of terror on 500 innocent but now proud men.

They tried getting us on mayhem, but the law stated mayhem was 'depriving' somebody of a body part...and we had added a body part.

They finally got us on 'Drugging a victim with the intent to commit a felony,' but even that was specious as nobody could figure out what felony we were going to commit.

Still, that got us 3 years in prison. With time off for good behavior.

That's fine. I'm sort of a hero in here, and other inmates are always asking for advice on how to 'alter' their husbands. I'm glad to give advice, but careful. I don't want a conspiracy rap tied on to my sentence.

As for Ronnie, he kept taking the Depo, and his boobies are getting larger. He visits me as often as is allowed, and he can't wait for me to get out and play with him.

Incidentally, we've started a new company, 'Depo Lipstick,' and the company is growing like gangbusters. It seems there is a big market for Depo lipstick.

END

Have you read…

The Big Tease: The Book

Check it out at…

https://gropperpress.wordpress.com

Dr. Frankendick

ALYCE THORNDYKE

CHAPTER ONE
KIDNAPPED

Jane Monroe took careful aim and let fly. The small, potted fern flew through the air and smashed against the door frame. Bits of dark earth and leaf struck Derrick's shoulder, but most of the missile was wasted.

"Son of a bitch," snarled Jane, rushing after her cheating boyfriend.

He had let his dick wander into the pussy of Jane's best friend, and now she had lost a boyfriend and a BFF.

She rushed through the door and caught sight of the traitor's head as he descended the stairs.

"Fuck you, you fuck!" Tears came from her eyes and her words echoed down the stairway. "I was tired of your short dick, anyway!" she screamed.

Doors down through the apartment were being opened to see what the latest ruckus was all about.

"That's not what you said when he shoved it up your ass!" Darla was there! Waiting downstairs for her cheating, limp-dicked son of a bitch boyfriend!

"And you, you fucking slut! Your cunt stinks!"

Derrick hadn't said a word when she had berated him in her apartment, but now he bleated, "Yeah, it stinks of my dick."

Darla laughed. "Yeah, you hear that you dried up old excuse for a pussy! We'll be thinking of you next time he porks me with that giant woody!"

On the landings people were poking their heads out and listening to the exchange.

"Fuck," whined Jane, backing into her apartment and slamming the door. "Fuck," she whispered her back to the door.

For a long minute her tears slid down her cheeks. Her mind was a black, cesspit whirlpool, obsessed with the idea that she had been dumped.

Finally, long minutes later, she bent and picked up the remains of her fern. She had bought it two years ago, and it had sat on her counter, an air freshening friend of no words, and now she had destroyed it. For what? A cheating, no good, short-dicked asshole.

Whimpering, she took the remains of her friend to the garbage and deposited it. Then she walked towards her bedroom, and stopped.

There she was, in the door mirror. She had curves and long hair, and everybody said her face was angelic. She turned slightly and studied the outline of her full breasts. She advanced closer to the mirror and studied her pretty face, now disfigured by tears and betrayal.

Fuck.

And from here on out…no fuck.

"That did it, my friend," she spoke to herself in the mirror. "No more boyfriends for me."

Then she fled to her bed, throwing herself facedown and sobbing. No boyfriend. And she didn't want a girlfriend. So what did that leave her?

Alone.

She cried herself to sleep.

The next day Jane awoke at 8 o'clock in the AM. Feeling like shit that's been steam pressed and hung out to dry, she struggled up from bed and out of her clothes. She took an extra long shower, hoping the hot liquid would sluice her soul as well as her body, but when she got out of the shower she felt just as depressed.

She pulled on some running tights and a short shirt for exercise. She tied the ends of the short shirt together in the front, which emphasized her ample and most bounteous breasts.

"How?" she asked of the mirror before leaving. She held up her tits to the mirror. They were large. "How could he fucking leave these?"

But there was no answer, and Jane crossed the living room, opened the front door and—

SPRITZ! Somebody in a hazmat suit advancing towards her, hand up with a sprayer in it.

The spray hit her in the face, making her blink before large tears welled up.

"Wha—" she tried to speak as she backed away.

"Stop."

And, unbelievably, she did. A mental fog descended upon her and she heard the invader speak again.

"Stop moving, stop talking. You will comply cheerfully."

Standing in the middle of her living room, tears flowing freely, totally alarmed, she began to cheerfully comply.

"I want you to go to your room and pack for a long trip." The voice was high, like a woman's, but a bit gravelly, like an old woman's.

"Okey, dokey," agreed Jane. She walked into her bedroom, and took her rolly bag out of the closet. She then opened drawers and ransacked her dresser for underwear, and her closet for clothes. The hazmat intruder leaned against the door and watched. When Jane had sat upon the bag and zipped it tight, the intruder said, "Go get your make up from the bathroom."

Jane cheerfully walked into the bathroom. She wondered how she could be so cheerful when somebody was upending her life.

She took out her little kit from under the sink, then filled it with lotions and creams and lipstick and eye curler and mascara and all the things a girl would need for a long trip. Finally, she was done.

"Okay, we're going down to a van. If we see anybody on the way you will tell them you are going to visit a friend, won't be back for a while. And don't be so damned cheerful."

"Okay," answered Jane soberly. She followed the hazmat figure out of her apartment.

The figure put a note on Jane's door. 'Out of town!' She locked the door, then led the way down the stairs.

Inside her mind Jane was trying to figure out how to tell somebody she was being kidnapped, but nobody came out of any apartment, and shortly they were walking out the front door. A dark van sat next to the curb, the door yawningly wide, and the hazmat woman motioned Jane inside.

Jane sat down in the darkness.

"Stay there," the mysterious figure commanded, then she slid the door shut.

A moment, then Jane could hear the front door opening, and the van settling under sitting weight. The motor roared, and the van slid into traffic.

CHAPTER TWO
MEETING MRS. FRANKENDICK

Jane sat in a cage and wondered what was going on. She had been drugged, by a spray, no less, and she was just starting to think again. The van had taken her somewhere, but the windows being blocked out, and being commanded to not move, she had no idea where. There were no smells to give her a clue, no sounds, nothing but dank darkness and the bars of a cage.

The cage seemed to be in a basement, and there was only one light at the far end of the basement for light. There were a couple of windows high in the walls, but these had been boarded over.

Suddenly, the lights went on, and she was better able to inspect her surroundings.

Yes, a basement. A lot of boxes stared along one wall, and then the common bric a brac one might find in a basement. A child's pink bicycle, an ancient record player, one with an over-sized spindle, a stack of kitchen chairs, spring mattresses stacked against a wall.

Jane's attention was drawn away from her surroundings by the sound of footsteps on stairs. At the far end of the basement a pair of skinny legs descended, and grew into a skinny, old woman.

"Help," croaked Jane. She swallowed quickly, got her throat used to working again, and said, "Help me!"

The skinny woman walked towards Jane. She was holding a bowl from which steam arose and a spoon stuck out.

"No use calling for help, dearie." It was the hazmat figure! She wore a grey dress that covered her from ankle to chin, and she had no boobs to speak of, just little nipple spots on the front of her sack-like dress.

"Who are you?"

Up close the woman had a skinny face and pinched eyes. She looked like she liked kicking kittens for fun.

"My name is Martha Frankendick." She placed the steaming bowl on a ledge just outside a small opening in the side of the cage, then stood back.

"Why am I here! Let me out!"

Mrs. Frankendick smiled a yellow grin. She was missing a tooth, and the smile was more like a grimace than a hearty greeting.

"Why don't you eat your supper, and I will explain your situation."

"I'm not hungry."

Mrs. Frankendick held up the hand sprayer, "You can eat, or you can eat cheerfully."

Jane was caught, and she knew it. She moved forward and took the bowl and sniffed it.

Delicious! Meaty with vegetables in a thick broth. Her look betrayed her and Mrs. Frankendick laughed. "What? You thought I was going to poison you? Why would I go to the trouble of kidnapping you and then poison you?"

Tentatively Jane sipped the broth. It was hot and she could feel the warmth of it penetrate to her bones. She thought about throwing it in the woman's face, then thought again. She was in the cage, and the woman would just use the spray and still her ability to resist, or even make a plan. She began eating.

Outside the cage Mrs. Frankendick pulled up a chair and began talking.

"I'll start with the spray. It always make things easier to understand when the girls know what it is."

Jane swallowed a marvelous piece of beef and thought: *girls...I'm not the first.*

"This is a Rohypnol spray Dr. Frankendick invented. Roofie in a mist. The date rape drug. It is just one of Dr. Frankendick's many wonderful inventions."

"I'm going to be raped." Something was loosey goosey in Jane's mind. It was like a haze had happened over her...and she didn't care.

"Yes," answered the woman, simply. "And you will love it."

Jane looked at the bowl and realized the Rohypnol was in the broth.

"Continue eating," Mrs. Frankendick commanded.

Jane slurped up some more broth.

"Yes, more roofie, if you will. You will obey all commands, but you may ask questions."

"Why can't I go home," asked Jane, swallowing the delicious stew.

"Dr. Frankendick needs an heir. You really must understand, Dr. Frankendick has overcome the secrets of life and death. He, and I, have been alive for over three hundred years. In that time he has conquered diseases and elongated life. Unfortunately, he has had an accident, and he requires a youthful mate."

"Myself."

"Yes. I can't have children, I went through menopause 250 years ago. But we need children. There have been side effects for poor Victor, his brain is starting to rot, and we need progeny to pick up where he is leaving off.

"Mind you, he is still able to think, he has the most marvelous brain in the history of mankind," it was obvious in the way Mrs. Frankendick was talking that she was enthralled by Victor Frankendick's mind. "But his thoughts are lacking vigor. He is able to maintain, but his creative phase is coming to an end. He needs a child, one with his type of mind, able to think outside the box."

"So you need me."

"Yes, dear. What I can't do you will be able to."

"When can I go home?"

Mrs. Frankendick just laughed, "The Rohypnol will fix that."

Jane knew, with that statement, that they weren't going to let her go home. She was going to have to figure a way out of this by herself.

"Now, are you ready to meet the good Doctor?"

Jane started to say 'no,' to shake her head in the negative, but Mrs. Frankendick merely raised a finger and bobbed it up and down. Jane found her own head bobbing up in down in time with the scrawny digit.

CHAPTER THREE
MEETING DR. FRANKENDICK

After commanding Jane not to try to escape, Mrs. Frankendick undid the lock on the cage.

In her heart, Jane wanted to rush forward, conk the old bitch on the head and make her escape. What happened in reality was she came docilely out of the cage and followed Mrs. Frankendick up the stairs.

The house was old. The staircase up from the basement was rickety and creaked alarmingly. The sink had an ancient faucet and the flooring was 100 year old linoleum. The walls were covered with ancient wallpaper.

Jane followed Mrs. Frankendick through the kitchen and down a hallway, then they ascended stairs to the second floor.

They passed a window and Jane caught a glimpse of the outside world. Treetops as far as the eye could see, no sign of another house. They were somewhere in the country. Even if Jane managed to escape, she would be lost in an endless forest.

Down the second floor hallway and into a bedroom. Jane was commanded to stop, so she did, and she had a moment to take in the room.

It was a bedroom, ancient trappings, including wallpaper and a round, threadbare carpet over a floor so old the boards rippled.

There was a window, but it was closed, the drapes drawn.

The bed was a big four poster affair. Curtains were drawn back to reveal a scrawny, old man half covered by a comforter and reclining like an odalisque. He was on his side and one arm supported his head. He had but fringes of tufted hair on an oversized head. His neck was skinny with folds of old skin. He was grinning like a 16 year old caught jacking off, and he eyed Jane like he was sizing up a steak at the supermarket.

Mrs. Frankendick commanded Jane: "Stand there until you are told to move." Then, to the wheezed, old skeleton in the bed, "This is Jane, honey, your new girlfriend."

"Thank you, Martha." The old man's rheumy eyes glittered hungrily.

"Jane, you love Dr. Frankendick, and you want nothing more than to satisfy him completely and utterly. Do you understand?"

Jane was frozen, wanting to run, but unable. In her heart she was revulsed. The grey folds of skin over a bony structure, the teeth crooked and yellow. And the hungry look in his eyes was enough to put anybody off.

Jane found her mouth answering: "Yes, ma'am."

She was caught. She wanted to run, to scream, to be anywhere but in this terrible bedroom torture chamber. She stood quietly, praying for a way out, and following instructions exactly.

Martha frowned. She knew Jane was resisting. She snarled, "You will believe that you love Dr. Frankendick."

Instantly, Jane's revulsion yielded to a desire to go to the man, to embrace him and love him, to feel him, to fuck him.

Martha watched the expression on Jane's face change from dislike to fascination. She smiled and stepped back. "She's all yours, dear," and. to Jane, "You can move now."

Martha turned and exited the room, closing the door with a soft click.

Jane stood motionless, She wanted to go rape the old toad, in spite of the terrible feeling in her heart.

Dr. Frankendick studied her. "Ah, yes. You are quite beautiful, my dear. Hold up your tits."

Jane placed hr palms under her mammaries and lifted them. She was proud of here full bosom, and now this pride undid her. She squeezed them and moaned and wanted to push them in the face of the old man. She wanted him to suckle her large, pointed nipples.

And, inside, she wanted to vomit.

"Blow kisses to me."

Jane made kissing motions as she held her tits out.

"Tickle yourself with one hand."

Somehow, Jane managed to lose her clothes, then she was massaging her pussy with one hand, holding her tit and squeezing the nipple with the other hand, and blowing kisses to the foul, old man.

Gleefully, Dr. Frankendick clapped his hands together. "Martha has really outdone herself this time. Do you want me to fuck you?"

Jane found herself moaning and saying, "I need your big dick plunged into my pussy. I'm wet, all wet, and your dick is the only cure."

Dr. Frankendick sat up then, cross legged with his legs under the covers. "And you shall fuck me, long and hard. And you will eat my sperm and get pregnant and love every minute of it. But first…you need to see my dick."

Jane was shivering now, wanting to dive forward and begin loving the man to death.

"You see, I had an accident. I was preparing dog food for my Poochie. I had reconstructed him out of dead bodies and he was the most lovable doggy. He was half Bulldog and half Shih Tzu which made him a Bull Shit….anyway, I was pushing body parts through the meat grinder…don't want to waste all that good meat, right? Good enough for my little Poochie, right? And, somehow, my dick got caught. Before I could flick the switch the meat grinder ate my dick right up. Ground it into bits and pieces. It hurt an awful lot, and my Poochie didn't realize what had happened, he thought everything coming out of the grinder was edible, so he ate my ground up dick right on the spot. "BUT..." Dr. Frankendick held up one finger. "My darling wifey has no doubt apprised you of my most marvelous abilities. I invented myself a new dick!"

Jane was now shaking with the desire to attack the old man, to lay waste to him and his reconstructed dick, even without knowing what that dick looked like.

"First, I scoured the world for appropriate parts. By that I mean it had to be appropriate to a human cunt. It had to fill all the spaces and rub the hot spots and all that. I examined elephant dicks, mosquito dicks, whale dicks, mouse dicks. Did you know that a sea turtle has a dick twice the length of his body? That's right...if it is 6 feet long it has a 3 foot dick.

"Second, I had to choose the right material to construct the penis. It had to be not too hard, not too soft...just perfect so that it would shape to the contours of the cunt without being too rigid.

"Third, it had to have massive balls to hold the right amount of sperm to insure pregnancy. This meant I had to reconstruct my balls, which didn't make it into the meat grinder.

"Fourth, I had to...well, don't let me bore you with all the scientific foofaraw. Let me just say there was a fourth, fifth, sixth, and so on.

"But the point is this..." Dr. Frankendick leaned forward, his pale eyes bulging, a bit of drool dripping from his mouth, "...my dick is the best, largest, most massive, yet tenderest cunt filler in the universe.

"Well, maybe the world. Haven't been off this planet, you know, but I simply can't imagine even an alien species having a bigger and better cock than I.

Jane felt her whole body blushing with heat, the desire to launch herself on Dr. Frankendick. Inside her heart of hearts, she was terrified. She didn't want some alien monstrosity of dick entering her, let alone impregnating her. But the Rohypnol developed by Dr. Frankendick was too much for her to resist.

"Can I...can I see?" She managed to sputter.

Slowly but proudly, Dr. Frankendick lowered the comforter and exposed his penis.

It came into view first as large as a baseball, but that was just the head. And the head had four segments, each with a piss slit.

"Don't worry, you'll be able to take the head," Dr. Frankendick explained. "The reason there are four sides to the skull is I wanted to be able to spray the sides of the cunt equally, it's the best way to make sure the little spermies have the best chance of swimming up your little cunnie."

He lowered the comforter more, and the shaft of the beast was slowly revealed. It was thick as a baseball bat, but triple twined.

"The triple twine feature insures that my dick gets enough rubbing. Each part of the dick rubs against your walls, and against the other two pillars in the trunk. That afford me the best pleasure, and makes sure I won't ever get bored fucking."

He pushed the comforter aside and revealed the largest balls Jane had ever seen. They were massive, as big as softballs.

"They swell a bit, you'll feel them, before I ejaculate, which gives my sperm a big shove up your canal. Do you want to see them up closer?"

Terrified within, Jane found her head nodding helplessly.

And, sad truth to tell, there was a part of Jane that was overcoming even her hidden revulsion. There isn't a woman on the planet, not a one of the female species, that hasn't wondered what a bigger cock feels like.

Just as 16 year old males can't be kept from hiding in the bathroom and stroking themselves silly, there isn't a woman alive who isn't on the hunt for that big whammer slammer of a penis. *What does that giant feel like? How much sperm is it going to squirt? Can my little pussy take it all?!*

Jane moved closer to the bed. She bent down on her knees and got eyeball close to the massive Frankendick.

Up close it was even more impressive. The head was shiny and swollen and dripping with pre-cum. The three shafts writhed against one another, and she could feel the heat being generated. And the balls...Oh. My. God!

She reached forward a hand and touched one of the balls. The testicle pulsated in response to her touch, it was hungry to spew its batter, and the pulsing made the ball grow noticeably larger.

"Take them in both hands, my dear."

Jane slid a hand under each ball and hefted them.

They were raw and red, filled with juices that swirled, and the veins on the outside rippled with waiting baby juice.

"Unnn!" moaned Dr. Frankendick.

Jane shifted her grip to the shaft. She felt the three individual poles twist tighter, then relax. She knew that if she stuck a finger between the rippling poles they would crush her finger.

"Gah hah!" drooled Dr. Frankendick. "Stroke...stroke!"

Using both hands, Jane stroked the triple pillar. Up and down went her hands, and the poles began to shorten then elongate. The three shafts, twined as they were, were like a massive spring. At one point Jane placed her palm over the head of Dr. Frankendick's dick and pushed it. The dick gave way, shortened, then sprang outward.

"Hoo! Ah Ah!" Dr. Frankendick's scrawny chest heaved and panted. the four sides of the head of his dick spurted a steady stream of pre-cum. Blood pulsed up the triple shaft, making the veins ripple and writhe against one another.

Jane leaned forward and licked up some of the pre-cum.

"Ahhhhahahah!" Dr. Frankendick responded to the feel of her tongue lapping at the head.

She licked up more, and swallowed greedily. It was obvious that Dr. Frankendick had made his pre-cum, and probably his sperm, delicious to the tongue.

Jane tried to get the head into her mouth, and, surprisingly, it slipped in!

"Ahhhh!" groaned Dr. Frankendick.

Jane realized that the substance of which the dick was constructed was soft on the outside and hard on the inside. It filled and touched everything in her mouth, yet she could feel, as she sucked, the bony structure inside the soft.

Dr. Frankendick was really moaning now, his hips were moving back and forth, and Jane sucked the head in deep, then spat it out. Sucked and spat, swallowing more and more of the delicious fluid spewing from the head.

"Gah gah gah!" Dr. Frankendick groaned, then, without warning, he came.

Sperm flooded Jane's mouth, filled it completely. She tried to draw back, to not be drowned by the massive amount of ejaculate, but Dr. Frankendick had a hold of her head.

Thick, milky fluid spurted out the sides of Jane's mouth, she gagged, but still the fluid kept coming. The dick was pulsing like a jackhammer, the balls had swollen and now were palpitating, and slowly, ever so slowly, growing smaller.

Now Jane's whole face was covered with the creamy batter, and she realized: *This is good!*

But, all good things must come to an end, the stream of cum became a trickle, then a dribble, and finally ended.

Dr. Frankendick released her head and she drew back. Her eyes were wide as she wiped the massive amounts of sperm off her face.

"Pretty impressive, eh, my dear?" Dr. Frankendick grinned mightily.

Jane nodded, couldn't keep her eyes off the giant headed triple column cunt fucker.

"Aren't you worried that I might have shot my wad? No more? That you won't get to sample my delightful but devious dick?"

Jane looked up at the ugly, little man with worry in her eyes.

Dr. Frankendick laughed. "Not to worry. I managed to give myself almost instantaneous powers of regeneration. Look!"

The doctor pointed between his legs, Jane looked and saw that the monster was already resurrecting.

"The secrets of life and death, my dear."

Jane watched in awe as the massive member became larger and larger, maybe even larger than it had been before.

"Now, I'll lie back and let you have your pleasure with me."

Dr. Frankendick laid back and his dick popped upward, pointed towards the ceiling like a spaceship ready to blast off. In this position it was truly stupendous, red and veined, rippling and pulsing, the balls surging as they refilled.

"Come, my dear."

Slowly, almost afraid, but too in love to resist herself, Jane stood up on the bed and put her feet on each side of Dr. Frankendick.

Slowly, cautiously, terrified but wanting it more than she had ever wanted anything in her life, Jane lowered herself until she felt the big ball of the head touch her thighs.

She used her hands to spread her labia. She pushed her pussy onto the big, baseball-sized head. It was so big, scarily big, but she already knew, from the blow job, that the outer part shrunk under pressure.

She grunted and lowered, and she felt the spongy head contract, slip into her pussy with a pop.

"Gah," she muttered, scarcely believing that she had the whole head in her slit.

Then she began to descend on the shaft.

"Hunh hunh hunh," she made guttural sounds of lust, feeling the springy triple pillar give way slightly, become spring loaded for the return trip.

And, most surprisingly, she could feel the triple columns grab her on the insides. Yes, they could have broken a finger, but when cushioned by the spongy outer covering, and compressed by the gentle walls of Jane's canal, the sides of her pussy were squeezed and threaded, kneaded and palpated, and every nerve inside her sex was caught and explored.

"Huh, ga ga, hunh!" She moaned and whined, losing all thought and becoming receptive only to the unbelievable pleasure being twisted out of her innards.

"Ha ah hunh hunh!"

She bottomed out.

She was so filled, her every fiber so aflame, she wasn't aware of Dr. Frankendick grunting in pleasure.

Then the fun really started.

Jane lifted slightly, and settled, and lifted and settled, and inside her the triple penis gave way, then shot forward. The sides of her cock holster were gripped and slipped, and the head began banging back and forth. Massive amounts of pre-cum aided the endeavor, and a frothy foam began expelling out of her pussy, squirting down the sides of the huge triple cock.

Unbelievably, Jane felt even more pleasure. She bounced and bounced, until the huge balls under Dr. Frankendick's cock were filled to the max, then those balls became something for her to bounce upon.

Jane's head began flopping back and forth, her big breasts bounced up and down.

Dr. Frankendick grabbed her tits with his bony hands and kneaded them.

Jane leaned forward and Dr. Frankendick placed his thin lips about the nipples and sucked hard.

Jane arched her back, which tilted her hips slightly and gave even more access to the huge dick pummeling her.

"Gah gah!" She shouted.

Underneath her, Dr. Frankendick was giving similar shouts of of pleasure.

"HUNH HUNH FUUUU!"

"AGH AGH FUUUUU!"

They came at the same time.

Jane just felt herself thrown aloft, across the blue sky and into the sun. Everything turned white hot and time stopped.

Dr. Frankendick shot his fluids deep into the beautiful woman riding him. Massive amounts of splooge squirted far into Jane's rumpled slit skin.

For a long minute they were frozen, her wafting away on clouds of pleasure, him emptying his sizable gonads with great pulses of his giant and most pleasing dick. Then they were done. She collapsed on him, and he simply went to sleep. Didn't even tell her to get off or clean himself up. Just went to sleep.

CHAPTER FOUR
SEX AND SLAVERY

And was rudely woken up.

"Get up!" hissed Martha Frankendick.

"But it's only been a few—"

"Shut. Time to do your chores."

Confused, dazed by the total and utter satiation of her every sexual desire, Jane followed the skinny witch.

In the kitchen Mrs. Frankendick told her to: clean the dishes, sweep and mop and wax the floors, clean the windows...and be quick about it.

Helpless under the influence of the Rohypnol, Jane began scrubbing dishes. The sink was piled high, a weeks worth of encrustation, and she had to put her whole weight and all the hot water the old sink was capable of into the task. By the end of an hour everything was sparkling, but her poor hands, once the envy of hand models everywhere, were raw and shaking.

Then came the floors. Sweeping was easy, and mopping wasn't too bad, but the waxing was brutal. Jane had to strip the old wax, and then apply the new wax by hand (Mrs. Frankendick insisted it be done on hands and knees and by hand) and rub it until it shone.

Now exhausted, Jane cleaned the windows, and this, too, was done by old standards. Jane had to use vinegar and newspapers. By the time she was done she was sobbing with the scent of vinegar and her hands were a mess. Her nails were chipped and broken and the skin was raw and even bleeding in some places.

And, if that wasn't enough, the old biddy came into the kitchen every half hour and inspected the work, demanding redo after redo after redo, even when to Jane's senses the job was perfectly done.

At last, done and ready to die, Mrs Frankendick threw her a crust of bread and said, "Squat in the corner and eat. And don't say a fucking word."

Mrs. Frankendick then began to prepare lunch. She might be the skinny bitch from hell, but she knew how to cook. Shortly the kitchen was a cauldron of delicious aromas. Jane, finished with her crust of bread, stared at the old lady. Drool flowed freely from her mouth, and her eyes were filled with a look of hunger.

"Jesus," muttered Martha at one point, "Can't you control yourself?" She tossed Jane another crust.

Jane pounced upon the crust and jammed it into her mouth. She was starving, and all the pleasure jammed into her pussy by the bad Doctor was a memory.

Mrs. Frankendick placed dishes upon the table, then leaned out the kitchen door and bellowed, "Lunch is ready!"

A minute later Dr. Frankendick entered the room. He was wearing a tattered robe, fuzzy slippers, and a pair of boxers. The boxers looked over sized on his skinny frame, and his monster dick hung out the bottom of one leg.

"Mmmm," smells good, my dear. Then, he noticed Jane squatting in the corner. "Who's this?"

Jane blinked. It was obvious the doctor didn't know who she was, didn't remember that he had filled her pussy with love juices just a few hours previous.

"This is Jane, dear," Mrs' Fraendick spoke cheerfully, but cheerful for her was like running a rusty razor over one's finer sensibilities. "She's our new maid."

"Well, hello," Dr, Frankendick sat down and started eating.

For a few minutes there was nothing but the sound of Dr. Frankendick's skinny, little lips smacking, then the meal was devoured. He had eaten half a pig, a rack of ribs, two steaks and a watermelon. And he was still skinny!

He stood up and smiled at his wife, "Thank you, dear." Then he left the room.

Martha Frankendick had been leaning against the sink the whole time, her face revealing her sour outlook on life. Now she jerked her head at Jane. "Well, clean up this mess."

Jane stood up and began cleaning the dishes off the table. Such a lot of dishes for such a skinny, little fart of a man. She began scrubbing the plates in the sink, and Martha stood to one side and watched her.

Finally, a half hour later, Jane was done. And she was tired and worn down. She had been kidnapped, raped by a monster dick, forced to be a slave, and she was tired.

"Smile," said Mrs. Frankendick.

Jane smiled brightly.

Mrs. Frankendick nodded and was satisfied. "Sit at the table."

Jane, smile stuck stuck across her puss, cheerfully sat at the old kitchen table. Mrs. Frankendick sat down opposite her.

"I don't know why I bother talking to girls like you. Dirty sluts that can't control their stupid pussies. I guess I just get lonely. The only time I'm out of this house is when I have to pick up a bitch like you. Oh, well. Go ahead. You've got questions?"

Jane couldn't help it, questions poured out of her like sperm had poured out of her pussy a few hours ago. "Why me? How did you find me? How long do I have to do this? Doesn't Dr. Frankendick really remember who I am? He just fucked me!..."

Jane poured out her questions for a long minute. Finally, Martha held up a hand to stop the outpouring.

"Okay, big mouth, my turn. I'm not going to answer all your questions, they're too stupid for me to answer. But...no, Victor doesn't remember who you are. One of the effects I noticed after he created his big dick was that it seemed to interfere with his memory. And the more he fucks the less he remembers. He'll probably fuck himself into terminal stupidity."

"But...but can't you limit his fucking?"

"Not as long as I have stupid girls like you to do it for me. Believe me, you'll eventually get tired of his big, super dick. I did. And, like I say, I'm too old for babies, anyway. No. As long as I can get girls like you I can keep him satisfied, and I get the added bonus of having a perfectly good maid."

"You say other girls...why didn't one of them have a baby?"

"Don't know. Maybe when he invented his dick and reconstructed his balls he didn't get something right. But we keep trying." She shrugged.

Then Jane had an idea: "Maybe if he didn't fuck so much he would be able to remember things!"

Martha Frankendick gave a big sigh. "Go get me some coffee."

Jane went to the stove and poured a cup of coffee for the older woman, then sat back down.

Martha took a sip, smacked her thin lips, and said, "Bring me the sugar bowl."

Jane did so, and watched while Martha poured a half a dozen spoonfuls of the sweet stuff into her cup and stirred.

"You certainly are stupid." She shook her head in dismay. "When Victor became stupid it was like being released from slavery. Now I'm in charge. I just keep him rutting like a pig, he doesn't remember anything, and I don't have to put up with his maleness. Haven't you figured out how stupid man is? Even when he was a genius Victor would get excited about the latest football score, want to play cards with other stupid men on Saturday night, and drink beer for breakfast. No. Men are stupid, and the stupider we can make them the more free we women are. Well, I am. You...you're as stupid as Victor."

Jane didn't say anything for a few minutes. It was obvious that the old lady was suffering her own case of the stupids. The things she was saying didn't always make sense. First she's all about babies, then she just wants to get out of fucking, and the Doctor is a genius...but stupid, and Jane realized the truth of the matter: Martha Frankendick was just a power mad, fuckless fuck.

"Now, let me tell you how the afternoon is going to go."

Jane paid attention.

"You've broken your fingernails, your hair is a mess, how do you ever think you'll be able to keep a man interested?"

"But...but—" Jane wanted to complain that it was her having to be a slave that had made her this way.

"Shut up."

Jane shut.

"Across the front room there is a small room. There is a shower there, and everything you need to make yourself beautiful, and let me tell you this," Martha leaned forward. "When you stop trying to be beautiful...when you lose interest in that big dick of my husband's... when not even the Rohypnol will keep you interested, then you'll go the way of the others."

"What way is that?" asked Jane fearfully.

Martha leaned forward and snarled, "I planted them in the garden out back. You want to end up like that?"

Jane shook her head.

"Then do your work, stay happy, and enjoy bouncing on my husband's cock. Got it?"

Jane nodded. "Yes."

"Good. Now go make yourself presentable. Victor will be ready for his afternoon fuck pretty soon."

Jane stood up and went towards the swinging door that led to the living room. Just before she reached it she managed to turn around. "Can I ask you something?"

"What?" Martha sipped on the dregs of her coffee and it was obvious she was just about out of patience and therefore answers.

"Why did you choose me? How did you find me?"

Jane lifted up a thin lip and showed a skinny smile. "We've got an ad on Craigslist. 'Gonna dump your girlfriend? Let us help!'"

Martha didn't say anything, just waited, grinning, for Jane to understand.

And Jane did understand, like lightening bolts make carcasses of old oaks. "Derrick."

Martha chortled then, a wheezing sort of gasp that was her laughter. "That's right. Your boyfriend did this to you."

Martha laughed and laughed and laughed, actually turning a little red in the face. Jane merely turned and went through the swinging door.

CHAPTER FIVE
AN ENDLESS LOOP

For the next hour Jane tried to repair herself. She scrubbed herself clean in the shower and applied her make up, and all the while thought about the girls in the garden.

She had no reason to believe that Martha Frankendick wasn't telling the truth, and that there wasn't a variety of used up girls under the soil of the garden. And she had no reason to believe that she wouldn't end up there herself.

What to do? What to do?

She thought of plans by the ton, but nothing seemed feasible.

The main point seemed to be the Rohypnol. So she thought about what she knew and searched for a way to overcome the drug.

That it worked she knew. She was forced to follow commands, and even alter her mood accordingly.

Martha had indicated that it would eventually wear off. And that she would be re-spritzed.

So the trick was to force herself to be cheerful and follow directions and try to take advantage prior to the re-spritzing.

But how long did it last?

Fortunately, the good news for her was that when she wasn't working frantically, being forced to slave to the point of exhaustion, she could actually have her own thoughts. She could ponder, while she put on her makeup and slid into lingerie and sexy dress, on how to break free from her situation.

Finally, appropriately beautiful, wearing a dress that showed her large and delicious bosoms, Jane laid down on a bed and closed her eyes. There must have been something in the mattress that alerted Mrs. Frankendick when she laid down, for the old biddy was into the room in a flash.

"Let's go," snarled the old harpy. "Time to get fucking."

Cheerfully, as per command, but with a core of worry and dread hiding on the inside, Jane followed Martha up the stairs and down the hall to Dr. Frankendick's bedroom. Then occurred one of the most happenings of the whole experience.

The bed was a big four poster affair. Curtains were drawn back to reveal a scrawny, old man half covered by a comforter and reclining like an odalisque. He was on his side and one arm supported his head. He had but fringes of tufted hair on an oversized head. His neck was skinny with folds of old skin. He was grinning like a 16 year old caught jacking off, and he eyed Jane like he was sizing up a steak at the supermarket.

Mrs. Frankendick commanded Jane: "Stand there until you are told to move." Then, to the wheezed, old skeleton in the bed, "This is Jane, honey, your new girlfriend."

"Thank you, Martha." The old man's rheumy eyes glittered hungrily.

"Jane, you love Dr. Frankendick, and you want nothing more than to satisfy him completely and utterly. Do you understand?"

Jane was frozen, wanting to run, but unable. In her heart she was revulsed. The grey folds of skin over a bony structure, the teeth crooked and yellow. And the hungry look in his eyes was enough to put anybody off.

Jane found her mouth answering: "Yes, ma'am."

She was caught. She wanted to run, to scream, to be anywhere but in this terrible bedroom torture chamber. She stood quietly, praying for a way out, and following instructions exactly.

Martha frowned. She knew Jane was resisting. She snarled, "You will believe that you love Dr. Frankendick."

Instantly, Jane's revulsion yielded to a desire to go to the man, to embrace him and love him, to feel him, to fuck him.

Martha watched the expression on Jane's face change from dislike to fascination. She smiled and stepped back. "She's all yours, dear."

Martha turned and exited the room, closing the door with a soft click.

Stunned, Jane realized that she had just repeated, exactly, word for word, move for move, her first introduction to Dr. Frankendick!

He really did forget, and he was meeting her all anew.

And, as the next few minutes to hour proved, everything was exactly the same as the first time.

It was like she was caught in a time loop!

And, after it was all over, she was woken up, as she had been before, and taken to the kitchen and given a list of tasks to do.

Thus, the days passed. Slave, fuck, slave fuck, day after day, week after week.

And, after about a month, Jane got sprayed with Rohypnol.

She was just starting to feel good, able to think, feeling the revulsion starting up as the Rohypnol wore off, and she got sprayed.

Desperately, she wondered why. What had she done? Or not done, that tipped off Mrs. Frankendick to administering the free will suppressing spray?

After much thought, she figured it out. After much thought and another month.

Mrs. Frankendick sprayed her on the first of the month. The old bitch didn't even wait for the substance to wear off! She just sprayed and didn't take chances.

Thus, the days passed. Slave, fuck, slave fuck, day after day, week after week, and Jane realized that she might have a chance.

The end of the month was when she got sprayed. That was when she would have the most free will, that was when she would have a chance.

The end of the month came. It was a 31 day month, and Jane summoned up all her wits and got ready for the monthly spritz.

The last couple of months the old bitch had sprayed her right after she had done the dishes. She had simply commanded Jane to turn around, and sprayed her right in the face.

The first arrived. Jane was doing the dishes, thinking, listening, and she heard a creak behind her.

"Turn around!"

Jane did, and got the Rohypnol right in the face!

She blinked...and held her breath. She knew she was still going to get some of the spray, and she did. It touched her eyeballs, she got some on her lips and tried not to lick her lips. But she didn't breath it in.

Mrs. Frankendick smiled a mean, nasty smile. She folded her arms in satisfaction. "Go get yourself ready for fucking."

Jane did so, and prayed that she had managed to limit the intake of Rohypnol and thus undo its effects.

She made herself pretty, taking her time, and inside was the worm of a victorious feeling. She actually felt a bit of herself wiggling around, trying to make itself felt.

She fucked Dr. Frankendick, for the first time, as usual. And she felt a deep revulsion working its way through her. The skinny, little fuck with the big balls and atomic dick was so stupid-ized from his dick, however, he didn't notice anything.

She fell asleep, and almost instantly the skinny, old bitch roused her.

"Come along. Time to get the dishes done." She had just spritzed Jane, and was confident, and that confidence was her undoing. As Jane followed her down the stairs she felt...exultation!

Without looking back Martha pointed at the sink full of dishes. "Do them, and be quick ab—"

Jane picked up a heavy metal skillet from the stove and smacked Martha Frankendick right in the eardrum.

The old bitch hit the floor like a sack of dead Frankendicks, but she wasn't dead. She lay on the floor and held the side of her head. "Wha... ow...who..." But she was dazed to the point of being no problem.

Jane grabbed Martha by an ankle and dragged her to the basement stairs. She dragged her down the steps, counting the steps by the bump!

Bump! Bump! of her head hitting the planks.

She dragged her to the cage and shoved her in. Mrs. Frankendick was just coming to as Jane snapped the lock.

"Wha—! What are you..." The skinny old fuckless shook the bars of the cage. "Let me out!"

Jane stood for a long moment, listened to the rantings of the crone. finally, when Martha dried up a bit: "I'm really going to fuck you up."

Martha blinked, astonished at the rage in the beautiful girl's voice.

Jane turned and left the basement.

Jane found the Rohypnol in a cupboard in the kitchen, and with finding the Rohypnol came a bonus.

In the cupboard was a gallon container with a handwritten label.

Pure Rohypnol:
dilute 1 to 10

Next to the gallon container was a small booklet, in which was the formula for making more.

Next to the booklet was the little spray bottle that Martha had used on Jane. There were a half dozen empty bottles next to the full one.

From the color in the full bottle it was obvious that the stuff was diluted, and that meant that it had been diluted for use on Jane!

But why?

Why had the old witch used a diluted form of the substance on Jane?

And Jane immediately knew, it was so obvious...because if she used the pure stuff on somebody it would make them...stupid!

Like Dr. Frankendick had been made stupid! Martha had used it on her husband in full form, and the result was an endless loop of stupidity!

Jane smiled, emptied out the small spray bottle and filled it with the pure Rohypnol.

CHAPTER SIX
JANE'S REVENGE

Dr. Frankendick was reclining like an odalisque, on his side with one arm supporting his head. If he hadn't been so fucking ugly it would have been laughable.

He blinked. He only had enough awareness to understand that something was different, that a loop had been derailed, before Jane sprayed him right in the face. He blinked.

Jane said: "Stay here. Your wife is coming. Ugly is now beautiful, and you will fuck her senseless. After you fuck her you will spray her in the face with this bottle and say the following…" and Jane told the Doctor what to say. When she was done, and confident that the Doctor would do as told, she said, "Now resume waiting."

Dr. Frankendick went back to his reclining position and waited for his ugly wife, who he now believed was forever beautiful.

Jane went down to the basement.

"When are you going to let me go?" snarled Martha, her face twisted into hate.

Jane spritzed her right in the face.

Martha knew what had been done to her, the knowledge was in her eyes, and the shock and the panic, right before Jane said, "Shut up."

Martha Frankendick clamped her vile, twisted lips shut.

Jane unlocked the door. "Come with me."

Jane lead the docile biddy up the stairs to the kitchen. She pointed her at the sink and said, "Do the dishes, then read the bottom of the sink."

Jane sat back and watched as Martha did the dishes. She had herself a bologna sandwich while she was waiting. She didn't bother checking the old crone's work because the woman was so anal Jane knew she would pick her own self to death.

At last, the last dish washed and dried and put away, Martha leaned over the sink and read the words carved into the bottom. "Spray yourself in the face with pure Rohypnol and tell yourself you need to go fuck your husband."

Jane had put a mirror on the cupboard and Martha took out the spray, sprayed herself in the face and told the mirror to: "Go fuck your husband."

Jane followed Mrs. Frankendick up the stairs and down the hallway. She followed the skinny slattern into her husband's bedroom.

Dr. Frankendick was waiting. "I want to make love to you, my beautiful wife."

Jane watched while Martha took off her clothes and crawled into bed.

The old lady's pussy was tight, probably hadn't been used in 250 years, and the insertion of the giant Frankendick, in spite of the super lubricating pre-cum, was a painful affair.

"AH! NO! AH!"

Jane moved up and whispered in Martha's ear. "You like pain."

Instantly, the old shrivel changed the cries of pain into moans of lust. "Ahhh, yeah...okay!"

An hour later Dr. Frankendick was done. His emotions were spent, his cum had splattered everything for a yard around, and Mrs. Frankendick collapsed forward.

And, as previously ordered, Dr. Frankendick reached for a bottle of pure Rohypnol on the side stand. He grabbed Martha by the hair and raised her head and sprayed it directly into her face.

Martha blinked and sputtered, and Dr. Frankendick gave her her orders.

"You will sleep for two hours, and two hours only. You will arise and fix me a feast. then clean the house. Then retrieve my dirty dishes and wash them. Then read what is written in the bottom of the sink."

Martha zonked out for her two hours of rest. Two hours, and then she would be back on the loop, rested enough so she didn't die, but never rested enough to think her way out of the mess.

Jane smiled, then went back to ransacking the house.

Interestingly, there were some real prizes. In fact, she was going to have to get a van to move some of the stuff.

A coin collection that had been building for 200 years.

A stamp collection, again, 200 years.

A book collection. First editions for more than 200 years. Martha was a real reader. Well, was a reader. By the time she managed to break the Rohypnol loop she was going to be so stupid she didn't even understand what a letter was!

Antique furniture in prime condition.

A safe. Fuck! A real safe, not one of those wall things that were good for fire resisting, barely, if that, but a huge six foot square monster made hundreds of years ago.

Jane went upstairs and interrupted Martha long enough to get the combination, then she put her back on the loop.

The safe was loaded, with a capital LOADED!

Money. Bonds. Deeds. All sorts of things. And all easily deeded to Jane. Just a little spritz here, a little spritz there, and Martha would be so elated that she had finally managed to get rid of all that nasty money!

Over the next couple of weeks Jane emptied out the old house of all valuables. When she was done there were only dishes, a bed, and a full bottle of Rohypnol.

Standing at the door, quite happy with herself, Jane knew that there was only one thing left to do. She gently closed the door and left the key under the mat.

Derrick and Darla were fucking. Some might call it making love, but, really, it was just animalistic, over the top fucking.

Thrust it in, pull it out, repeat until squirt.

Finally, exhausted, they lay on their backs and stared at the ceiling.

They loved each other, and that was obvious. They went to work, and at work all they could think of was getting home and fucking. So they returned home and fucked their brains out.

In truth, they were kindred spirits.

And they spent a lot of time laughing at how stupid Jane had been.

Jane, of course, found this out through the services of a sleazy security service. She had the couple followed for a month, and she knew when they fucked, how much they fucked, and what they even talked about before, during, and after fucking.

"So they think I'm stupid, eh?" Jane's eyes narrowed as she finished reading the latest report. "Well, it's time to find out how stupid."

Derrick thrust forward, his dick widening Darla's gaping hole, then pulled back.

Darla gasped at the sensations. She thrust her hips forward, trying to capture him, trying to make the impalement last.

Suddenly, they froze. They each felt it, a presence in the room.

Derrick spun over, hitting Darla in the chin with his shoulder, and stared at the dark figure outlined in the bedroom doorway.

"Who the fuck are you?" he snarled.

Jane waited. She was wearing a trench coat and a floppy brimmed hat. The hat was pulled low so he couldn't see her face.

"Hi Derrick," she spoke throatily, disguising her voice.

Derrick realized from the tone of the voice, and the shape of the shadow, that the intruder was a female. He climbed off Darla, who was rubbing her chin and trying to figure things out. He stomped across the bedroom towards the mysterious figure.

"I don't know who the fuck you think you are, but—"

Jane raised her hat and smiled.

"You!" Derrick stopped, mouth opened in surprise, which was perfect because Jane...SPRITZED!

"Don't move, lover," Jane smiled sweetly. She walked past the now immobile figure and approached Darla, who had finally figured out that there was an intruder in her bedroom!

"Who the fuck are—"

Jane lifted her hat and smiled.

"You!" And, like her boyfriend before her, Darla opened her mouth and gaped.

SPRITZ!

They sat at the kitchen table, happy as three monkeys in a barrel. Derrick and Darla had been commanded to be happy at anything Jane told them.

"Tomorrow," said Jane, "I want you to go to the address written on this piece of paper." She shoved Dr. Frankendick's address towards the grinning couple.

"Oh, goodie!" Darla clapped her hands.

"You will dig up all the bodies in the garden, then you will call the police and confess that you killed them all."

"Fantastic!" Derrick rocked back and forth with joy.

"When the police don't believe you, and they won't once they get a close look at Dr. Frankendick and his wife, you will turn on each other, even growing violent, and do your best to convince them that you, Darla, know that Derrick killed all the girls, and Derrick, you will do your best to convince them that Darla killed them. Do you understand?"

In turn, Jane had them each explain what they were to do. Happy, bubbling with joy, they repeated their orders, so glad to be given something that was so much fun to do.

Finally, Jane gave them their last order. "You both love me. You will do anything for me. Because you love me so much you will never, ever even remember that I was involved in this at all."

They especially loved this command. To be in love with such a wonderful, beautiful girl as Jane was a blessing beyond belief. They jumped for joy and laughed merrily and couldn't wait for the morrow.

fin

A Note from the Author!

We hope you liked these little gems.
Please take a moment to rate me five stars.
That helps support my writing,
and lets me know which direction I should take
for future books.

Thank you

Grace & Alyce

Six volumes! Over 40 stories!

Come on, baby…give in to your desires!
You *know* you want to!

https://gropperpress.wordpress.com

Five Star Gropper Stories on Amazon!

I Changed My Husband into a Woman
Sissy Ride: The Book
The Feminization Games
The Stepforth Husband
Revenge of the Stepforth Husbands
Too Tough to Feminize
The Horny Wizard of Oz
The Lusty Land of Oz
My Husband's Funny Breasts
My Neighbor Feminized Me
I Gave My Man Boobs
The Day the Democrats Changed the Republicans into Girls
The Sexual Edge
The Lactating Man
I Changed My Nephew into a Girl
Feminized for Granny
The Feminine Vaccination
The Were-Fem
The Feminization Curse
We Made Him Our Fem Boy

https://gropperpress.wordpress.com

The Best Erotica in the World is at...

GROPPER PRESS

Read the best full length novels ever written!
Sex, Feminization, chastity, bondage...
everything you could ever want in a novel.
click on the following link...

Big erotic novels!

The BEST Erotic novels in the World!

Full Length Books from Gropper Press

A classic of feminization.

Alex is ensnared by an internet stalker. Day after day he is forced to feminize. His neighbor finds out and the situation becomes worse. Now his wife is due home, and he doesn't know what to do. What's worse, he is starting to like it.

Sissy Ride: The Book!

Sissy Ride: The Book
The Complete Saga: All 10 Stories!

Grace Man

Randy catches his wife cheating, but a mysterious woman is about to take him in hand and teach him that when a woman cheats…it is the man's fault.

This story has female domination, spanking, male submission, male chastity, pegging, cross dressing, feminization

The Big Tease!

The Big Tease: The Book
A 'how to' novel on how to
Train a man to know his place!

Grace Mansfield

Full Length Books from Gropper Press

I Changed My Husband into a Woman

Roscoe was a power player in Hollywood. He was handsome, adored, and had one fault - he liked to play practical jokes. Now his wife is playing one on him, and it's going to be the grandest practical joke of all time.

I CHANGED MY HUSBAND INTO A WOMAN!

A delightful novel of total power exchange!

GRACE MANSFIELD

Too Tough to Feminize

Sam thought he was a tough guy. He was cock of the walk, a real, live, do or die Mr. Tough Guy.

Then he made a mistake. He took on the wrong … woman.

This is the story of what happened when Sam finally met his match and learned who the really tough people were.

TOO TOUGH TO FEMINIZE

Until he messed with the wrong woman!

GRACE MANSFIELD

Full Length Books from Gropper Press

The Feminization Games

Jim Camden was a manly man, until the day he crossed his wife. Now he's in for a battle of the sexes, and if he loses… he has to dress like a woman for a week. But what he doesn't know is the depths of manipulation his wife will go to. Lois Camden, you see, is a woman about to break free, and if she has to step on her husband to do it…so be it. And Jim is about to learn that a woman unleashed is a man consumed.

My Husband's Funny Breasts

Tom Dickson was a happy camper. He lived a good life, had a beautiful wife, then he started to grow breasts, his hair grew long, and his body reshaped. Now Tom is on the way to being a woman, and he doesn't know why.

MY HUSBAND'S FUNNY BREASTS

It's not so funny when
it's happening to you!

GRACE MANSFIELD

Full Length Books from Gropper Press

Silithia: The hope of All Women...the Bane of All Men

In this amazing story Grace Mansfield has crafted a true classic.

Silithia is a Gypsy. Small in stature, diseased, looked down upon by the whole world, she yet rises to heights never imagined by man. And now man has to pay the price.

What is the true value of a woman? What are her true abilities? Silithia will show you.

Womanland: Whatever you do...don't unlock the Warlock

Sam and Shiela have a vacation in a resort named 'Womanland.' It is supposed to be a little 'slap and tickle' resort, but it's more. It is a place where Witches thrive and men don't survive. Sam, however, has a little secret, and Womanland is going to be fighting for its life!

The Best Erotica in the World is at…

GROPPER PRESS

Save money with big collections.
All your favorite novelettes.
Kinky, nasty, naughty.
click on the following link…
Big Erotic Collections!

The BEST Erotic collections in the World!

BIG COLLECTIONS!

The Electric Groin!

Save money

SEVEN sexy stories

A sorority that feminizes, 'Tootsie' goes all the way, National lipstick day and all the men in Hollywood start growing breasts, learning to be a man by being a woman, and more, more, more.

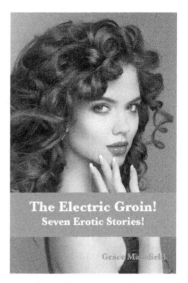

The Electric Groin!
Seven Erotic Stories!

Grace Mansfield

The Shivering Bone!

Save money with SEVEN sexy stories

A sorority that feminizes, 'Tootsie' goes all the way, National lipstick day and all the men in Hollywood start growing breasts, learning to be a man by being a woman, and more, more, more.

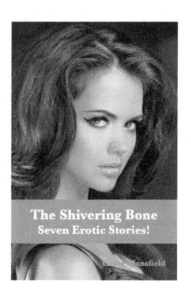

The Shivering Bone
Seven Erotic Stories!

Mansfield

BIG COLLECTIONS!

The Girl in Me

Save money

SEVEN erotic stories

A woman gives her man boobs…a scientist figures out how to lose the Y chromosome…a young man will get free college, if he lets them give him boobs…and all sorts of stuff!

Quivering Buns

Save money

SEVEN erotic stories

Men turning into women because of the vaccine…a woman makes her husband wear a chastity device, then they swap bodies…feminization training…feminized by his sister…and more, more!

BIG COLLECTIONS!

Tainted Love!

Save money
SEVEN erotic stories

A curse makes him lose his package and grow boobs...the latest medical device has side effects...a man dominated by a gang of women...and much, MUCH more!

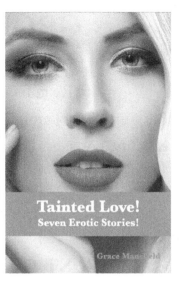

Stories to Pump your Heart

Save money
SEVEN erotic stories

A nephew changed into a girl... emasculating a cheating husband...a feminized cop...sentenced to feminization...and a LOT More!

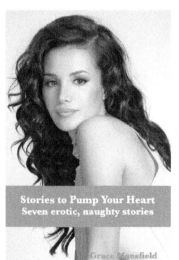

The Best Erotica in the World is at…

GROPPER PRESS

Read the best novelettes ever!
Sex, Feminization, monsters, curses,
chastity, bondage, enslaved husbands, dominant women!
click on the following link…

Big Novelettes!

The BEST Erotic novels in the World!

Big Novelettes

The Day the Democrats Turned the Republicans into...Girls! ~ A note from Grace...I got tired of all the politics on TV, everybody yelling at everybody, and everybody knowing they are the only ones that are right...it's enough to make a girl pick up an erotic book. You know? So, are you ready for the 'transgenderment' of half the country?

The Lactating Man ~ Jessica is about to have a bay, the only problem is she can't produce enough milk to nurse. Solution? Her husband, Robert, is about to go on the wildest trip any man has ever gone on.

This book has feminization, cross dressing, hormones, breast growth, lactation, small penis, pegging.

Big Novelettes

The Were-Fem ~ Rodney is a hard working lad who stumbles upon a beautiful girl in the forest. The girl turns out to be a demon, and Rodney is cursed. By day an honorable man, by night a man sucking demon.

The Half and Half Man ~ Jesse is forced to have his hands manicured, which causes an orgasms. Now he is faced with full feminism. Will Jesse survive the trip?

Big Novelettes

<u>Feminized for Granny</u> ~ Underwear is disappearing from Joanna's department store. She catches the culprit, and a spanking reveals that Eric is a cross dresser. Joann realizes there is something very hot about cross dressing, but how far can she push Eric?

Feminized for Granny!
Revenge, lust and...Grandma?

Grace Mansfield

<u>Feminized Cop</u> ~ He wasn't big enough to be a real cop, so he became T-Rex, a feminized cop. He infiltrated a dangerous gang and got the goods, but now he has to get out.

Feminized Cop
It was a job a man couldn't do

Grace Mansfield

Big Novelettes

<u>Feminized in 100 Days</u> ~ Tom loves his wife, but he doesn't feel worthy. She is so beautiful and powerful. Tammi learns how Tom feels, and comes up with a plan to make Tom feel beautiful and worthy, and It only takes 100 days.

    A wonderful tale of erotic sex and the exchange of power.

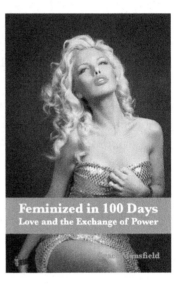

Feminized in 100 Days
Love and the Exchange of Power

<u>Dominated for a Week: He was Caught and Punished!</u> ~ Brandon is a kinky, little boy. He wears dresses, has a chastity device, and lives for when his wife is working as a stewardess. Then he is caught, and five women take control of him. He doesn't know who they are, but his wife is due home any time!

Dominated by a Gang of Women!
He was caught and punished!

Grace Mansfield

Big Novelettes

My Wife Dominated Me: He asked for a little, she gave him a lot! ~ Jerrod and Janice have a strange relationship, he gets to make love to her when he makes a million dollars. What he doesn't know is that the end of one agreement is the beginning of another, and she has incredible plans for him!

A Month of Feminization: He never thought he'd like it! ~ Roger received a mysterious present, now he's locked into a chastity belt, and somebody has hacked it! His wife thinks it's funny, her friend thinks it's hilarious, then his wife goes away and the fun starts. Will Roger ever be free from the clutches a mysterious internet hacker and…his wife's best friend?

The Best Erotica in the World is at…
GROPPER PRESS

Novels, short story collections, novelettes…
Men and women dealing with a world gone mad.
There are new books and stories coming out almost every day!

Gropper Press

The BEST Erotic novels in the World!

If you liked
'Mad Scientists and Feminization'
you will really love...

'I Changed My Husband into a Woman'

A full length novel by Grace Mansfield

Here is an excerpt...

"What the fuck!"

I roused myself from a deep and very deserved sleep, only to see Roscoe standing next to the bed, looking down at his feet and cursing.

"Wha..." I mumbled, pulling the covers over me and trying to look like I was still asleep. In truth, though I was tired, I was as awake as I had ever been.

"Did you do this?" His voice was going up. "Is this your idea of a joke?"

"Shut up," I whined. "I wanna sleep!"

"No! Wake up! Why'd you do this?"

"Do what?" and I finally rolled over and made my eyes sleepy and tired.

Oh, baby, was I acting. And I was acting in front of the fellow who had created a half a dozen Best Actor Oscar winners. This was going to take all my prowess to pull off.

"My toes! Look at my toes."

I blinked, and edged towards the side of the bed so I could look down to where he was pointing. And I exulted. He had felt he had to explain that it was his toes, so he was just working off emotion and blaming whoever was closest. He didn't have any clue as to why his toes were red.

"What the fuck!" I opened my eyes wide and stared at his tootsies.

"Why'd you do this?"

I looked up at him and put a tiny edge of anger in my voice. "I didn't do that! Why the hell would I paint my sissy husband's toes red?" Very important to get the word sissy into the conversation as quickly as possible. "Do I look like I'm the kind of girl who'd marry a sissy?"

He kept trying to look fierce, but I could tell that my arrows had hit the mark. In some odd, almost invisible way he shriveled. He withdrew slightly into himself. I had met the challenge and acted my way out of being the culprit.

"Okay, okay," then he tried again. "You did this because I jacked off on you the other day."

"First, I just said I didn't do that!" I pointed at his toes. "And, I already got you back, and, husband of mine, practical jokes aren't my forte." At least they usually weren't. I was enjoying this; I was thinking of a career change. Sandy Tannenbaum, Practical Joker Extraordinaire!

"So who did this?"

Now I looked at him suspiciously. "There's only two people in this room."

He sputtered in outrage, so I kept up the attack. "So why did you paint your toe nails red?"

"I didn't!"

"There's nobody else here!" I was pushing him now. I had been accused unfairly (he thought) so I had to act the outrage. I narrowed my eyes. "Are you going pervert on me?"

"I didn't do this!" he wailed.

"Well I didn't, and I didn't figure on waking up next to Bruce Jenner."

Oh, Jesus!" he almost ran to my make up station and started looking for polish remover. "Where is it!?"

I got out of bed, and went to him. I didn't want him making a mess, so I handed him a bottle of polish remover. He grabbed at it like a sailor grabs a life preserver after jumping off the Titanic. He sat down and lifted his foot up to the edge of the chair.

"Hold on," I said. I took the remover out of his hands. "I don't want you making a mess. Come here."

I led him into the bathroom. "Put your foot here," I pointed to the john. He placed his foot on the toilet and I sat cross legged in front of it. I giggled.

"What?" he groused.

"It is sort of cute. Hubbie gives himself a peddie. Make a good TV series."

He let his breath out in disgust. "I'm a man's man, not a girly man."

Yeah, that's right, you like to get young girl's pregnant. how manly. But I didn't say that, I just thought it, and kept manipulating him.

"Well, you might say so, but Roscoe Junior says otherwise."

Now, truth, he wasn't really all that hard, just sort of a morning half woodie, but I reached up and grabbed his meat and in a second he was throbbing in my hand.

"Hey!" he said. But he wasn't really protesting. What man would object to a pair of sexy hands fondling his man pole? "Take the polish off."

"Oh, okay." but the damage was done. He was now erect, and associating that erection with nail polish. Manly man. Huh!

So I hummed a tune and stripped the polish off and returned his toes to their 'manly' state.

"Okay," he said. Standing and looking down at his repaired

manhood, uh, nails.

"Not even a thanks?"

"Thank you," and he did sound abashed. "But I have no idea how... somebody must have broken in and done it."

"While you slept? They painted your nails and you didn't even wake up?"

"Well, I was pretty drunk."

I'll say.

"Not that drunk," I lied. "You never get that drunk."

"Well, yeah. But somebody did it." We left the bathroom then and re-entered the bedroom. He walked over to the double windows, which led out to a small patio. He tried the doors. "See! they're open!"

"We're on the second floor."

"He had a ladder."

"He?"

"Well, you don't think a woman did this?"

"Those nails were done pretty well. Men don't know how to apply polish that well." Then I cocked my head and it was obvious what I was thinking.

"Don't look at me that way! I didn't polish my own nails."

I shrugged. "Okay. So Spiderman left off fighting crime for one day so he could paint your nails."

He made a grimace.

"Or maybe somebody just walked in because our door is unlocked." I swung the bedroom door opened.

"Well, I don't..."

"Forget it, Roscoe." I use his name when I am angry with him, or irritated, and he took notice of that. "just admit that you did some sleep walking." Then I giggled, "Or sleep toenail painting."

"Oh, shut up." he brushed past me and headed down the stairs. It was a mark of how irritated and upset he was that he had forgotten to get dressed.

"Ahem!" I cleared my throat.

He turned at the top of the stairs and looked at me. Oh, the look on his face. Irritated, confused. Priceless.

I looked at his groin, placed an elbow in a palm and wiggled my index finger in the air.

He looked down at himself, mumbled a curse word I dasn't dare repeat, and stomped back into the bedroom.

This has been an excerpt from

I Changed My Husband into a Woman!

Read it on kindle or paperback